ANDRE GONZALEZ

Followed East

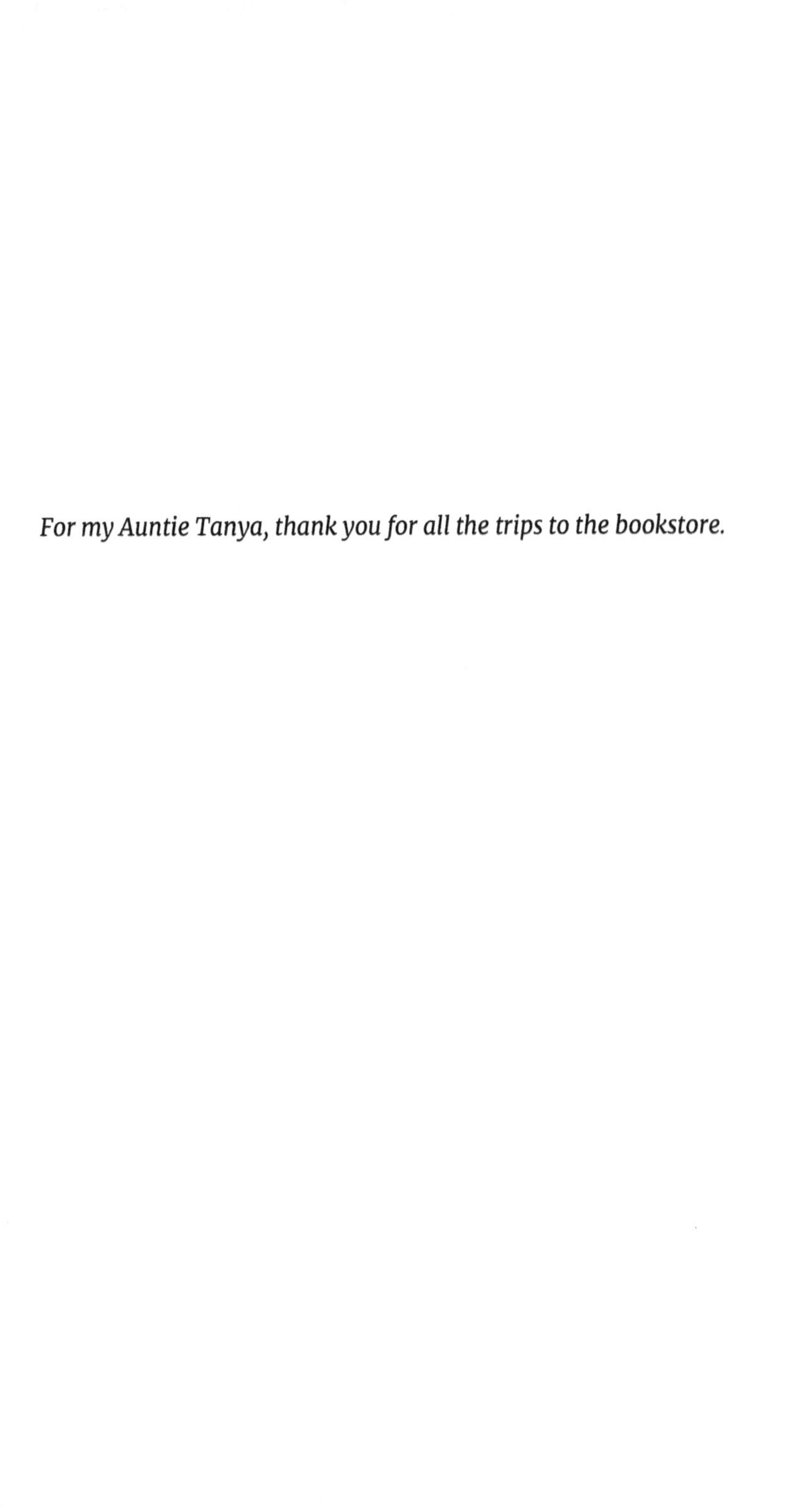

For my Auntie Tanya, thank you for all the trips to the bookstore.

Contents

1

Chapter 1

Kyle stared Colonel Griffins in the eyes, his bushy eyebrows splayed out in every direction. The colonel had just asked Kyle to move to Washington, D.C. to officially enter the training program to join The Crew.

"You know I just turned seventeen years old two weeks ago, right?" Kyle asked, expecting the question. Why else would the busy colonel of a top-secret military organization fly to Denver for lunch? They had kept in touch via email since the tragedy at Kyle's grandmother's house where, at the age of twelve, he had witnessed her death at the Exalls' hands, his friends and father by his side.

"Son, we know everything. We're not concerned with your age."

"But I'm not even old enough to serve in the military."

The colonel smirked, his eyes never breaking from Kyle. "You remind me so much of her. She's still probably the only person who ever stormed into the Oval Office without giving a shit who sat behind the desk. You have that same kind of confidence—she was right about you." Griffins sipped lemonade through the straw pinched between his grinning lips. They were having lunch at D'Corazon, a Mexican restaurant in downtown Denver, the scattered remnants of chicken fajitas and cheesy enchiladas the only food remaining on the table. "For the record, the minimum age to join The Crew is sixteen. Kennedy believed if you're old enough to make life and death decisions behind the wheel of a car, then you're old enough to make those same decisions with our team."

"Death?" Kyle asked, the word slipping through his lips beyond his control. "I thought they don't come back for thirty years."

Colonel Griffins was gracious enough to leave all of Susan's belongings in her house following her passing. Protocol was to remove any trace of The Crew, but he swore Kyle to secrecy, and left all of Susan's textbooks, notes, and equipment behind. "Don't ever leave the house with any of this stuff," he warned. "You can have it all, but it stays within these walls until further notice."

Kyle thought back to this moment and wondered if Griffins had already known this current conversation would one day occur.

"Correct. The mass invasion comes around every thirty years. It's not precise—I've heard as early as twenty-five years and as late as forty years. It's more a window of time that we prepare for."

"Then why do I need to come now? Why not after I finish high school?"

Kyle had just entered his first serious relationship three months earlier and had no interest in leaving his new girlfriend, Jessica, behind to live on the other side of the country. He didn't have any romantic experience, but understood that long-distance was not the way to go.

"Your education continues at an even higher level. You'll have plenty of classroom time and will learn about theories that are often taught in Master's programs from Ivy League colleges."

That didn't sound fun at all. Kyle wanted a regular, senior year of high school: lunch with his friends, pep rallies and football games, spring baseball, and prom with his high school sweetheart. How was he supposed to do any of this if he was studying Exall transportation theory on Friday nights?

"I don't know, Colonel. I'm not ready to give up my life to do this. I'd rather finish high school here, then go join you guys. It can be like my college."

Griffins nodded. "I can appreciate that. We know you have a much higher maturity level for your age than your peers—and that's why I'm here. It's rare for someone your age to know what they want in life. If you really do have an interest in joining us at any point in your future, it's imperative you begin as soon as possible. The window of opportunity can close at any time. We're not always on the search for recruits, but right now we are."

Kyle pursed his lips as he looked over the glob of cheese on his plate. "I just don't think I can commit right this second. Can I have some time to think it over?"

"Of course. I was never expecting a decision from you today, although I was hoping you'd be so overwhelmed with excitement that you'd ride back on the jet with me this afternoon." Griffins let out a hoarse chuckle.

Well, that was never *happening,* Kyle thought, returning a nervous laugh.

"Take a week or two—let's say, June 14th, to let me know.

Talk things over with your parents—I've already filled them in on the situation. When you decide what you want, give me a call and let me know. We'll be waiting."

"I can do that."

The two leaned back in their chairs, finishing the food and sucking down the rest of their soft drinks.

"Tell me one thing," Colonel Griffins said, his smirk leaving his face. "Have you checked out that gift I gave you at the funeral?"

Kyle felt the blood leave his face. That was the one object he had never been told rules about using. It was given to him far outside of his grandmother's house—at Arlington National Cemetery—therefore, he kept it among his personal belongings. And yes, he looked at that damn thing every single day. It fascinated him, and he knew one of those red dots on the screen of the Exall Tracking Device belonged to his old friend, Brian.

Only it wasn't Brian any more, and Griffins had made it plenty clear that even if they were to capture him one day, there was no guarantee that their special medicine would return him back to his human form.

Kyle wanted to lie, and make it sound as if maybe he looked at the device every couple months or so, but the technology was too advanced. It likely registered on a private server at the Pentagon every time it was in use, and Griffins already knew the answer to the question.

"Yeah. I look at it a lot," Kyle finally said, as if ashamed to admit to a guilty addiction.

"Mind-blowing stuff, isn't it?"

"It is. Sometimes I open it at night and stare out my window, wondering what they're all doing out there. It makes me feel so small."

"We are merely specks of dust in this universe. We have no idea how many of them are out there. Some of our scholars argue that there are millions, while others insist it's only the ones who come around every thirty years."

"What do you believe?"

"Me? I don't know as many facts like our historians, but I believe they inhabit a planet lightyears away. Billions of them just like us, living their lives and working for the weekend. They clearly have technology beyond our understanding, and we just want to study them, learn from them. Anyway, I should get going. Did you have any last questions for me before I head back?"

"I don't, but... thanks for coming out. I'll let you know what I decide after I think it over some more."

"Please do. Take your time, and if you do have any questions, you know how to get ahold of me."

Griffins stood, his joints popping. Kyle couldn't recall ever seeing Griffins outside of his solid green uniform, but today he wore a flannel button-down tucked into jeans. "Have a good rest of your day, and say hello to your parents for me."

"I'll walk out with you," Kyle said, standing from the table. He followed the colonel as they weaved through the tables toward the exit.

It was a scorching summer day, highs expected in the mid-90s, and the rush of heat greeted them as they stepped outside.

"I'll tell you this much, Kyle," Griffins said. "Susan insisted you'd be ready and that we needed to do everything in order to get you to join the team." He raised his hand in the air as if taking an oath. "I swear on her grave. She wanted this life for you. Told me off the record that she believed you would be even better than her." Griffins stuck out his hand for Kyle to shake. "Call me."

Off he went, back to his private government jet to fly back to D.C., where life chasing Exalls continued every day.

Kyle felt sick to his stomach. Would his grandmother really have said those things? He thought back to the many summer days he spent at her house. She had kept a BB gun in the garage and liked to shoot at the squirrels threatening the wellbeing of her garden. When Kyle was six, she had set up empty Coke bottles along the top of the backyard fence, and asked him to shoot them.

Like any six-year-old, the gun was nearly as big as him, but she taught him the proper way to hold it, how to line up a shot, and how to ignore everything else in the world before pulling the trigger. By the time he was eight, Kyle could shoot at least nine out of ten bottles with ease, and in rapid succession.

He never thought anything of it, just going with the flow of what his grandmother asked him to do. If shooting bottles was her idea of fun, then that's what they did every day.

Was that all preparation for this? How could she know so early that I'd even have an interest in joining The Crew?

Kyle returned to his car and drove to his grandmother's house.

2

Chapter 2

Kyle walked into his grandmother's old house, now the residence of his father, Travis. His parents had finalized their divorce a few months after the tragedy four years ago, throwing Kyle's world into further chaos.

Kyle alternated nights between here and his mother's house two blocks down the street. His mother had dated a handful of men over the past couple of years, but nothing ever turned steady. Travis had dated no one—at least to Kyle's knowledge—but often disappeared to bars on Friday and Saturday nights.

The first few months of Travis living on his own had consisted of cheap microwaveable dinners and piles of pizza boxes. Kyle didn't mind, but it hurt to see his father living such a sloppy life. The phase passed, and Travis settled into a healthier lifestyle, actually learning to cook for the first time in his life.

Travis spoke to Kyle many nights about the secrets he had been sworn to since he was a child. Travis, his brother, and their father, had all played second fiddle to Susan's life as a high-ranking Crew member. Travis understood the lifestyle and had answers to many of the questions Kyle brought to the table. It was impossible for them to not discuss the Crew, as everywhere they looked in the house was a sign of Susan's past life. New hidden cameras were discovered in different corners, while secret compartments with hidden pistols were found in every room.

After a year had passed, Travis decided it was time to renovate the house and rid it of the old secrets buried within. Everything from the walls and flooring were ripped out and redone, modernized with new paint, furniture, and appliances. Susan had left him millions of dollars on top of an already generous life insurance policy from The Crew. Travis put the money aside for Kyle's future, and the rest into the renovations.

As Kyle pulled into the driveway on this particular hot summer day, the house looked nothing like the one he had watched his grandmother get slaughtered in. That was probably for the best. He parked under the tall oak tree that shaded the entire front yard, and climbed the front steps to enter.

Travis sat in the living room recliner, feet up with a cold beer in hand as he watched TV in front of a blasting fan.

"Hey, Ky, how was it?" he asked, getting up from the chair.

"It was fine. Colonel Griffins says hi."

"Come sit down and talk to me. I'm sure you have more to tell me."

Kyle dragged his feet into the living room and sat on the couch where Travis joined him.

"He wants me to join The Crew. Says grandma wanted me to, and that I'm ready."

"You don't sound excited about it."

"I am. But I don't wanna move across the country, away from you and Mom. I'm not ready for that."

"You know he came and spoke with us yesterday—your mom and I."

"He mentioned it. What did he say?"

"Well, as your parents, he needed our permission before even sitting down with you. He told us all about the program you'd be joining, and we couldn't deny how special of an opportunity it would be for you."

"Are you kidding me? You *want* me to drop out of school to learn how to kill aliens?"

"You wouldn't be dropping out of school. You'd be doing the opposite, in fact. Their education program is nothing like regular school – it's years more advanced. Even if one day you decide you don't want to continue with The Crew, you'll have such a strong background, you can do whatever you want in this world."

"That's a lie!" Kyle barked, now fully on the defensive. He wasn't expecting to come home to find his parents in agreement with the colonel. Surely they would have wanted him to stay home and finish what he had started at Larkwood High School. Instead, it was just him against the world. "It's a lifetime commitment—there's no getting out of it. *You* of all people know that."

Travis frowned. "That's true, yes, but that's not the point."

"It *is* the point. You're all asking me to make a decision that will dictate the rest of my life. I just wanna hang out with my friends and play baseball. I don't give a shit about any of this!"

His eyes welled with tears, but he wiped them away before they rolled down his face.

Travis cleared his throat before speaking in his most gentle voice. "Ky, no one is going to force you into this decision. It's yours to make. We're just making sure you understand the full perspective of both sides. You know your mother and I will support you in whatever you decide. One thing you need to realize, though, is that you already lost your innocent high school years when all of this drama happened.

"You were only twelve and got thrust into the middle of this mess. We've tried to keep your life as normal as possible, but we know it's unrealistic to think it doesn't eat away at you every day. I've seen you look at that machine. You have the same look in your eyes as my mom. Like there's something growing inside of you, and you need to let it out."

Kyle looked down to his twiddling thumbs. "I want to do it, I just don't want to do it *now*."

"I'm afraid that part of the decision isn't up to you."

"If they think so highly of me, why can't they take me on when I feel ready?"

"It doesn't work that way, Ky. This is the military, and it's directly overseen by the president. They have the strictest procedures in place for good reason. There were times your grandma had to go on trips to D.C. at the last second, and they kept her there for months. That's just the way of life in this group. They have to adhere by their rules to keep the public in the dark."

"Do you think they really know when we talk about it? The colonel said they always know."

"They know. You're always being watched. This is our government's biggest secret. Even if you decide to not join them, you still know about the secret. They're always listening. That's why you and your friends should never discuss it, pretend it never happened."

"We already do that. I think they *want* it to have never happened. It never comes up, but sometimes if a kid at school makes a joke about aliens, we all look at each other. It's a secret that lives between us and always will. We all miss Brian."

"I'm sure."

"I don't know what to do, Dad." Kyle slouched, his rage gone, giving way to anxiety.

"Take your time and sleep on it. The answer will come when you least expect it. It's a unique opportunity that people don't even dream of—because they don't even know it's real. You can always talk with me or your mom. Trust yourself to make the right decision. Why don't you go to your grandmother's room and reflect?"

They had moved all of Susan's belongings into the pantry in the basement. The same freezer that served as a secret passageway to the underground panic room remained in place, a gentle reminder of what they had all gone through on that fateful day. Kyle often went down there anyway, sifting through the boxes of her old Crew notes and files. He had educated himself on the Exalls and the workings of the Crew. The history was rich, and reading through those six-inch-thick textbooks always kindled a flame in his soul.

I actually do love this stuff, he thought. *I've never felt this way about anything.*

"I'll do that," he said. "I'll go down there right now. Thank you."

"Any time, son. I'll be here if you need me."

Kyle ran down the stairs to the old pantry, boxes and tubs piled to the ceiling. In the back corner, on top of the freezer, was the box he looked through most. It had Susan's personal journals, with her handwritten notes in sharp cursive. She had written in her journal on a weekly basis in the early 1970's, and he flipped one of the journals open to a passage he recalled skimming over in the past.

The entry was dated June 3, 1972.

I'm terrified. The training has been grueling. I feel like a truck ran me over. There's no end in sight, and I'm wondering if I made the wrong decision. I'll see it through the end, though – I can't quit in the middle of this program. The work is too important for the future of the world to ever stop. I've never had this much purpose in my life, or been so in demand. My life is taken care of. My future kids' lives are taken care of. Even my grandkids will be set. I suspect my doubts are personal. I miss my husband, as we only see each other for a few hours each week. They promised it will change when training ends, but I imagine I'll just have more work to do. Thankfully it's meaningful and gets me out of bed in the mornings. Next week I'll probably be laughing about all of this – my dream life is just a few days away. I know it will all work out for the best.

Kyle ran his fingers down the old, crisp pages, feeling his grandmother's presence in the ink. She had written this particular note before Travis had even been born. He didn't know her exact age, but she was definitely at a point in her life where making such a decision would have changed her entire future.

Deciding between a regular life and a set future as a Crew member seemed a no-brainer on the surface. He was just becoming observant of his parents' stress of balancing jobs and life, although much of that had vanished after the inheritance.

Kyle still planned on taking his time to think the decision over, but the choice appeared to be leaning in favor of acceptance. He just needed that final push to convince himself that it was okay to give up the rest of his teenage years to have a life like no one else.

3

Chapter 3

The sun set later that night, bringing a cool breeze over the eastern plains of Colorado. Dr. Hudson Klemens and his friend, Brian Carsner, had been hiding since destroying Brian's middle school in 2016 and killing all of those pesky preteens in the process.

"It's time," Dr. Klemens said, an evil grin spreading across his gray face, black teeth revealed under the moonlight. "Time to ride."

He howled, loving the solitude they possessed in the middle of nowhere. They had lived in a tent thirty miles north of Stratton, Colorado, no longer requiring food or sleep, just spending their days dreaming of the future.

They were glad to have found each other, undergoing their complete transformations together. They had to learn their new way of life, mold new abilities that made them feel like their heads might explode any second. If they stepped into a crowded area like a restaurant, the sounds of dozens of voices screamed within their heads.

It had happened to them on the first night they decided to go out after learning how to morph their bodies into their original human versions. They had driven down to Stratton for dinner at the only diner in town. For a town with a population of 600, a good five percent of that crammed into the small restaurant to chow down burgers and malts. When they stepped in, the voices hit them like a water balloon to the face and they immediately turned around and left.

"What the hell was that?" Dr. Klemens asked, rubbing his temples.

"You heard that, too? There weren't that many people to make that much noise, were there?" Brian replied, both hands grasping his head.

"No, of course not. That sound was coming from within. I could *feel* it in my head."

They headed back to their tent, fortunate to not *have* to eat thanks to their new Exall bodies. They didn't require food or air, but that didn't stop them from craving the old foods that they had grown fond of during their lives as humans.

It wasn't until they were visited by a fellow Exall—by complete surprise—later that week that they learned of the other gift they had inherited. The voices in their heads belonged to all of those people in the restaurant, and Brian had damn near shit his pants learning he had the ability to hear everyone's conversations. Their visiting friend, who opted to not share his name, gave them insight on how to manage the voices when stepping into a full room. It took many brain exercises to learn how to compartmentalize their minds, creating a filter of sorts that pushed the voices aside, yet still allow them to zone in on specific conversations.

The Exall, who insisted his name wasn't important, assured them more knowledge awaited, but would come in due time.

"You just need to stay under the radar for now," he told them. "The humans have ways of tracking us, and they definitely know about those of us who remain on this planet in between our Explorations. For some reason, they leave us alone. I've wandered this planet for more than 200 years and have never been bothered. But once the others land, they decide it's time to break into war. I'll never understand the aggression."

Brian reminded the doctor of this particular encounter, stressing the need to not make any moves until they received word to do so.

"You can sit here if you want, Brian. But I'm not gonna wait around for thirty years until they decide they want to have some fun. Besides, did you miss the part when he told us they want to plan bigger things for those of us on Earth? We know this world, it's ours. I take that as an invite to do whatever we want. I don't know about you, but I've never felt so strong. So *pure*. I feel like I drank 100 gallons of adrenaline—and I feel that way all the time. Don't you want to go fuck shit up?"

"I feel it too, but I don't want to disobey him. We don't know if they're watching us, or what they'll do if they catch us."

"That's very cute of you. I guess I can't be surprised – what are you, ten years old?" The doctor threw his head back and howled again. "When you shot that old lady, you made your choice. You're in this whether you like it or not. And I know you feel what I feel. Don't you love not ever having to sleep or eat? What a waste of time those things were."

"Sure, but we don't do anything with our time."

"Aha!" The doctor raised a finger in the air. "And that's why I'm ready to head out and spread our good news."

"Good news?"

The doctor's grin returned. "We need to let the world know

that the Exalls are here and we're not going to play nice."

"You're going to get us killed. You know they have special bullets to kill us? Did you not read any of the information he left for us?"

"Why would I read anything when I feel like God? Brian, we can turn ourselves into our human selves and walk around like nothing ever happened. You could go home and raise all kinds of hell just by walking down the street. People will think they're seeing a ghost! I can read and control people's minds. Why the fuck do I need to read that giant folder he left us?"

Brian shook his head. "You know, I thought you were the adult among us, but I wonder sometimes. You're stupid like a teenager. You act like I should, not like an educated doctor."

"Get off your high horse and have some fun, kid. You think I *liked* being a doctor? Giving sixteen or more hours out of my day just to save people's lives? It killed me from the inside out. I was a walking zombie. And now . . . I'm a zombie who can't be killed."

"WE CAN BE KILLED!" Brian snapped. "Stop thinking we're invincible. They will hunt us down and kill us."

"You can live here in fear. But I'm going out into the world." Dr. Klemens jumped up from the small lawn chair outside of their tent. "I suggest you come with me, and channel that beast living inside of you. There's no need to hold back. That Exall told us they want to increase our population, so let's go make it happen."

The doctor lunged into the tent and returned with the car keys in hand. They had stolen a pickup truck in Denver shortly after the attacks in Larkwood, and parked it in the field. They were a good five miles away from the nearest road where no one could ever find them. The closest ranch was ten miles away as they nestled into an area of land deserted of vegetation, animals, or people.

"We're going tonight. Let's just head into town, see what kind of action we can find, and have some fun. Think of all the possibilities we have now with our abilities."

Brian chased him to the truck. He had no intent on staying overnight by himself. Even though he trusted his body's new capabilities, his mind still belonged to that of the 16-year-old boy who had been jerked out his life at the age of twelve, and used like a remote-controlled robot to kill his best friend's grandmother. Somewhere back in Larkwood his friends continued on with their lives, scarred by the tragedy, but living as humans. They would all be on summer break between their junior and senior years, probably playing baseball all summer, dating girls, and making out with them in the backseat of their cars. He often looked up to the stars, knowing that in some alternate universe where none of this happened, his life carried on with them as well.

"Let's go!" the doctor shouted, firing up the engine of their Ford pickup. Brian climbed in and strapped his seat belt over his chest by habit. They no longer felt pain. They could get in a car accident, fly through the windshield, and not feel a thing. Just stand up and walk away like they had tripped on their shoelaces. He understood why the doctor felt the urge to live a carefree life now that they had been liberated from everything that made being a human so painful, but he still feared what the humans could do.

He had escaped from Susan's house that day just in time. Had he hung around any longer, The Crew would have captured and killed him. Lights out for Brian, ladies and gentlemen.

But it hadn't happened in their four years hiding out. As

much as he didn't want to admit it, the doctor was right. They were likely safe from any attacks. Even in the middle of nowhere, they had been left alone. Killing the two of them would be easy—no one in the general public would ever know. Their remote location could have worked against them, but the only person—or thing—to visit them was the other Exall.

The doctor drove out of the field, screaming, "We're going to tear this town to fucking pieces! LET'S GO!"

Dr. Klemens had many moments that reminded Brian of a person with Turrets Syndrome, especially when he drove, all fear dissipated, pedal to the ground as they sped down the country roads at 120 miles per hour.

This night was no different as they skidded onto the main road, the quiet town waiting a short fifteen-minute drive away.

$$4$$

Chapter 4

Every Wednesday night locals packed the Eagle's Landing Sports Bar and Grill in Stratton. The bar offered their best drink specials on this day: two-for-one shots, three dollar beers, four dollar well drinks. Most people stopped by for a quick drink after work before returning home to their families, but there were always a dozen or so who stayed all night to take full advantage and obliterate their minds.

This group grew close over time, to the point they expected to see each other every week for this ritual. They all sat around the bar, leaving the dining room open for anyone who wasn't part of this alcoholic cult to sit and not disturb their good time.

A handsome man, probably in his early forties, walked in with a tall, skinny teenage boy. The bell above the door chimed, causing everyone at the bar to look over their shoulders and see who was barely arriving at 10 P.M.

John Chambers, the owner of Eagle's Landing, came out from behind the bar to greet his guests. "Evenin', folks. Were you looking for a late dinner?" John, who would turn sixty later in the year, looked the pair up and down, moving a toothpick from side to side below his thick, black mustache. Most of the locals dressed like John: jeans, button-up shirt, boots, and a cowboy hat. These two men were clearly from out of town in their athletic pants and t-shirts. Likely some uppity father and son from Denver, passing through on a road trip to some other big city like St. Louis or Dallas.

"Good evening, sir," the presumed father said. "Yes, my son and I are looking for a quick bite. We saw your neon lights from the highway and thought we'd give it a look-see. It's been a long day."

"Where you folks coming from?" John asked, laying out a couple of menus on a table.

"We were visiting some family in Nebraska, headed back to Denver tonight."

"I see. Well, our kitchen is still open for another hour, so please take a look and give me a shout when you know what you want. Can I get you a drink from the bar, sir?"

"I'd love one. Pour me your finest scotch."

"And for you, young man?" John turned his attention to the teenage boy.

"Coke is fine, thank you."

The boy seemed to not want to be there. Perhaps he was just tired – sitting in a car for hours did no good to young people who had so much energy to expel on a daily basis.

"Very good. I'll be right back with those drinks for you gentlemen."

John returned to the bar to top off everyone's drinks and pour the fresh ones.

The father and son sat at their table, the boy glancing suspiciously around the room.

"Why are we doing this?" the boy whispered to his pretend

father. "These people are just minding their business. Leave them alone."

"We're doing our job, expanding our brand. Don't you want there to be others like you and me? Or do you want just the two of us forever? Because that's what I think *their* plans are for us."

"You know where we are. These people probably have guns."

"Let them shoot us – nothing happens! You worry too much, *son*." The father cackled as he slapped the top of the table, getting the attention of everyone at the bar for a brief moment.

John returned with their drinks. "Did you gentlemen decide on something to eat?"

"Yes, sir," the father said. "We just want a couple orders of burgers and fries. Put all the good stuff on it. Also, is that a real jukebox over there?" He nodded to the far corner of the room where an obvious jukebox stood, its lights flashing and tempting the man to come over.

"Sure is. Do you need any change?"

"I have some. We don't see too many of those in Denver, and the ones we do have are all electronic. You still have a classic one with actual records. I'm impressed."

"Yeah, they don't make 'em like her anymore. She's from 1968 and has all the classics. Still runs like she's brand new, too."

"I'll definitely give it a look," the father said, grinning, winking across the table.

"Perfect, I'll get those burgers started right away."

John left them, and the father leaned in toward the boy. "What do you say we have a little fun before the party starts?"

He stood from the table, chair screeching against the floor, and skipped across the room to the jukebox. He didn't give a shit about the music inside; he only wanted to see how loud the machine would go. Currently, a TV behind the bar blared Fox News as the only noise in the building.

He placed his hands over the glass case, telepathically flipping through the books of records until he landed on Frank Sinatra's "Luck Be A Lady", and started the machine. Sinatra crooned the opening line, and he cranked the volume dial as far right as it would go. When the trumpets started blaring, the song boomed through the bar, getting the attention of every single person who had swiveled around to see the strange man swaying side to side in front of the jukebox.

"Hey, buddy!" one of the patrons yelled. "Some of us are trying to have a conversation over here."

The man at the jukebox looked to the bar, but couldn't hear a thing they were yelling at him. The music drowned out every other sound in the world. Out of the corner of his eye, he watched as the boy stood from the table and ran to the opposite side of the room toward the bathroom door. The father cupped a hand behind his ear, craning his neck as if trying to hear the screaming patrons.

John burst out of the kitchen, his hands in the air, shouting, "Shut it off! Shut it off!"

The man grinned, showing pearly white teeth, shaking his head. He turned back to the jukebox, placed his hands on the glass, and raised the volume to the level of an outdoor concert. Silverware vibrated on the tables, and one of the neon beer lights hanging on the wall fell to the ground with a crash that would never be heard.

"What the fuck are you doing?" John screamed, his words falling on no one's ears. He crossed the bar and was making his way to the jukebox.

The father pivoted to see John's hands balled into fists, charging for him. A fat man from the bar had jumped out of his seat and trailed behind John. "What the fuck is your problem?" someone shouted, and although the actual words were lost behind Sinatra's singing, the father could hear them in his head.

John lunged at the man with his fist leading the way, swinging and missing, sending him flailing off balance into the jukebox. His fingers fumbled across the dials, but caused no changes to the volume.

The fat man jumped forward, arms extended in front of him like a drunken bear. The father lowered his shoulder and rammed it into the fat man's belly, pushing him back. One thing he had recently learned was how to rally together all of the strength in his body and focus it on one target; in this instance, placing the bullseye on the fat man's gut. It felt like hitting a trash bag full of water balloons, his shoulder sinking into the man's stomach, pushing the years of food and alcohol out of place as he flew backward like he had been tasered.

John regained his balance and continued to fiddle with the knobs on the jukebox. The father grabbed him from behind, one hand pulling his head back, and thrust his skull through the machine's glass. The shatter was faint, but satisfying. The blood that immediately trickled from John's crown and sprayed all over the records was even better. Sinatra held a long note, his angelic voice now the soundtrack to this horrific scene unfolding.

"I don't fucking think so!" a woman from the bar yelled, hopping off her barstool and reaching behind her back, pulling out a pistol. "Get the hell out of here!"

The boy burst out of the corner like a ninja in hiding, growling as he leaped toward the woman, his mouth snarled like a rabid dog. He was on her within a second, chomping on the woman's arm like a rack of ribs.

"Would you like some barbecue sauce with that, son?" the father shouted, only for himself to hear. He fell back against John's body, head still stuck in the machine like an ostrich with its head in the ground, and howled manic laughter.

The woman's pistol fell out of her grip and dropped to the ground with a heavy thud. Blood squirted from her arm, creating a red abstract splatter painting on the walls.

The song faded to silence, leaving the only sounds to be the TV and the woman screaming on the ground, squeezing her arm with her free hand, shouting, "Help me, Jesus Christ, it *fucking hurts!*"

Nine other people sat at the bar, seven men and two women, gawking at the woman on the ground.

"Rebecca!" one of the women shouted. "Rebecca, hang on!" She whipped out her cell phone so fast it flew across the bar, sliding across the floor and out of sight under one of the booths.

"Think you city boys are tough?!" a voice growled from behind the bar. A man, who reminded the boy of Vin Diesel due to his bald head and bulky frame, stood in the doorway that connected to the kitchen, a greasy apron draped over his monstrous body, a double-barrel shotgun clutched in his grip, pointed directly at the father's face.

"Oh no, please don't shoot me," he mocked, giggling like a little girl. "Please don't—"

The shotgun burst out its two rounds, the sound ricocheting off the walls and causing everyone at the bar to throw their hands over their ears in reflex.

The slugs caught the father directly in the throat, and he

reached into the hole with a wide smile. A stream of black liquid oozed before his hand waved over the hole, new skin filling the open space, patching up like it had never happened.

"I don't like being shot," he said, his voice completely unaffected by the blast. "You're all mine. The doors are locked, your tires are flat. No one is leaving here until I'm done with you all. Brian! Where did you go?"

The boy had vanished after biting Rebecca like a crazed zombie. He stood up from behind the bar, causing the large cook to jump back in fear, knocking a couple bottles of alcohol off the shelves.

The father grinned. "You people can call me Dr. Klemens; we're going to be the best of friends. We can do this the easy way, or the hard way – just let me know. If you don't want to end up like this poor lady over here, I suggest you remain seated and wait for me and my 'son' to come around. You can thank me later."

5

Chapter 5

"We have a situation, people, and it's not good."

Colonel Griffins spoke to a crowded conference room at the Pentagon, six levels underground where two dozen Crew members listened to the information about the attacks in eastern Colorado. He turned on the projector to show images of the crime scene.

"The local police are trying to piece all of this together. There are no witnesses, and the one camera in the bar had been wiped clean. They don't know what to think, but we do. We've seen this before. Investigators concluded there were at least ten people—that's how many spots were occupied at the bar. Not one person remains. This was apparently a weekly routine, many regulars there for happy hour. Local authorities are contacting the families of those they believe were there, but we haven't heard anything back yet. When this many people just disappear after a bloody scene, I think we all know what that means."

"Has anyone checked the highway cameras to see?" a man asked from the back.

"Yes. There's nothing. We suspect whoever carried out this attack was living close by and still does. Although there are many side roads in this rural part of the state, so they could have realistically escaped in any direction."

"If it's what we think, did nobody see the ETD's going berserk last night? That many new Exalls in one location would have surely set off some alarms."

"Nothing hit our radar. We rewound the footage and found nothing out of the ordinary."

"So then why do we think this is an Exall attack?" a woman asked, an accusatory undertone in her voice.

"Because the victims are nowhere to be seen. We've seen this play out before and—"

"If we have no proof, I don't think we can call this an attack by the Exalls." That voice belonged to Damien Kurtz, and made Griffins's blood boil. The two had knocked heads over just about any topic that arose within the Crew, going back the last ten years. Kurtz was the head of technical research, his group studying the advances of the Exall species. "But I may have some proof of a different possibility," he said with a teasing grin.

Always trying to one-up me, Griffins thought, his fists subconsciously clenched.

"And that is?" Griffins asked, all eyes in the room turning to Kurtz at the middle of the table.

"We may have discovered that our friends have found a way to go undetected on our ETD's."

He spoke the words slowly and let them hang in the air. This was their biggest fear, a disturbing possibility that no one ever spoke out loud due to fear of it coming true.

"Major Kurtz, I don't think this is the time or place to bring this matter up," Griffins said.

"With all due respect, Colonel, I think it is. We have the heads of every department here and a crisis that we cannot yet say with confidence happened due to a breakdown in our technology."

The others around the table whispered to each other in shock.

"Very well. Please share what you have learned."

Kurtz stood, brushing his salt and pepper hair with stubby fingers before adjusting his glasses. "Our suspicion arose two months ago. We started to see a decrease in the Exall population all around the world. I reached out to some of our international department heads to check that it wasn't just faulty information on our side, but they confirmed to see the same thing."

"And you didn't think this information should be shared?" Griffins asked, his arms now crossed as he leaned against the wall at the front of the room.

"We didn't want to jump to any conclusions. And it's not as if there was an increase in the Exall population. We showed it going *down*. We did let the intelligence department know of the trend, and they have also been looking into the matter."

"Grady?" Griffins asked.

A young African-American man sitting across the table from Kurtz stood up. "Yes, sir, we have been looking into it and have not found any evidence of Exalls leaving Earth. It practically confirms that they have fallen off our radar, but further missions are being carried out to verify this."

"Why was I not informed?" Griffins asked. "Actually, never mind that right now. What are we doing about this?"

"Our technology team is examining our coding to make sure we haven't missed anything," Brandon Grady continued.

"Remember, Jonathon Browne had screwed with all the coding in our system years ago. We did our best to patch things back together, but every now and then we find something that is still off."

A woman stood up next to Grady. This was Felicia Lewis, head of the Crew's technology department that overlooked the Exall Tracking Devices. "Colonel, we have been hard at work as Major Kurtz mentioned. I have a crew working twelve-hour shifts, seven days a week, combing through our coding. It's the equivalent of an 8,000-page textbook, and we can only have the same team working on it to avoid any confusion. It's a slow process, and we should be wrapping up in another month."

"Jesus Christ, people. We can't have any more secrets, especially if this attack is real. Are we clear?"

Everyone nodded around the table.

"Lewis, if this is indeed confirmed, is there a plan in place to fix it, or are we out of luck?"

"I already have a different team looking into this, just in case. It may be early, but I believe it's true they have found a way to avoid our radar. Some of them, that is. Intelligence hasn't reported a decrease in population in a couple weeks now, but that doesn't mean it won't continue at some point. The Exalls may just be learning this and are trying to find a way to implement it across their population. Our preliminary theory is that they have found a way to elevate their internal temperatures. We don't think they've interfered with our technology, and instead have once again improved themselves to circumvent our capabilities."

"Grady, did we ever track those two from the 2016 attacks in Colorado?"

"No, sir. We believe they were part of the population who

fell off the radar."

Griffins sat down at the head of the table and crossed his hands, staring at his thumbs. Sure, he was frustrated, but he had the best minds in the world working on this issue, and so far, there was nothing too far out of the ordinary. Exalls came and went all the time, and there had been a handful of coding issues since the incident with Jonathon Browne. But something about this entire situation in Stratton felt off, especially once combined with this new information.

"I've been following the Susan Wells disappearance very closely since it happened," Griffins said. "I think there is something bigger at play. They took her, people. They took her right from us, and I've always believed they did it to study us. Never anything malicious. I saw the video – they took great care of her body, like it was a fragile piece of china. They wanted to study us, and now they have. Here we are, four years later, and they're back with their newfound knowledge."

"Colonel, we've looked into that incident from every angle. There's nothing left to study."

"You didn't know Wells like I did. I worked by her side for more than thirty years. Half of you in this room are barely thirty years old, so don't tell me this nonsense. She had more information in her brain about the Exalls than anyone who ever existed. She should have been in my position, but she refused it, wanting to stay in Denver with her family and protect them. Which is why I think there is something about the Wells boy. She went out of her way to protect him, more than even her own son."

"Are we going to get him under our protection?" Grady asked.

"Protection? He's going to be part of our team. He'll

probably be in this conference room in the next five years if he decides to join us, which I think he will. I promised his parents the world if they helped nudge him our way, and I also warned them the danger he would be in if he stays on his normal life track. All the Exalls would have to do is wait until Wells gets drunk for the first time at some high school party, and they'll easily take him away. We have eyes on his family's houses and school, but we can't follow him everywhere he goes."

"If this is true," Grady said. "We need to get him. We can use him as bait."

"I've already thought about it, and yes we can. But I'm not going to do that without telling him. I'd never send a Crew member into danger without him understanding the risks. I'd never sleep again if something went wrong. But yes, we can lay a perfect trap to capture some of these bastards, and just maybe get one of them alive. That's actually what Wells was working on before they took her. I told her she didn't have the proper team to execute it, but she insisted on trying to ambush them. Now we'll be ready next time, and no one will go missing."

6

Chapter 6

June 14th arrived and Kyle lay in bed on Sunday morning in his mom's house. Colonel Griffins had sent him an e-mail confirming Sunday as the deadline for a decision. His mind had been made up since last Monday, but he wanted to wait until the deadline before finalizing anything, in case he realized a reason to stay.

After plenty of reflection, Kyle decided his life in Larkwood was over for the time being. His grandmother was gone, Brian was still missing, his relationship with Jessica was too new, and his parents were well into their new lives as single people.

Kyle had met with psychiatrists following the drama at his grandmother's house, mental health services provided courtesy of The Crew. Some people, they said, had a spontaneous combustion of the mind after learning about the Exalls and witnessing their wrath up close. Aside from a bout of heavy grief following Susan's death, they deemed Kyle perfectly fine. Too fine, in fact. They questioned his parents, wondering if Kyle had shown any signs of post-traumatic stress or paranoia at home, but they had nothing different to report.

Thinking back to that time, Kyle wondered if that was when The Crew had decided he'd make a good fit to join them. Colonel Griffins had stayed in touch, checking in with him every few months, bringing small talk of how school was going and the patterns of Colorado weather. It always struck Kyle as strange for him to reach out, but it all made sense now. This plan had been four years in the making.

Kyle sent a text message to Travis, asking him to come over to his mom's house. His dad responded that he'd be over in five minutes. His parents had fortunately remained cordial in front of Kyle, especially over the last week while he debated this life-changing decision.

He rolled out of bed and got dressed. It was almost ten o'clock, but he'd been awake since six after a long night of tossing and turning, terrified of what the future held. He had so many questions about life as a Crew member, but none whose answer would change his mind. Would there be other kids his age there, or would he be the youngest by far? Even if there were only older people, had any of them gone through the same experience in leaving their teenage years behind to pursue this new life? Would they mentor him, or was he expected to learn things on his own? Just how grueling was the training program? His grandmother made it sound out of this world in her journal, but that had also been over forty years ago. Surely the program had undergone changes since then. And what was he supposed to tell his friends? And Jessica? His closest friends, Mikey and Jimmy, at least knew about The Crew, while Jessica had been left completely in the dark.

There wasn't an explanation for a student to leave before his senior year, moving across the country without his parents. He couldn't even lie and say he was joining the military because everyone knew the minimum age for that was eighteen. *Except for The Crew.*

He also wanted to know how much free time he'd have, and where he'd live. He understood this new life required an unwavering dedication, where The Crew's needs came before his own, but surely they had to let people out into the real world to blow off some steam.

A knock on the front door broke him out of his thoughts.

"Mom!" Kyle called from his room, his mother's room only two doors down the hallway. "Dad's here. I need to talk to you both."

"Be right out," Lori called back, so Kyle rushed down the hallway into the living room and pulled the door open for his father.

"Good morning, Ky," he greeted, stepping in and examining the house for any changes that had been made since he was last inside. The previous meetings with the three of them had either been at Travis's house or at public locations.

"Morning," Kyle said. "Let's sit down, please."

Kyle's mom came from her bedroom, dressed and ready for the day with her makeup and hair ritual complete.

"Hello," she said, joining them at the kitchen table. "So, have you made your decision?"

It was no secret what this discussion was about; they also knew about the Sunday deadline.

"I have," Kyle said, his voice trembling, and his stomach churning into tight knots. "I'm going."

He said those two words, leaving a long pause, expecting his mother to cry. But she never did. She only stared at him blankly while Travis nodded quietly to himself.

"Are you going to say anything?" Kyle asked.

Travis and Lori locked eyes for a brief moment before Travis spoke first. "We kind of thought you might go—can't say we're surprised."

Kyle looked to his mother, her eyes now welling with tears. "We saw all the signs, Ky," she said. "It's like this life was... made for you. They're going to take care of you. They assured us that we can come visit, and that one day you'll be relocated back here. They still haven't filled your grandmother's spot because they expect you to take it over."

"From the day you were born," Travis said. "Grandma always told me you were special. She had that sort of ability, you know, to read people's souls. It's like she put her hands on you and saw your entire future play out in her head. 'He's the one,' she told me. And I knew what she meant."

"What do you mean by *special*? I'm just a regular kid." Kyle shifted in his seat, uncomfortable knowing his parents had kept a secret hidden from him all this time.

"These people in Washington claim there are people in this world who are destined for this sort of life. They have a sort of sixth sense, I guess you could say. A level of awareness that goes beyond what your eyes can see. And these people can supposedly sense it in each other. That's how your grandmother knew way before you could even speak a word."

"Awareness? I don't know what you're talking about."

"Hey, neither do I, but they will be able to help you figure it out."

"Did you know about this, Mom?"

Lori nodded. "I tried to pretend that I never knew about it. I heard the stories of some of the situations your grandmother went through, and I told myself I'd never let you get into that sort of danger. But, here we are."

"If you were to stay, you'd be wasting your life," Travis said, lowering his head. "You see, The Crew always has its eyes open for people to recruit. Once you start excelling in life is when they come knocking."

"But I'm only a B student. I've never been an overachiever."

"It's not about grades. Grades have nothing to do with how smart you are – they're about discipline in school and playing the game right. You write essays in an hour that take some of your classmates three nights to complete—and it's still B-quality work."

"You're not challenged enough," his mom added. She then broke down, burying her face into her hands and sobbing.

Travis gestured for Kyle to do something since he no longer could. Kyle stood up and embraced his mother. "I'm going to be okay, Mom. I promise."

"I know," she cried. "I'm supposed to have you for eighteen years, though. I'm not ready to have a few months taken away."

"You're going to do great, Ky," Travis said, tears forming in his eyes.

Kyle waited a moment for his parents to gather themselves before asking, "So what do I do now?"

"Call Colonel Griffins. He'll have your travel arrangements ready for you," Travis said. "You're leaving tomorrow."

Kyle leaned back and pursed his lips, the weight of the world suddenly squeezing his skull.

7

Chapter 7

The next twenty-four hours passed in a blur for Kyle. His parents had arranged a farewell dinner for Kyle and his two best friends that same night. He insisted they not invite his girlfriend, Jessica, who he planned to deliver the news to in person.

His parents and friends agreed to publicly share the lie that Kyle was moving to the east coast to enter military school, not out of disciplinary reasons as many people assumed, but because he wanted to join the armed forces on the day he turned eighteen.

The dinner with Mikey and Jimmy was full of laughs and memories. Not once did the topic of Exalls or their near-death experience at the extraterrestrials' hands come up, which provided much-needed relief for Kyle to take his mind off his pending future. Dinner was followed by a short drive across town to breakup with Jessica at nine o'clock. She had questioned why he wanted to come over so late on a school night, her cranky father surely berating her with questions of his own. But Kyle assured it was too urgent to wait until the morning. While they both shed tears after a thirty-minute chat on her front porch, they hugged and went off on their separate ways. Kyle returned home needing to pack his bags, emotionally stunned and empty.

Colonel Griffins nearly jumped through the phone to thank Kyle for joining, promising it would be a decision he'd never regret. He sent an email while they were still on the phone with Kyle's travel arrangements for the following day.

When he finished packing at one in the morning—with the help of his mother, who refused to spend a second away from him—Kyle looked around his bedroom, memories of his childhood screaming out, and cried himself to sleep. He didn't know the first thing about living on his own. His cooking skills consisted of Kraft macaroni. Sometimes cereal.

Was he expected to find a place to live on his own after the training program? How much were they going to pay him? All they ever told him was to not worry, that everything would be covered, but what the hell did that actually mean? The stress weighed down as he slept, causing him to wake up at least once an hour with a new worry he hadn't considered before.

When the sun broke through his blinds at 6:30, his eyes felt puffy, and his brain itched with exhaustion.

I'm in no shape to start a new life today, he thought. His parents had a final breakfast planned for just the three of them before they'd drive him to the airport for his flight at noon. Everything had moved so quickly that he wondered if he'd ever have a moment to process what was happening. When he rolled his suitcase out of his childhood home, a tinge of despair ran through his body as he wondered if he'd ever return. There were no guarantees when dealing with Exalls—he'd learned that much from reading his grandmother's journals.

Life was now a movie running on fast forward, Kyle merely watching from the audience. Never had a two-hour breakfast passed in a matter of ten minutes. Destiny was tugging him to the next chapter of life, no matter how hard he dug his feet into the ground to try and prevent it.

"It's about that time," Travis said, checking his watch at quarter to ten. Kyle's mom clenched her lips together as she fought off fresh tears.

Kyle's body numbed as he felt himself going through the motions. Just a couple months ago he was a regular kid attending Larkwood High, giddy to have just received his driver's license. Today he was boarding a plane to the nation's capital with no idea when he'd return.

His parents joined him all the way up to the security checkpoint where they gave their final goodbyes. His mother sobbed uncontrollably, while Travis gave a bearlike hug. As Kyle passed through security and looked over his shoulder, he caught sight of his dad embracing his mom, an image he thought he'd never see again. His leaving clearly took a toll on both of them too large to individually handle. They'd probably return home and resume their separate lives, but for this one moment it was heartbreakingly beautiful, and Kyle was grateful to have the image to keep in his heart.

It left a wide grin on his face, even two hours later when he boarded the plane, and he trusted that everything was going to be alright.

* * *

Kyle slept heavily on the flight, his body demanding it catch up from the last week of shoddy sleep. He was snoring before they even took off, and didn't wake up until the wheels touched ground, jerking the entire plane awake. Between the flight and the time change, it was already six in the evening when they arrived at Dulles International Airport.

Colonel Griffins was to personally pick him up and escort him back to his new living quarters at the Pentagon, only he never mentioned it was going to be in such style.

Kyle found the colonel waiting for him in the pickup area outside of baggage claim, standing in front of a shiny black town car, waving him over.

"Welcome to Washington!" Griffins greeted, his hand stuck out firmly for Kyle to shake.

"Thank you, sir. I can't believe I'm already here."

"Well, we can, and we're so excited to have you on board. Are you hungry for some dinner?"

"Sure am."

"Let's pick up some food on the way, and I'll see you get settled into your dormitory."

"Sounds good."

Kyle had gone on a few family vacations, but had never traveled alone. Being responsible for himself in a new city provided an unexpected boost of energy. No one here knew him with the exception of the colonel, but even Griffins didn't *know* him on a personal level. All the toxins of home—his parents' divorce and his grandmother's death, mainly—were in the rear-view mirror. Now he had an open road to the future, and for the first time after all of his skepticism, he realized he was free from his parents. Not that they were strict to begin with, but he no longer had to check-in regarding his whereabouts.

The Crew must have truly thought highly of him to trust a 17-year-old boy to live on his own in a brand new city.

"Tonight will be low-key," Griffins said as they settled into the backseat. The front seat hid behind a thick black screen, where only the silhouette of a driver's head could be made out. "I'll show you around the Pentagon – well, our areas of it. Then you can get your room set up as much as you'd like, or go to sleep—I'm sure you're exhausted. Tomorrow I'll give you a tour of the city so you can get familiar with it, and Wednesday we'll jump right into the training program."

"Do I have a roommate?" Kyle asked.

"A roommate? Of course not. We don't expect you to share your living space with anyone. We want you as comfortable as possible. You'll see that when we get to the Pentagon. We reside many levels underground. Even have fake outdoor areas, in case you need a quick break in the sunlight. You're going to live inside, but we have everything you can imagine. It's literally an entire underground city."

"I see."

The thought of living underground bothered him, but he'd hold his final judgment until he saw the living spaces for himself.

"Just to give you an idea of what the next week will look like, Wednesday is the start of your training. We open with a raw skills test. We'll give you basic tasks to complete, both mental and physical, without any training, just to see where you stand. Don't feel pressured to achieve some sort of success. Just do your best. It's strictly for us to formulate your training program for the following weeks. Thursday through Saturday will be actual training. Lots of classroom time to take you through the history of The Crew and the Exalls, and how we're all interconnected. It sounds boring, but really is fascinating stuff."

"I don't doubt it."

"Sunday is always an off day, so you're free to do as you please. Just let us know if there's anything in particular you'd like to do in town and we can arrange it."

"Anything?"

"Yes. If you need a ride, tickets to an event, reservations at a restaurant, just let us know at least two hours in advance and we'll get it taken care of. You'll meet our concierge team—they're the best."

Kyle gazed out the window as they passed Arlington National Cemetery, and chills broke out on his back as he remembered that's where his grandmother's gravestone stood, even though her body roamed somewhere in space.

"Can I ask you something, Colonel?"

"Of course."

"Were those attacks in Colorado done by . . . them? I saw the story on the news, and I couldn't help but wonder."

Griffins stared at Kyle, first in amazement, but then in acceptance that he was now part of the team. "We are looking into it. We haven't found any evidence yet that it was an Exall attack, but we can't rule it out, either—it definitely has the characteristics of one."

"And that would throw everything off that we already know, right? Since they're only supposed to attack every thirty years."

"You sure do know a lot already."

"My grandma took very detailed notes on just about everything. Every week in her journal was like a new discovery, even up to her final days."

"I see. You're right, though – if the attack is confirmed as Exalls, we have a big problem on our hands. We're already preparing for that possibility, but I pray every day it's not true."

"Would I already have to go into battle?"

"Not until you're fully trained."

Kyle wanted to ask how long it would be until the training program was completed, but decided he didn't want to know. Having a defined countdown would send his mind into a frenzy that he couldn't afford. He kept his gaze out the window, letting the conversation with Griffins fade away, and he remembered what his father told him about having an ability to sense things.

When he had watched the news about the bar attack in Stratton, the thought of Brian throbbed in his mind, nearly taking over his body. Every time he blinked he saw flashes of his old friend. And now again, just talking about the attacks created similar mental flashes. Brian grinning. Brian laughing. Brian staring into Kyle's soul, promising to come find him.

8

Chapter 8

They pulled into the Pentagon's parking garage, and that's when reality slapped Kyle across the face. This was his home now, the place where his future would mold his legacy. He felt his grandmother's presence, knowing she had spent a lifetime in this same building, carving out a legacy of her own.

The car entered the garage, cutting off the outside world as orange lighting splashed along the walls to guide the way. They drove down one level, then another. Four levels down they approached an armed gate with a giant stop sign and a booth with a solider holding an M5 rifle. The soldier nodded and pushed a button to raise the gate, and down they went to the sixth and final level.

"This is so cool," Kyle uttered, staring out his window. It had been nothing but a typical garage, but he noticed the cameras lining the walls, not even trying to hide. Guards stood in every corner, guns cocked and ready.

The car stopped at steel double doors where two soldiers stood watch. They immediately raised their hands in a salute when Colonel Griffins stepped out of the car.

"Good evening, gentlemen," he greeted them as they parted ways to clear a path. "Follow me, Kyle."

Kyle had hesitated, momentarily terrified of the two soldiers who may or may not have known who he was. He was with the colonel, though, so had nothing to worry about.

Colonel Griffins pulled open the door and led them into a lobby and whole new world. The dungeon-like feel of the garage gave way to a pristine office setting, glass walls, crystal chandeliers, and TV monitors behind an oak reception desk.

"Good evening, Colonel," greeted another soldier who appeared just as intimidating as the two standing outside. "Is this Mr. Wells?"

"It sure is. Kyle, this is Jack. He splits the duty of manning our front desk with Rachel McDowell. You'll meet her another time I'm sure, but these two will always be here if you need anything. They are our concierge team I had told you about."

"Jack Bridges. We have all the fun around here," Jack said, reaching over his desk to shake Kyle's hand. He had a buzz cut and a pair of glasses that seemed too small for his large face. "We know every little secret about this city, so if there's anything you ever need, just let us know, Mr. Wells."

"Thank you," Kyle said, returning the handshake and feeling how he imagined rich people must felt checking in to some exotic five-star hotel. "Do you get Nationals tickets?" he asked, making sure his baseball needs would be met.

Jack chuckled. "How does front row behind the Nationals' dugout sound?"

Kyle gasped, not meaning to, but the genuine surprise and shock forced the sound out of his throat. Griffins and Jack looked at each other and started laughing.

"It's refreshing to have your basic joy of life around here, kid," Griffins said, slapping a hand on Kyle's back. "We sure could use it. Let's head up to your dorm, but you can always come back down and see Jack."

"Nice meeting you, Mr. Wells, and welcome to The Crew."

"Thanks again."

Griffins led them into a bullpen area where hundreds of empty desks and a handful of workers filled the room.

"This place is *huge*," Kyle said, unable to see the back wall. "This many people work here?"

"Yes," Griffins replied. "And this is just Washington. We have a few remote offices around the country and tons of agents working in the field. As for our main office here, we have over 600 members who will come through over the course of a week. This place is chaos during the workday, but right now you can see there are only a few people still at their desks. Mostly everyone has gone home for the night, but there will always be someone here at any time of day, monitoring the activities going on around the world."

"Is this where I'll be?"

"No, the training program is a different part of the office. Keep in mind we have sublevels four through seven. Seven is below us and is our infirmary. We're on six right now, the heart of the office, where the majority of the work gets done. All of the department heads have offices down here, myself included. You might spend some time down here during your training to see how different teams work, but most of your time will be on the fifth floor. That's where we have our training room, gym, cafeteria, and outdoor patio. The dorms are on the fourth floor. So let me take you through five first, show you where you'll need to be on Wednesday morning, then we'll head to your room."

Griffins led the way, zigzagging through the labyrinth of desks until they reached the back wall a minute later where a stairwell led up to the fifth floor. Griffins's boots clapped and echoed on the stairs as they worked their way up, stepping into a long hallway that stretched as far as the office space below them on the sixth level.

"Up here, everything is divided into its own room. You'll see each door is labeled with what's inside."

Kyle gawked down the hallway. There had to be at least twelve doors on each side.

"You'll be getting a schedule every morning delivered under your door. It'll have your class times for the day and which rooms they'll be in. It will always be on this floor. Let me show you around. This first door is the cafeteria."

Griffins pushed open the door to the sight of dozens of rectangular tables in neat rows. A handful of people ate dinner while others stood at the counter placing their order.

"You can order anything you want," Griffins said. "You can actually create your own personal menu ahead of time – our chefs like that so they can prepare."

Kyle noticed a salad bar, vending machines, and a fountain machine, the modern kind with a touchscreen, and hundreds of random flavors to add to your Coke.

"This is free?" Kyle asked, his jaw hanging open.

"Free to you. Everything is free to you. Our department is treated the best in all of the military. Our budget is off the books, for obvious reasons."

"So if I wanted to order a steak with a side of mashed potatoes, I could go do that right now?"

Griffins laughed. "You could, but we must be moving on – that's why we stopped for the burgers in the car. They're open until ten, so if you really want to come back later you can." He turned and led them back into the hallway. "The next three doors across the hall are all part of our gym. Door one is our swimming pool and sauna, door two an indoor track with a weight room in the middle, and door three is the combat area where much of your training will take place, fully equipped with punching bags, a shooting range, a boxing ring, and all sorts of fun."

Kyle had never been in a fight, and the thought of training to be an alien-killing machine both excited and stressed him out.

"You'll see those in time, but let me show you the outdoor room." Griffins charged down the hallway, clearly excited to see it for himself. They reached a door labeled as "Outside" and Griffins pushed it open.

They stepped in—or out, it seemed—to a park. A pond sat still in the distance, birds flocking around a fountain in the middle. Grass rustled beneath their feet as an orange glow filled the ceiling above them. Kyle looked up and around, unable to see walls or lights of any sort for at least 100 yards.

"Welcome to Outside," Griffins said. "We've used some of our most advanced technology to create this room. Special lighting you can't see will reflect the current time of day. If you come back in a couple hours, this room will be dark, lit up only by the moon and the lamp posts in this park."

"Is this all real?" Kyle asked, taking a deep breath of what felt like natural air.

"Aside from the lighting, yes. The grass is real, the trees are real, even the birds are real. The vents suck in the air from outside the Pentagon and blow it into this room. There are about 100 different vents hidden in the ceiling, each performing a different function to mimic the exact temperature, humidity, and precipitation as outside. So if it starts snowing outside, it will snow in here, and you'll even feel the temperature drop."

"This is insane," Kyle said. "But why would anyone want to sit in here in the cold? Why not just make it like being at the beach all day?"

"We have members from all around the country, and visitors from around the world. Not everyone cares for the beach and sunshine, just like everyone doesn't want to live in a snow globe every day of their life. Washington gets enough of the different seasons that we decided it was best to give the authentic experience of walking around outside the building."

"Does this mean I'm not allowed to go outside?"

"Of course not. You can go outside whenever you please, but it is a bit of a hassle. Leaving by car is the only way to get out, even if you just wanted to go for a walk around the building. We made this room to make it easier for people. You'll see them in here all the time, jogging, reading on the bench, taking a nap under a tree. It's peaceful on a nice spring day. The only time you'll see the weather change is if we are training our soldiers to prepare for combat in drastic conditions. It's rare, but we've had to prepare for war in Antarctica and the middle of the Sahara Desert. We created those climates in this very room to get them ready."

"Very cool."

"Now, let's finish up on this floor so you can get settled in. Your bags should be arriving any minute now."

Griffins led them out and continued down the hall.

"The rest of these rooms are different classrooms and a movie theater. We have all the same movies that are showing in theaters across town, and can accommodate most requests if there is a particular one you want to watch. Our classrooms, though, are named after important figures we've had in The Crew." He walked faster to the end of the hallway and stopped in front of the last door. "This one is my favorite."

Kyle caught up and felt goosebumps spread across his body. His hands trembled as one reached up to touch the silver plaque that read *SUSAN WELLS TRAINING ROOM*.

"We had this put up a week after she passed," Griffins explained. "Wasn't sure if anyone in her family would ever get to see it, but here you are." He placed an arm around Kyle's shoulder, who was still staring at it like a rare bird.

"I always knew she was important, but I've never grasped just *how* important." Kyle said through his swelling throat.

"She was a pioneer. The first woman to join The Crew – did you know that?"

"No, she never mentioned that in her journals. But it wasn't like her to brag about anything."

"I know it. She didn't lay the groundwork for just women, either. She still remains the highest scoring individual to complete our test at the end of the training program. She set the bar for *everyone* who comes through here. That's why we wanted to bring you here, because anything she said was as good as gold. And she told us we needed you on to the team."

"I don't understand, Colonel. I don't *feel* special."

"Sometimes you just have to roll with the flow, son. Your grandmother believed that, and she ended up having dinner with every president since Nixon, always personally invited. During her prime in the 80's, she was the most valuable person perhaps in the entire government, but no one could know about her."

"She never said a thing to us, and we'd never have known, either. . ."

"Welcome home, Kyle," Griffins said. "This is exactly where she'd want you to be."

9

Chapter 9

Colonel Griffins returned to his office after showing Kyle to his new dorm. They had his bags delivered, and Kyle hung back to relax and get his things set up.

Grady waited outside of Griffins's office, pacing frantic circles.

"Colonel!" he shouted when he saw him emerge from the stairwell. "Colonel, I have some news."

"Let's go in my office." Griffins kicked open his door and slammed it as soon as Grady trailed in behind. "What's going on?"

"Sir, we found the hideout for the two Exalls who went missing four years ago in Colorado."

"The doctor and the boy?"

"Yes, and we think they were the ones responsible for the attack at the bar. They had a tent thirty miles north of the scene, in the middle of nowhere. Our team located the campsite from a helicopter, but there was no one there when we touched down."

"How do you know it was them?"

"We're assuming one of them is the doctor, but we know it's the boy. We found his old student ID inside of his abandoned backpack. But there were definitely belongings for two people. Who else would the boy be traveling with? The doctor turned him into an Exall; it only makes sense."

Griffins sat behind a cluttered desk. He hadn't spent much time in his office the last few days, yet the work continued to pile up.

"Is there any update on the ETD situation?"

"Not yet, but sir, we might have a bigger problem."

"What?!" Griffins barked. *Why the hell does everyone seem so content on beating around the bush lately?*

"We think they're coming for the Wells boy."

"What the hell makes you say that?"

"We went through their tent and found some things. They had pictures of Wells, and maps of his parents' houses. They even had a copy of his class schedule. It looked as if they were planning to make a move on him soon."

"Jesus Christ. How would they even have gotten that sort of information?"

"That's what we're still looking into, but it would seem they both have the capability to shift their bodies to appear like regular humans."

"Both of them, huh? Well, fuck."

The ability to transform wasn't universal across all Exalls. They all had different abilities, no different than humans. Some humans can jump over a moving a car, some can't. For the Exalls, their abilities went way beyond that sort of nonsense. If one couldn't transform their body, they could probably read your mind, or force you to jump off a bridge by hijacking your brain.

"We examined the bar, as well. We did find two drops of Exall blood on the ground to confirm it was an Exall attack."

"What else did you find?"

"Not much. We were able to piece together some of what had happened, and have matched up the different blood samples with their victims. It appears the owner of the bar, John Chambers, had his head slammed into a jukebox; his blood was all over the records. A woman named Rebecca Burns lost a ton of blood by the bar. We found a pistol registered to her name under one of the booths. We presume she pulled it out to shoot at the attackers, but never did. There were no rounds found besides two from a shotgun that was registered to the bar owner. We assume he was either attacked after firing off the rounds, or someone else who worked there may have tried. We pulled samples off the spent rounds and it matches the same black blood of the Exall."

"These attacks are going to continue, aren't they?"

"We don't know for certain, but these two are definitely not sticking to the thirty-year trend. And we still don't know where all of these people are. My team believes they are all traveling together. We found tire tracks leaving the tent site, would be the size of a decent pickup truck. None of the cars from the diner are missing, at least from those we have confirmed were there that night."

"I need to tell the president He needs to know that attacks might be coming."

"We don't know that for sure. In Stratton, the people are saying it was a random attack on the bar. Everyone there knew each other, so they claim it was an outsider driving through to have a little fun."

"But a random attack like this would leave bodies behind.

No one is going to haul out ten corpses in the middle of the night. To do what with? Dump them all in a lake?"

"I know that, but *they* don't know what to think. They're just a small community trying to make sense of it. The sheriff down there even said there could have been a fight that broke out, someone accidentally got killed, and they all fled the scene. Where to, I have no idea. It's nothing but small farm towns two hours in any direction."

"I wish that were the case, but the goddamn black blood." Griffins shook his head. "Your team did quick work finding all of this out. I'm going to hold off on alerting the president and give you one more day to see what you can find. If we find nothing, I'm still going to let him know that we have evidence the attack was done by the Exalls."

"I doubt another day will turn anything up; we got very lucky with this find today, but we won't stop."

"Thank you. Now if you'll please excuse me, I have to get back to this pile of paperwork."

Grady nodded and saw himself out of the office.

Griffins leaned back in his squeaky chair and pulled open his bottom desk drawer, retrieving a flask of whiskey and an envelope. He took a quick swig of the booze, his racing mind welcoming the tingle of relaxation, and opened the envelope, unfolding a hand-written letter across his desk. It was from Susan Wells, given to him a year before her death:

Colonel,

I don't know how much time I have left. I sense that my end is near, but I don't know when or how it all ends for me. Sometimes I feel like they're standing in my backyard watching me, but every time I check, nothing is there. I think one of these nights I'm going to turn on the outside lights and see a dozen of them coming for me, and that will be how it ends. I don't know – maybe enough years in this work is making me lose my mind. Maybe nothing will ever be there, but my instincts have never been wrong.

My grandson is in danger. They promised to make my family pay for what I did, but I know my sons will be fine. Kyle is still too young to know any better, but you need to believe me when I tell you he has my gift. I've seen him shoot a gun, and he can shoot with his mind, not his eyes. He doesn't know it yet, but he has all the signs of a future Crew member, and a key one at that. I've already told this to Travis, and let him know you'll be in touch. Don't waste a day – they'll be coming for him. We've traded lots of favors over the years (don't forget that time I saved your life in Tallahassee), but I have one final favor to ask.

Protect Kyle. Train him, challenge him, and you won't be disappointed. Don't hold back on anything, give him the full training and see how he responds. He's ready.

With love,

Susan

Griffins folded up the note and put it back in the envelope. Susan had never been wrong – even when her foresight wasn't perfectly clear, she still had a sense for what would happen. He had come this far, managing to get Kyle into the Pentagon, and did so without having to scare his parents by letting them know this little tidbit of information that Susan had left behind.

Kyle was already bait, whether The Crew planned to use him as such or not. The Exalls clearly knew something about Kyle that not even the government did, and this made Griffins queasy. Building security had gone under a complete revamp after the Jonathon Browne incident, but these bastards had already shown the ability to bypass their radar.

"This is a mess," he grunted to himself. The Exalls could

transform their bodies to look like whoever they wanted, alter their body temperature to bypass the Crew's thermal surveillance systems, and also no longer fit into their trends of attacking humans once every thirty years. "I just might have to fight this to my death."

He had always imagined his golden years spent at a beach-side cabana. The money was already set aside to purchase a residence somewhere on the Mexican Riviera. A life free of gray aliens and full of fruity cocktails would have to wait. He couldn't back out of his promise to protect Kyle Wells.

10

Chapter 10

Kyle woke on Wednesday morning to a blaring alarm. The training program had a strict schedule and set its own alarms that required Kyle to get out of bed to turn off on the mounted tablet near the bathroom door. They gave him an hour to get dressed, eat breakfast, and head down to the Floor Five classroom named after his grandmother.

The day's schedule was indeed slipped under his door, like a hotel leaving the folio before checkout, and he studied June 17th to see a packed day. Eight to ten was a "brief" history of The Crew. Ten to noon was more history, this time on the Exalls. Lunch ran from noon to one, and the rest of the afternoon looked like more studying, with Exall Technology, Tracking Devices, and Psychological Warfare filling his afternoon until his day ended at six.

He had spent yesterday wandering around Washington like a tourist, even taking his professional-grade camera to snap photos of all the historic monuments. He called his parents who were together awaiting his call, both excited to hear from him and wanting to know about his stay so far. He told them about his dorm and how everyone around the building had been so welcoming, but didn't go into any further detail, not wanting to get in trouble for saying anything against the rules. To anyone passing by, they would have thought Kyle was just a college student calling home to check in with his parents, not an undercover alien hunter.

Tuesday was long gone by the time he woke on Wednesday, and he rushed down to the cafeteria to enjoy a plate of eggs, bacon, and potatoes. The cafeteria was crowded with dozens of Crew members, but he returned to his room with the food. Colonel Griffins had told him to avoid any conversations with other members until his training was complete, so he made sure to honor this request.

His new training uniform had been delivered to his bedroom while he went down for food. Solid black pants and shirts of stretchy, athletic fabric stood in piles of five each on the foot of his bed. A note left on top requested he put any dirty laundry in the hamper in his closet to be washed over the weekend.

This isn't real life, he thought, but every day he learned of some new accommodation that The Crew simply "took care of." He'd never have to cook, clean, drive, or do his own laundry. He wouldn't receive a salary until he passed the test at the end of the training, but was told if he needed anything within reason, to let the concierge team know. But he couldn't imagine what he'd possibly need, considering the all-inclusive amenities already offered everything. When he wandered the halls Tuesday evening, he had discovered a gaming room complete with a bowling alley, billiards, darts, video games, and a ping pong table. He wondered why the colonel would have not shown him that room.

He passed it en route to his very first training session

and promised to stop in there that evening to enjoy some PlayStation before heading back to his room for the night. His only complaint about his new digs would be that there was no TV in his room.

He reached the training room, brushed his grandmother's name on the silver plaque and pulled open the door to an empty classroom, minus a short bald man sitting behind the desk in the front of the room.

"You must be Kyle," he said in a squeaky voice, standing to cross the room and shake Kyle's hand.

"Am I in the right place?" Kyle asked, looking at the thirty empty seats facing the front of the room.

"You sure are. My name is Gerard Palmer, and I'm the head of our training and education department. It's a pleasure to meet you."

Gerard had broad shoulders and beefy arms protruding from his uniform. Kyle shook his hands that felt like rocks.

"Nice to meet you. Is there anyone else training with me?"

"I'm afraid not. We brought you on outside of our normal recruitment schedule, so you'll be going through the training program all on your own. But don't worry. Even though it's not ideal to not have others around, this means we can move through the program as quickly or slowly as suits you."

"How long is the program supposed to take? No one has given me an idea."

"The average trainee takes six months from start to finish. We have three months of full on training. After that, you'll have two weeks to prepare for the test. From there, it's just a matter of how many times you have to take the test to pass. It can take some people months to pass it, others a couple of weeks. Once you do, you'll meet with the president for final approval."

"The *president*? Why would *I* get to meet the *president*?"

Gerard chuckled. "Relax, kid, it's part of the process. Everyone who's ever been a part of The Crew receives final approval from the president. It's not so much approval—by then you've already gone through hell and back—as it is an introduction. President Kennedy started the tradition, wanting to know the faces of every person working to protect the entire planet. And that's really all it is: a tradition. You'll have passed the most difficult test in this country, so as an honor, you get to meet with the president in the Oval Office for about 15 minutes."

"Wow," Kyle said, unsure what else to say.

"Let's get started, shall we?"

***

The next two weeks felt like one long, horrendous day for Kyle. He spent every waking moment in the classroom, with occasional breaks in the Outside Room to gather his bearings. Otherwise, between the hours of eight in the morning and six at night, Kyle sat in the classroom learning everything under the sun and moon about the Exalls and The Crew. His brain felt like an overflowing file cabinet having more documents stuffed into it. The desire to play in the gaming room after dinner faded to the way of an urge to sleep. He slept at least ten hours every night, but still woke up exhausted. He lost track of the days, only knowing it was Sunday when an alarm didn't sound off in the morning. Even on his only day off, he opted to sleep in until noon and lounge around in his pajamas all day.

After the two weeks of strict learning, Kyle's training shifted to the gym. He was expected to get into shape while learning basic combat techniques in the mornings, a brief classroom session after lunch, and then finish the day with cardio workouts.

For someone who typically loitered in the weight room during baseball's preseason workouts, the days in the gym steamrolled his body like an 18-wheeler. Fortunately, The Crew provided a special ointment for him to apply to his muscle aches each night. The ointment, devised in the laboratory by government scientists, tingled when first applied, then turned the affected areas completely numb. By the time he woke the following morning, all pain and soreness had vanished as if someone had just zapped it away.

And so his body grew, gaining muscle every week as he lifted weights, swam, ran, and learned the art of different fighting techniques like Krav Maga, Brazilian Jiu Jitsu, wrestling, and boxing.

"Even though the Exalls cannot feel pain, you can stun them with these techniques," his instructor, Ira Yung, had told him. "A foot to the throat will still send them sailing backward and buy you a few seconds. I've heard plenty of stories where one of our own survived because they escaped after physically fighting off an Exall. It's not the ideal situation to be in, but it can happen. And you must be prepared."

Somewhere in the midst of the training, Kyle had filled out a consent form for a psychiatric evaluation. They wanted to make sure his mind was okay after the grueling start to the program, but they also wanted ammunition to shout at him during a sparring session.

Some days Ira would blurt out random things in the middle

of a fight. "Your parents' divorce is all your fault. So was your grandmother's death! Brian is an Exall now, and he wants to come for you."

Kyle let the words get to him, sparking instant rage as he fought out of control. Ira promptly ended the fight with a series of combinations that left Kyle on the ground panting for his breath, Ira's foot held firmly over his throat.

"Get up!" Ira barked. Kyle flailed to his feet, blood rushing in every direction. "Unacceptable! You can't ever let your emotions get the best of you when dealing with these monsters. You think what I'm saying is bad? They will fuck with your mind one hundred times worse. You have to be ready for the foulest things, and keep your focus."

"I'm sorry."

"Sorry doesn't cut it, Wells. There is no 'sorry' out there. You make that mistake in a real encounter with the Exalls and it will be the last mistake you make in your life. Remember that. They know how to fight, but they're not that great at it. They rely on mind games to make you snap. You need to learn how to seal your mind from their words, put a wall up around your head that only you can see through. Does that make sense?"

"Yes, sir."

Ira panted for breath still, the exercise providing him with a good workout as well. "We're gonna get you into some psychology classes. We have doctors who can teach you how to zone out all of the noise and give you complete focus. They can even show you how to keep an Exall from hijacking your brain—it's not as hard as you'd think. It's a great course, really. I'll see if our doctor is free to begin with you tomorrow."

They returned to one final sparring session, Kyle nagged by the constant wonder of what the Exalls could possibly say that was worse.

11

Chapter 11

Dr. Klemens and Brian enjoyed their time on the road together. At a gas station near the Colorado and Kansas border, they upgraded their truck to a black 2018 Ford F-150. It provided so much space that Brian reclined his seat and put his feet up for most of the trip.

This was also where they let their new friends out of their watch after they all hid together for two weeks in another open field 100 miles east of where the attacks had taken place in Stratton. They spent their time learning about their new abilities with the guidance of Dr. Klemens and Brian.

"Be free, my friends," Klemens had told them, standing in the bed of the truck while everyone gathered around at one in the morning. "Go out and spread the news about our kind. Show them the light as I have shown you, ladies and gentlemen. Bring your friends to us, your neighbors, even your family. With enough of us, there will be no stopping what we can do."

The group, who had all watched their skins turn gray and their eyes blacken over the last day, howled in appreciation. Then they left the gas station, walking through the night as silently as a cemetery security guard doing their rounds, death hanging in the air.

"Where are they going?" Brian asked.

"Looks like everywhere," the doctor replied, admiring the group of ten new Exalls scattering every which way. "They'll be near civilization in the morning and we'll have doubled our numbers again. But you and I must be going – we have a long trip to D.C."

"I told you I don't want to go. I'm not going to hurt Kyle."

"That's precious, but we don't have a choice. I can feel it tugging at me—that's where we need to go."

Brian had debated running off on his own at least two hundred times, leaving this madman to do whatever he needed, but he also felt the tug, like a mystical rope pulling them to Washington, gradually inching them closer. And even though he said he didn't want to hurt Kyle, his subconscious—or his inner Exall, whatever it was—said differently. It was as if he had two minds, one wanting to return to his normal life as a high school student, the other wanting to go to D.C. to find Kyle and slash open his throat.

If you don't kill him first, he'll kill you. Brian remembered the words the doctor had eerily whispered one night as they sat around their campfire. *He only sees you as an evil creature now. As far as he knows, his friend is dead and you're just the gray piece of scum responsible. He'll shoot you so fast—*

Brian had to continually shake his head free of these thoughts. Kyle could be reasoned with—that's just the way he was. He wouldn't shoot Brian on first sight.

"But I want to gut him like a fish," Brian blurted, slapping his hand directly to his mouth as if the words had come out on their own.

The doctor howled. "That's the spirit. Let's go."

Even if Brian did run away, the doctor would just come find him. He had a sense for the events at hand and seemed hellbent on following this internal tug.

They returned to the truck, its owner dead in the dumpster behind the gas station, and got back on I-70 headed east.

* * *

"Do you feel what I feel?" Klemens asked after a long stretch of silence where Brian daydreamed, staring out the window as the sun chased the moon across the sky.

"Where are we?" Brian asked, stretching his arms above his head, yawning. "Was I asleep?"

The doctor cackled. "You sure were. I feel like you're not embracing your new self, Brian. You know, with these new bodies we don't actually need any sleep. You must be clinging to your human self."

"I wasn't planning to sleep; it just happened."

"We've been on the road for six hours. It's 7 A.M. and we're about to arrive in Kansas City, Missouri, the home of the best barbecue. Or so I've been told."

"Okay?"

"Do you not feel the tingle inside of you like I do? We're supposed to do something here, recruit more people."

Brian had felt a lot of things within his mind, body, and soul since becoming infected with the Exall blood. But the doctor seemed to have more of these "feelings" that always ended with some sort of violent outburst. He reminded Brian of the televangelists on TV who claimed to be overtaken by the Holy Spirit, flailing around on stage with their tongues out like a seizure victim. They were all full of shit, and so was the doctor, but he could never say that to his face – just like the poor clergy members who handed millions of dollars over to the same televangelists.

"Can't we just get to D.C. without killing any more people?" Brian pleaded.

"Killing people?" the doctor gasped. "How dare you, young man. We don't kill people; we *convert* them. We share our gift of transforming their bodies to not require sleep or food. Think of how much more productive society will be saving on all that time eating and sleeping."

"We're going to get caught. That's what I can feel."

"That's called paranoia."

"No. I guarantee I *feel* it coming. Sometimes I have dreams about getting shot in the face by one of them."

"Again, that's why you shouldn't sleep. Any other nonsense you'd like to try?"

Brian shook his head. He really did have nightmares. And it was always Kyle who shot him in the face. It didn't bother him, either—he deserved it for killing Kyle's grandmother. It was only a matter of time before Kyle rose to the occasion to avenge Susan's murder. He'd never tell the doctor any of this, that would only speed up the trip to Washington, and he still needed to figure out what he was going to do once they arrived there. He had no plans on meeting with Kyle face to face, whether in his human or Exall form. For now, he had to go along with whatever the doctor planned, hoping the Feds wouldn't show up to crash their attacks on innocent lives.

The car slowed as they exited the highway. "Well would you

look at that, it's our lucky day," the doctor cackled. He pointed across the road where a billboard announced an outdoor concert called Country Jam. "July 2nd? That's tonight, don't you know? All the big names are going to be there, Brian. . . and so are we."

"We can't go to that. You have to be out of your mind."

"As a matter of fact, I *am* out of my mind. I'm in this doctor's mind. And body. And we're going to spread our joy all night long at the concert."

Brian shook his head as they pulled off the highway, the sun rising over a quiet Kansas City, oblivious to what the night would bring for the innocent concertgoers.

12

Chapter 12

Music filled the air, booming louder than the screaming fans packed around the stage. The Country Jam was held every summer at the Starlight Theater, an outdoor venue that seated just under 10,000 people, with more standing room behind the sections of seats. In all, this year's concert welcomed over 12,000 by the official count.

The seating area was separated from the concessions and restrooms by a tall wall, and this is where Tammy Bell waited in line for an ice cold strawberry margarita. The show had started at six, but it was already eight o'clock, meaning the names in the lineup became bigger with each new artist stepping on to the stage. Tammy came every year with her closest group of girlfriends, a collection of stay-at-home mothers who all knew each other through PTA meetings at their kids' school.

Tammy had gone off to get her third margarita of the night while two friends stayed in their seats, the fourth making a quick trip to the restroom.

She vowed to not talk to any men at the concert, her divorce only a couple months fresh with emotional scars that surely wouldn't heal for some time. She felt emotionally numb, like her heart had been cut right out of her chest and placed in a bucket of ice.

The men would surely come knocking once they noticed her naked ring finger. She kept a strict workout routine and knew she looked great for a forty-year-old mother of two. She had dyed her hair blond a few days after the divorce, needing anything that might make her feel like a new person with a fresh start. While it gave her confidence a boost, it all meant nothing when she crawled into bed by herself. The weekends were even worse when the boys stayed with their father, leaving the house lifeless and depressing. She couldn't lean on her friends during these dark times either, as they all had their own families to tend to. That's why she needed to make tonight count. And that's why her margaritas wouldn't stop at three. She was shooting for six, and just maybe she could fall asleep without crying.

She had loved her husband, and suspected she still did, judging by the tears shed every night. But he went behind her back with another woman, cheating not just on her, but on the entire family. He begged for forgiveness, which she eventually granted, but that didn't change the events that had happened. Tammy was normally easy-going, but the line had to be drawn somewhere, and her now ex-husband had crossed it.

The affair stayed in the back of her mind like a criminal hiding in the alley, waiting to pounce if she so much as looked at another man. All trust was broken with the opposite sex, and she didn't want to engage in conversation with a man until a sliver of it had been restored.

The line for margaritas stretched back about a dozen people, all shifting side to side in a half-hearted attempt to dance to the music that was jumbled bass and noise from their area outside of the concert stage.

"Is this line moving at all?" a voice asked from behind. A man's voice.

Tammy turned and shrugged her shoulders, offering a sideways grin, but not speaking a word. She was going to stick to her guns, and wished her friend would hurry up in the bathroom to keep her company. The man was good-looking: smooth face, strong jaw, and dark hair slicked to the side, streaks of gray peppered in. But that didn't matter. Not now, at least.

Just keep looking forward and pretend he's not there.

"How are you liking the show?" he asked from behind.

Blood rushed to the back of her head, right where she felt his eyes staring. She didn't want to come off as rude, but managed to ignore him, pulling out her cell phone to fidget with and appear preoccupied.

"Okay then, sorry I asked," he said.

She heard a slight waver in his voice and felt awful. It was just small talk, it didn't mean she was going to turn around and marry the guy. In ten minutes they'd each have their own margaritas and return to their separate lives to never see each other again.

"I'm sorry," she said turning around. "I didn't mean to be rude, I've just had a long day."

Holy shit, she thought as he grinned at her. She couldn't help but look him up and down, hoping he didn't notice the sudden movement of her eyes. The man looked like he could be a TV actor or a model in some middle-age prescription drug advertisement.

"No need to apologize," he said. "Just trying to make the time pass in this line."

Tammy's head spun, her third margarita finally kicking into full gear. She had reached the point where her face became numb, and that's when she knew she was officially drunk.

"I've been in this line all night; it doesn't get any better." She said this and immediately wished she hadn't, lowering her head in embarrassment.

The man chuckled. "Well these are some of the best margaritas in the world, right? Twelve dollars for eight ounces in a little plastic cup. How could you *not* stand in this line all night?"

Tammy burst into a short laughter, stopping herself when she realized the alcohol was making everything seem a bit funnier than it actually was. She was feeling loose and relaxed for the first time in weeks, and it created a sort of utopia in her current state of mind.

The line shuffled forward, and she returned to her cell phone to send a text message to her friend in the bathroom.

Hurry up, I think some guy is hitting on me.

She had her back to him, but still felt his eyes on her, *glued* to her, but not in the way most men did when they saw an attractive woman. This stare felt authentic, not superficial, as if he were trying to see into her soul.

"Where are you sitting tonight?" the man asked her.

"In the hundreds," she said over her shoulder, immediately returning to her cell phone.

"Oh really? I'm in 102. Which are you in?"

She debated telling him. He might come find her, but if he was crazy enough to do that, it wouldn't have mattered, anyway; he'd still find her as the sections weren't that big.

"102," she said, trying to play it cool.

"What?! I'm in 102, row 15, right in the middle seats. Which row do you have?"

Now her heart sunk, but she was already too deep into this conversation to lie. "Row 14."

"I'll be damned," the man said, a smile in his voice. "How did I miss you?"

"Well, I'm on the aisle with my friends—that's probably why." Tammy said this in a somewhat snooty tone, hoping the man would take the hint and not get any ideas about stopping by her seat that was now too close for comfort. Would that burning sensation of his stare continue throughout the concert? She hoped not, that would surely distract her from the rest of the show.

She could already see how the rest of the night would play out. He likely came with a group of friends, and they'd all make their way down to row 14 to introduce themselves, trying to get the two groups of people to hang out together. Only they'd all be barking up the wrong tree, seeing as everyone in Tammy's group was still married. Even still, her friends wouldn't tell them off. They'd been telling her for weeks to go out and have fun with a random stranger. They told her the best way to get over a man is to get under another one.

Maybe she should be the one staying away from her own group of friends; they would only egg on this situation to a point Tammy didn't want.

The line moved forward, down to two people in front of Tammy, with a counter of three bartenders. *This is almost done,* she thought, tasting the freedom that would come as soon as she had her fresh margarita in hand. *Twelve dollars for eight ounces in a plastic cup.*

She giggled at this again. Everyone knew the prices at any event were a rip-off, but this comment struck her as the cold hard truth, yet here she was buying her fourth plastic cup of the night.

"What's your name?" he asked, the line moving up one more person.

Just as a spot opened at the bar, Tammy lunged forward, shooting a look over her shoulder at the man. "I'm Tammy."

The man grinned before moving into his place at the other side of the bar, a person separating them in the middle spot.

Tammy ordered her drink and paid in record time, rushing away from the bar before the man had a chance to follow her. If he really was in the row behind her, he'd come find her anyway. He had a look in his eyes that suggested he wasn't done talking to her. She disappeared into the concert, working her way through the crowd of people toward her seat, texting her friend to meet her back in their section.

* * *

The hot summer night grew sticky with humidity, and Tammy's fourth margarita went down with ease. After so many, the flavor started to seem more like water, making it easier to chug the alcohol. Her head spun as the music boomed from every angle, the bass rumbling the core of her body.

She had forgotten all about the man from the bar, falling into a trance from the performance of Lady Antebellum on the stage. Tammy had the aisle seat, allowing her to see her three friends dancing, swaying their hips as they sung into the night sky with imaginary microphones held in front of their mouths.

The song ended, applause and screams erupting from the audience of 12,000 country music lovers. Tammy scanned the crowd, illuminated only by the bright lights of the stage, seeing thousands of cowboy hats, boots, and tight jeans, and knew this is exactly where she wanted to be. Away from her couch, her bedroom, her house. All of which had memories of her past clung to the walls like a dirty stain.

Then the tap came on her shoulder that changed everything. A quick, hard double tap from a stiff finger.

"Hey there, Ms. Tammy," the man's voice shouted from behind to be heard over the rowdy crowd.

She debated not turning around, pretending to not have felt the tap, but who was she kidding? Besides, the alcohol was in full force, so let this poor soul try whatever he needed; she was ready for it.

"Did you forget something at the bar?" he asked, prompting her to turn around.

There he stood, grinning that charming smile, with a fresh margarita held out to her.

Her eyes dropped from his face to the drink in amazement, like he had pulled a rabbit out of a hat. "How did you—?"

"I bought one for my friend, but he didn't want it." The man nodded his head in the direction of his seat in the row behind, right in the middle as he had said. Tammy looked over her shoulder, but didn't know who she was looking for in the cluster of dancing people. "I figured you probably wanted it."

He extended it all the way to her, damn near forcing it into her hands. Under normal circumstances she knew better than to take a drink from a random man, but she was four margaritas deep, and logic had already taken its final trip home for the night.

She snatched it out of his hands with a wide smile. "You're too sweet. You didn't have to do this."

"It's my pleasure. It's not every day I meet such a beautiful woman."

There it is. He was playing it smooth all along, making it seem like he wasn't interested, but these men won't actually let a moment pass without making a move.

"Well, thank you. Enjoy the rest of the show."

Tammy turned away to see her three friends gawking at her in amazement, stupid grins smacked on their faces as their eyes moved from her to the handsome man standing shunned behind her.

Talk to him, her friend, Leslie, mouthed to her.

Tammy rolled her eyes. This guy had done nothing wrong, he was just trying to be nice, yet here she was taking his drink and ignoring him. The least she could do was humor him. She'd even tell him about her recent divorce and make it crystal-clear that she wasn't interested in anyone at the moment. He'd probably hang around for a few minutes before wandering off to find another woman who might say yes.

She spun around, his wide grin stuck on his face. "So what's your name?"

The concert had just gone on a brief intermission to change the set for the next artist, leaving her no easy way out of this conversation for at least the next ten minutes. They no longer had to shout, only needing to speak in a slightly elevated voice to hear through their still ringing ears.

"Hudson. Pleased to formally meet you." He stuck out a hand and she shook it.

"And what do you do for a living, Hudson?"

You're doing great, just keep the small talk going. Next you can talk about the weather, then hopefully the show will start again.

"I'm a doctor."

"Dr. Hudson has a nice ring to it," she said, unsure what else to say. Her drunkenness made even a basic conversation like this one seem ten times more difficult. "Are you from here in Kansas City?"

He chuckled. "No. I'm from Denver, but always enjoy getting away to see different shows. Are you from here?"

"Born and raised."

"I see. Maybe you could show me around the city tomorrow? I'm only in town for the next couple of days."

Tammy was grateful the conversation was taking place away from her group. They had sat down, chatting among themselves, occasionally sneaking a look over their shoulders to see how she was doing. If only they could hear his words, they'd be egging her on as this was the perfect window of opportunity to "get under a man" who would walk out of her life forever.

No. Don't even start thinking like that. It's just the margaritas talking. Finish this conversation and end your night like you always do, alone in your king-sized bed.

"I don't think that's a good idea," she said, taking an extended sip from her new margarita.

"Why not?"

"Well, for starters I have to work tomorrow—tonight is Thursday, you know."

"You can always call in. Was there another reason?"

She took another long swig from her plastic cup, now halfway done with her fifth margarita. Her stomach churned, and she didn't see a way of her avoiding a long night of puking her brains into the toilet.

"I'm just not in a good place right now to be spending time with a man. I hope you can understand."

Hudson's grin wavered but didn't vanish. "I can appreciate that. I'm not looking for a relationship or anything. I genuinely want to be shown around town. I've never been here and don't know anyone who lives here. I'm sorry if I came across as anything more than that."

In her moment of growing sloppiness, she saw an innocent man looking for someone to spend time with. Nothing more. Nothing less.

"Sorry, I'm not gonna call off work to show you around. I can give you some suggestions on what to do though, if you'd like."

The stage was ready for the next performer and the lights cut out, leaving the venue in near pitch-blackness.

"One dance," Hudson said, his face invisible in the darkness.

"What?"

"Let me dance with you for one song and I'll leave you alone forever. Never have to see me again."

Tammy had certainly had worse offers before. "Okay, one song."

The spotlight flashed on the stage, revealing Jason Aldean strumming a shiny black guitar, singing the opening lines to his popular love song, "You Make It Easy."

The audience ruptured, the sound of thousands of women screaming into the night like loons.

Of course it's a slow song, Tammy thought as Hudson inched closer, clearly unsure if it was okay for him to dance with her. She nodded to him, prompting him to offer his hands to her.

When she grabbed them, all worries that had been weighing

on her mind vanished like a grain of sand in the wind. Inner peace spread throughout her core, and she felt as if she had taken some sort of happy pill that worked the instant you placed it on your tongue. She noted how his hands felt ice cold, but figured it was because he had been holding margaritas.

Tammy took one long final sip of her drink and placed the empty cup on the ground to hold Hudson with both of her hands. Her friends gawked like high school girls, giggling and whispering to each other. She loved the feeling of having no cares in the world, dancing under the moon with a handsome gentleman to a romantic song. The rest of the crowd, her friends, even herself seemed to blur into the background. It was just her and Hudson, his silvery eyes staring deep into hers.

His lips parted to show his perfect smile, and Tammy no longer felt in control of her own body. She supposed it was the alcohol. But she didn't feel drunk anymore, not in this perfect moment, as if simply touching Hudson's skin made her instantly sober. His grin hypnotized her as his face inched a little closer to hers.

He's going to try to kiss me—

She moved in to him, feeling tugged by his soul, completely out of her control.

—and I don't know what to do!

Time froze as their lips remained an entire two inches apart. Tammy's heart thumped wildly in her chest, seemingly the only thing moving in the whole world. Tequila oozed from his breath, but she didn't care; the taste was still on her tongue, too.

Just kiss him!

Tammy closed the gap and their lips locked, sparking an

instant—but brief—flood of emotions from sorrow and guilt to ecstasy and lust. She parted her lips and welcomed his tongue as her hands slid onto his back where she ran them up and down, enjoying the feel of his rock-hard body.

Hudson pulled her in closer by her waist, his hands gentle as they caressed the sides of her abdomen.

It was the moment she didn't know she wanted, and it was time for it to end. Nothing good would come from escalating the current situation, and she pushed back to end the kiss. Hudson tilted his head, but didn't release his grip from her hips, holding on tight like he never wanted to let go.

"You said one dance and you'll leave forever," she whispered. Not even the music could overthrow this perfect moment, drowning into background noise despite the thousands of people singing around them.

"Yes," Hudson said. "One more kiss?"

Tammy nodded and slung her arms around his neck, pulling his face into hers where they swapped tongues for another thirty seconds. She felt his teeth scrape her bottom lip, giving the slightest of tugs.

This time when she tried to pull away, she was met with resistance. Hudson kept his hands tight on her, not forceful, but refusing to let her end the moment. Her lip stayed between his teeth, and now that the kiss had ended for her, she recoiled back, but he didn't release her hips. Or her lips.

A sharp pain clamped down on her lip, his teeth digging into her soft flesh. It felt like someone was trying to cut her lip off with a pair of scissors, and then Hudson threw his head back, ripping a chunk of her lip off as blood spouted from her mouth.

Tammy's hand shot up to her mouth, her fingers instantly smeared in her own blood. Hudson grinned, the chunk of her flabby lip pinched between his teeth like a cigarette, wiggling in the air like a worm on a hook.

Her eyes looked from her bloody fingers to his mouth, and back to her fingers in disbelief. The music continued in the background, not a soul paying any attention to the gory scene unfolding. *Where the fuck are my friends now?*

She still had her back to them, but her body froze with shock, unable to do so much as turn around. Even the useless people in the row behind them were so entranced by Jason Aldean that they didn't see the blood oozing from her mouth like a goddam river.

She tried to shout for help, but it only came out as, "HELLL-LLLLL!" Her shrieking voice was lost in the cluster of music and other screams from the crowd, as inaudible as a mouse crawling along the back wall of a church.

Hudson remained in place, grinning, before tilting his head back and opening his mouth to swallow Tammy's lip. It reminded her of videos she had seen of people swallowing a gold fish. Just open up your throat and swallow it whole. And they always had their head tilted back just like he had.

The song ended, leaving a brief few seconds for Tammy to shriek as loud as her lungs allowed, and she didn't waste the opportunity. Her friends turned, their eyes dropping to the pool of blood on the ground, trying to piece together what had happened.

A man in a cowboy hat from the row behind them saw Tammy's bloodied face and lunged toward Hudson. "You son of a bitch!" he barked.

But Hudson remained unfazed, sticking out a stiff arm to hold the man a safe distance away. The cowboy pushed, jumping over the seat with a balled fist and swung it toward

Hudson's face. He dodged it with the reflexes of a professional boxer, grinning the entire time. The cowboy went tumbling into their row, taking out Tammy's legs in his fall, knocking her onto the ground in front of her friends.

Hudson kept his grin as the next song started, all eyes in the immediate area now focused on the unfolding scene. He reached down and pulled up the cowboy by his shirt collar. The man swayed on his feet, clearly a bit intoxicated himself, before Hudson stuck his face into the man's neck, mouth open as if ready to take a large bite of steak.

Tammy swore the teeth appeared fang-like, but figured her mind was playing tricks after having just lost a piece of her face to the same mouth. Hudson sunk his teeth into the man's neck, causing a howl that could have been mistaken for a pack of wolves.

Tammy lay on the ground, watching from below, but felt a surprising burst of energy. The music continued echoing as her friends huddled around, gawking at her with their bulging eyes.

"What the hell did he do to you?" one screamed.

"Are you okay?"

"Do we need to call an ambulance?"

Their voices all jumbled together, making no sense under the music and Hudson's howling laughter next to them, blood oozing from his mouth. The cowboy's blood.

The man he had bitten wriggled on the ground, hands grasping his neck as if that would keep all of his blood from spilling onto the concrete. Tammy imagined his throat was gurgling blood, but a sound that fine would never be heard in the middle of a concert. She wanted to help him. Help herself. Maybe sink *her* teeth into his juicy skin.

Tammy shuddered, the poison of a million negative thoughts flooding her mind as she tried to make sense of the last thirty minutes of her life.

Why did I have to go back for another margarita? she asked herself, wishing she could rewind the clock. Wishing she could—

—rip out someone's throat and have a great night!

She rose to her feet, crying tears of horror as she felt her body and mind undergo a transformation of which she had no control.

Come with me, let's have some fun, Hudson's voice said within her mind. She looked to him, terrified that she heard his voice, knowing the words weren't spoken because they would have never been heard over the concert. *Before it's too late, let's spread our love. The people behind us already ran away – let's take your friends with us.*

Tammy spun around to the row behind, where the six seats in the vicinity had indeed cleared out. She looked to the writhing cowboy on the ground and watched in amazement as he gathered himself and rose to his feet just as she had, a wide smile revealing his teeth above the gashed open throat that had somehow stopped bleeding already.

The cowboy and Tammy turned to Hudson, whose skin appeared a shade darker, turning gray.

He stared back at them, somehow splitting each of his eyes to look at both of them at the same time. He nodded.

The cowboy dashed across the aisle and jumped on top of a small group of dancing people.

Rage boiled within Tammy, spilling into her soul, as she pivoted around to her friends, her mouth parted with teeth that had become sharper in just the past few seconds. She growled and lunged for them, attacking all three of them within the next thirty seconds while the music carried on.

13

Chapter 13

Colonel Griffins thought he might vomit all over his office. Every morning he received a briefing of the prior day's events around the country, whether Exall-related or not. This morning's was particularly thick—at least 100 pages long, compared to the usual thirty. The majority of pages stuffed into it were from the Kansas City police department, hundreds of statements from a country concert that had turned deadly. Initially starting the report, Griffins thought it was another mass shooting that had taken place and wondered why a big sticky note had been left on the front demanding he read the entire thing. Then he saw why.

A man started the tragedy by biting a woman's face and another man's throat. The man who had been bitten was thought to have been dead, but shortly rose to his feet and started biting others in the crowd. The woman followed suit, attacking her own group of friends. And this was all in one particular section of the venue.

Out on the main concourse, a teenage boy snuck into one of the concession stand kitchens to steal a couple of chef knives, and slashed everyone behind the counter before eventually making his way back out to slaughter more of the concertgoers waiting in line for a brisket sandwich. A couple of security guards were able to detain him after he had killed seven people, but the boy bit them on the arms, turning them into some sort of possessed zombies who started attacking the innocent bystanders watching with their phones out, recording the incident, and sharing it to several different websites within five minutes.

By the end of the night, 1200 people had been killed or wounded, with another 300 sent to the hospital with serious injuries from being stampeded on by the panicked crowd. All of the madness had unfolded with only twenty minutes remaining of the concert.

Twenty fucking minutes, Colonel Griffins thought, slamming his fists on his desk, sending a couple of pens rolling over the edge. Twenty minutes between 12,000 people going home after a fun night out, savoring a memory to last a lifetime. Instead they would all be haunted for the rest of their lives, horrified at the prospect of even stepping foot into another concert. Or they'd be dead, or worse.

A full-on crisis was now brewing for The Crew, but Griffins didn't know it yet. It was still too early to say for certain that this had been a job by the Exalls, but the possibility throbbed in the back of his mind, growing louder with each passing second. He thought back to a briefing he had once read from Susan, stating her certainty that one day the Exalls would find a way to advance how they spread their "infection" to others. Before, they had to find ways to get their blood injected into a human's bloodstream, and they always seemed to do so. Colonel Griffins pulled up Susan's report on his computer and scrolled through it until he found a specific passage that had haunted him since the first time he read it.

The Exalls are continually looking for ways to improve their process for everything they do. We don't know what drives them, but they are always evolving like their existence depends on it. They have advanced exponentially over the past decade, and it's arrogant to think they won't continue that over the next decade, and the decade after that. They move at a pace we cannot keep up with. We either have to prepare to increase our presence, put all hands on deck to increase our intelligence, or prepare for Plan D.

Plan D, the two-ton elephant always sitting in the corner of the room. It was called Plan D, short for Doomsday, because that's exactly what it was. If at least forty-five percent of the United States population was deemed to be at risk of an Exall infection, Plan D would execute an attack on the entire country, essentially bombing civilization while The Crew and higher government officials were protected in underground bunkers. The Crew would plan to revive the country's population, having always kept men and women under the age of thirty to reproduce in case of this drastic emergency.

Plan D seemed light years away still, but if this attack was confirmed as the Exalls, it would prove a drastic step in that direction. There had never been a massive public attack like this. Most Exall attacks occurred within small communities, and were much easier to contain. But this was a concert with 12,000 people as possible witnesses or victims, the videos on the internet spreading like a wildfire during the hottest of summers. The briefing lacked many details that Colonel Griffins needed. Were there others who were bitten and revived? Were they being contained and studied? What would a doctor do if they came across traces of the black blood belonging to Exalls?

Please let this be a freak attack that has nothing to do with the Exalls. Please, God.

Colonel Griffins recalled another discussion he once had with Susan, right in this same office. He stared at the empty seat across from his desk and imagined her sitting there, her silvery hair tied into a bun, her eyes watchful, hiding the decades of horror she had witnessed.

"One day," she had said, "There will be an attack that goes way above what we are equipped to handle. They advance at a rate roughly eight times faster than we can. We can't keep up. It will be grisly, and potentially threaten the entire country. When the time comes, you have to think big."

Griffins snickered as he gawked at the empty seat. He just now realized that she had spoken in the future tense, assuming she wouldn't be around to help when the time came. She had always shown a disturbing ability to sense what would come. Griffins always assumed it was because she studied the Exalls' history and used the knowledge to predict the future—which he still believed. But he also *felt* that she had a sort of psychic ability to combine with her book smarts. It's what made her the ultimate weapon for the Crew, and a strong reason she was never tangled in a mess until her final day alive.

Did she know her death was coming that day? he wondered. The more he considered it, the more it seemed the event wouldn't have caught her by surprise. Perhaps she knew she had to sacrifice herself in order to save her family—most importantly, Kyle. She was always ten steps ahead, somehow staying on a level playing field with the Exalls.

"Getting captured was part of your plan," Griffins said to

the empty chair. "All so we could have the boy. But why?"

Kyle had excelled in the training course and would be ready to take his test in the coming weeks, but he hadn't yet displayed any of Susan's freakishly successful abilities. As of now, he projected to be an above-average soldier with potential to be one of their best. There had to be more to it, but Griffins didn't have time today to piece together the puzzle.

Just as he was about to pick up his phone to call the head of intelligence, Grady himself came bursting into the colonel's office.

"Colonel Griffins," Grady said through panting breath, clearly having just run across the building. "Have you read the briefing this morning?"

"I was just finishing it. I take it you have something for me?"

Grady plopped himself down in the chair while he gathered himself and the stack of papers he had tucked in his armpit. "The attack is confirmed as Exalls, but we have a bigger problem."

Griffins felt his stomach sink deep into his intestines. Whatever came out of Grady's mouth next would surely warrant a visit to the Oval Office.

"There were too many people infected by the Exall DNA, sir. We captured a couple of the victims from the bar massacre in Colorado, and found they were infected by a simple bite. Exalls no longer have to get creative to take control of humans. They can walk up to us and bite us anywhere on the flesh, and our bloodstream becomes infected within a minute. At that point, the Exalls have full control over any of those infected."

"Why are they still here, dammit?" Griffins slammed his fists on his desk again. He seemed to be doing that more lately. "I thought the next attack wasn't coming for another twenty years at least, long after I'm gone."

"It's the doctor and boy, sir. They never left, and they clearly don't give a shit about the Exalls' plans to strike us every three decades."

"What's going on in Kansas City?"

"We have some people in St. Louis who are on their way, should be landing in the next few minutes. They've already been watching the news, and word across the region is that this is some sort of zombie apocalypse. There have been dozens of witnesses saying they watched people biting each other at the concert, falling over, and getting back up to join in the attack. Our early reports suggest there are at least 200 new Exalls in that area, but we don't know for sure because the ETD's aren't picking up anything. We can only see the old Exalls who were already there, the benign ones. All two of them in Kansas City."

"Jesus Christ." Griffins buried his face into his hands and furiously rubbed his forehead. This was bordering on a state of emergency declaration, the first step before Plan D. The president would have to declare an emergency, and tell the people he was sending the National Guard. In reality it would be hundreds of Crew soldiers sent to execute any and all Exalls they came in contact with. "Let's get some people to follow the peaceful Exalls that we know of. Surely the new ones will eventually flock to them, don't you think?"

"We have no reason to believe that is true. The peaceful Exalls either want no part of all the violence, or are just people who don't know they've been infected with Exall blood."

"How the hell can they not know?" When someone became infected, their body temperature dropped drastically, their skin turned a shade of gray, even if slightly, and an unleashed rage filled them from the inside.

"Homeless people, sir. They might feel sick, but have nowhere to go, so they just live on not knowing what's wrong with them."

"I still want them tailed. We're kidding ourselves if we don't think the Exalls have been planting these 'peaceful' Exalls around the country for no reason. In fact, let's go take one and bring them here."

"You know we can't do that."

"Bullshit, it's time."

"It's in our bylaws to leave any peaceful Exalls alone."

"To hell with the bylaws. Those were written decades ago, and there isn't even a reason for it. Kennedy wrote the original bylaws, and he was a damn hippie. Of course he wanted to keep peace with this species who comes and kills us every few decades."

"You'll need presidential approval."

"I know the rules, Grady, I'm the colonel. Jesus Christ, were you the kid in school who reminded the teacher that the homework was due? I also have the authority to declare that we are under attack from the Exalls, granting me the power to execute any order related to the Exalls. Did you forget that rule?"

"No, sir, I just—"

"You just nothing. We're under attack. You said it yourself that what happened last night was the Exalls. We're at a point where the secret could get out to the general population. Then what?"

"Plan D."

"Plan D is a last resort. You kids like to throw it around like it's some sort of viable option. You do realize what that means right? Your own family will be wiped off the map. All of them, all your friends. The only family that is exempt is the First Family." Grady frowned. "They don't tell you that. Why would they? I personally think they should, and that's why I don't hesitate to tell Crew members that brutal truth. Maybe it would keep everyone working harder to prevent attacks like last night."

"There's no way of preventing an attack like yesterday. How could we ever know they were going to do that?"

"If our technology was working, it could have been stopped. What we need right now are the numbers. We need to know exactly how many Exalls are wandering around Kansas City. And Colorado, for that matter. We need to know how many others have been infected with their blood. And we need to prepare for a quarantine."

"Sir, a quarantine will make everyone suspicious – they're already calling it a zombie attack."

"Well then, it's a good thing zombies aren't real. Let them believe that; we can't let this spread beyond Kansas City. Now, as the head of intelligence, can you get me these numbers by the end of the day?"

"Yes, sir."

"Good. Get to work, and get this Plan D shit out of your head."

Grady nodded before leaving the office with his tail between his legs.

Griffins shook his head and returned to the briefing, knowing an inevitable war was looming with the Exalls.

14

Chapter 14

Kyle sprinted through an obstacle course in between ducking, jumping, and diving. There was even a quick dip into a swimming pool where he soared through the twenty feet like a shortfin mako shark.

The physical training had been the hardest trial, yet the most rewarding. His body begged for him to roll over and quit, but his mind kept pushing through the end. He had heard about the attacks in Colorado and Kansas City being tied to the Exalls, and couldn't help but wonder if Brian was somehow involved. Or even possibly his grandmother. The more he learned about the Exalls, the more he doubted his grandmother was actually dead. They could have taken her body and injected their blood into it, bringing her back to life in the form of an old, gray-skinned woman. It was more likely they were studying her body, seeing as they had never captured anyone who worked with The Crew, but Kyle held his reservations.

Today, however, was his final bootcamp-style drill with the obstacle course. He had excelled through it after weeks of gaining muscle and building his stamina and endurance. He never imagined his body could feel so strong, and start to show the chisel of a Grecian statue. But here he was in late July, feeling the best he ever had.

"Wells!" Gerard shouted. He had watched Kyle complete the course from a watch tower twenty feet high. "Let's call it a day. Come see me."

Kyle panted for breath, clasping his hands together behind his head, as he walked on the turf around the obstacle course that reminded him of the Ninja Warrior challenge they always showed on TV.

Gerard climbed down the tower's ladder and met Kyle at the base. "Good work today. How are you feeling?"

"Tired, but good."

"That's good. You look like a natural out there – your weight lifting has really paid off. I think we're going to call it a wrap on the physical training for the time being. You'll still have time in the gym to maintain your strength, but we won't be doing any more of the obstacle or field training until we get closer to your final test." Kyle stared at Gerard with a puzzled expression, unsure if he was in trouble or exceeding expectations. "We're going to focus more on your mind. You'll likely be ready to take your final test within the next couple weeks, and Colonel Griffins already has a special mission he'd like to assign you. It's going to require you take huge strides forward in your mental strength, something that's been your only real weakness so far."

"What kind of mission?"

"I can't go into those details—that's something the colonel will have to do, and he probably won't tell you until it's time. So for now, you'll be reporting directly to Dr. Barlowe. Have you met him yet?"

"No, I don't think so." Kyle had briefly met what seemed like hundreds of people over the last few weeks, but that particular name didn't stand out.

"He's a bit of a character," Gerard said with a smirk. "But I suppose that's the nature of the business when you're one of the world's top psychologists. I'm going to warn you: he'll try to break your mind. So take everything he says during preparation very seriously and you won't have any problems."

Kyle nodded, terrified at the concept of having his mind broken, whatever that was supposed to mean.

"He'll be ready for you tomorrow. You'll meet in his office on the sixth floor and will likely be spending the next couple weeks in that room with him. You'll have a new schedule delivered tonight to your room to reflect this new change."

"Thank you." Kyle wanted to ask if there was a projected date for his inevitable final test, but he didn't really want to know. The last thing he needed was a date circled on the calendar, pulling him closer to the next phase of his life where he would actually be a full-fledged member of The Crew.

Gerard wished him a good rest of the day before parting ways.

* * *

Kyle hadn't had a weekday afternoon free to himself since the first days of his life in the compound six weeks ago. It was only noon when Gerard had released him, and he wanted to spend the rest of the day doing something he had longed for, but hadn't the chance to do. Sundays had been for resting, and Kyle struggled to get out of bed in time for breakfast.

He had rushed back to his room, changed out of his training uniform in favor of his street clothes that seemed to never get used any more, and worked his way through the building to the front desk where Jack sat, staring mindlessly into the computer monitors.

"Kyle Wells," Jack said, perking up in his seat. "I haven't seen you since your first day. How are things going in training?"

Jack had the appearance of a man who could snap your spine in half with his bare hands, yet spoke and interacted with the gentleness of a nurse.

"It's going well, I think."

"I'd say so. You were a twig when I met you, and you already have guns for arms. Wait until you see your transformation after multiple months of our workout regimen."

Kyle chuckled nervously, not wanting to think of the physical training becoming more grueling than it already was.

"Is there something I can do for you today?" Jack asked, his eyebrows raised.

"Yes. I want to go out." Kyle spoke like a nervous teenager asking his parents' permission to hang out with his friends after school. He was still a teenager, but The Crew didn't view him as such. He didn't technically need permission to do anything on his free time, and the sudden realization made Kyle giddy with anticipation. Maybe his Sundays wouldn't be wasted in bed moving forward, after all.

"I can have a car ready to take you in five minutes. Where are you looking to go?"

"Arlington National Cemetery."

"You going to visit your grandma?"

Kyle nodded. She really had been a celebrity within this

organization.

"Very good. It's a beautiful cemetery – I'd suggest you give a full walk around it. You can visit JFK's grave, and see the changing of the guard at the Tomb of the Unknown Soldiers."

"I'll be sure to take a look, thank you. I was only there for her funeral and wasn't in the mood to walk around."

"Understandable. Is that the only place you'll be going? We like to know how to schedule our drivers' days."

"Yes, that'll be my only stop today."

Kyle had visited the main attractions, the memorials and parks, during a walk around D.C. on his first free day. Once he got into more of a groove with his schedule, he'd plan to see more of the sights.

"Perfect, I'll arrange the car to pick you up right outside these door in just a few minutes. Let us know if you change your mind and want to go anywhere else. Here's my number."

Jack handed over a white business card with nothing printed on it but a phone number.

Kyle took it and slid it into his pocket, returning his gaze to Jack. "Can I ask you something?"

"What's on your mind?"

"What do they say about me?"

"Who?"

"People here. I feel like I get special treatment. No one has ever *not* been friendly to me. I just wonder sometimes what they told everyone before I showed up."

Jack leaned back in his seat and clasped his hands behind his head. "We've never had a recruit show up with such high expectations. We've also never had one show up on a rec-ommendation. Did they tell you how the regular recruitment process works?"

Kyle shook his head.

"Our recruiters hack into college scoring systems—although *hack* is probably the wrong word since we're the government. We *access* the colleges' systems and start our search by finding top performers—and I'm talking the top one percent of students. From there we run background checks, study the person's social media accounts and emails, just to get a feel for the type of person they are and what their current situation is in life. If they've started a family, we'll leave them alone until maybe their kids are older."

"My grandma had kids. . . obviously."

"Probably not at the time of her recruitment. She might have been married at the time, but we hire people who have their availability and life paths wide open. If they decide they want to incorporate kids into their busy schedules after joining us, they certainly can."

Kyle felt queasy, thinking he had been one bad work trip away from not even existing.

"Anyway, once we narrow down that list of one percenters to another one percent, we will briefly follow the person from a distance to make sure there's nothing we missed. If everything checks out, we approach them in private and let them know about this special opportunity here at the Pentagon. When most people hear we're the government, they listen."

"So there have been people watching me?"

Jack nodded, smirking. "It's not as bad as you think. You've been treated differently from the start because of Susan. She left your name as a recommendation for us to recruit, and she was never known to have a bad hunch. The people following you were more there to protect you."

"Protect me from what?"

"Exalls," Jack responded, matter-of-factly.

"Why would the Exalls want me? I never did anything to them."

"That's probably a better question for the colonel. I only know what I hear—which is a lot in this position, but not everything. Your car is here, though."

Kyle pivoted around to see headlights waiting for him outside of the lobby doors. "Thanks again, Jack. We'll have to talk some more another time."

"Anytime, young man. You know where to find me."

Kyle left The Crew's offices, questions swirling about his past and future.

15

Chapter 15

Over the next month, Kyle graduated from the classroom sessions to spend more time practicing combat and stealth. While it was more entertaining to run through obstacle courses, shoot high-powered rifles, and learn espionage tactics that made him feel like a ninja, the physical toll wore him out by the end of each day. He was in good shape by this point, but after scarfing down chicken and veggies and showering at the end of each session, his body begged for him to lie down. Time became a constant blur.

Colonel Griffins had slipped into the room during random training sessions, whispering with whoever was leading that particular training, but never speaking to Kyle directly. That was until the evening of August 27th, when the colonel pulled him aside, letting him know his big test was scheduled for the following day.

"*Tomorrow?*" Kyle had asked. "All I get is one day's notice?"

"Of course. Do you think the Exalls send us *notice* before they attack our people?"

"No, sir."

"Good. You're ready, everyone says so. Just relax and do what you already know how to do."

Do what you already know how to do, Kyle told himself as he looked in the mirror the next morning before his life-changing test.

His stomach felt like an empty pit. He had forced down a cup of yogurt and two slices of toast, but had no interest in eating. The anticipation of the test gnawed at him both mentally and physically.

"Don't be afraid of failure," Griffins had told him. "There is no failing this test. If you don't pass, we just work on your weaknesses until they are up to par. Trust your instincts, don't overthink anything, and perform naturally."

Kyle slipped into his training uniform of athletic pants and a skin-tight t-shirt. "Let's do this," he said before leaving his room, his future awaiting.

He headed for the classroom named after his grandmother. The test started there with a written exam that covered his knowledge of the Exalls. He zipped through the pages that asked questions about their history and abilities, confident with every answer chosen, as these facts had been drilled into his brain over the last few months.

From there Kyle was taken to the Kennedy Room, an area he had yet to see as it housed a mazelike obstacle course of towering white walls, spanning the size of half a football field. The maze was filled with different checkpoints, each consisting of one physical task and one mental task. A bell chimed through hidden speakers once he successfully completed the tasks, prompting him to move on to the next checkpoint.

The challenges were supposed to start at an easier level and become increasingly more difficult, so his knees trembled as he approached the first checkpoint, a small round table with a tablet on it. He read the tablet to find he owed 30 pushups to begin the test, along with a word problem he had to solve.

Kyle dropped to the ground, did his pushups, and returned to the table to read the question:

A bus driver was heading down a street. He went right past a stop sign without stopping, turned left where there was a "no left turn" sign, and went the wrong way on a one-way street. Then he went on the left side of the road past a cop. Yet, he didn't break any traffic laws. Why not?

Kyle grinned as a fresh wave of confidence surged through his body. He enjoyed these types of riddles, or word problems, whatever the hell they were. He aced these during training because his grandmother would always ask him one every day after picking him up from school. And he remembered her asking this specific problem once. It was one of the first times she had asked one of these types of questions, and he remembered it vividly. They were waiting at a crosswalk as a school bus drove by, prompting Susan to ask him the question. Kyle was maybe ten years old, wondering why his grandmother was asking such an absurd riddle.

He searched on the tablet for somewhere to type the answer, but there was no space to type. He looked around, white walls surrounding him, seeing nowhere to make a move.

"He didn't break any laws because he was walking," Kyle said to the tablet. The speakers chimed, and the tablet flashed a message telling him to go to the next checkpoint.

He grinned and put the tablet back on the table before moving forward, working his way through the twisting maze until he approached a closed door. The walls towered above him, providing only a glimpse of the bright fluorescent lights in the ceiling. The door clearly led into another room, and as Kyle approached it, he noticed a rifle on the ground. It was the same type of rifle he had used in training, the one loaded with The Crew's special "choker" bullets designed to kill Exalls.

Kyle snatched the rifle, admiring its cool black metal as he brushed fingers along its surface. A magazine was already loaded, and he checked to see six rounds inside it, cocking the gun as he pushed the door open with the muzzle.

It opened to pure darkness, a black hole under the bright lights. He looked around to see if there was anything else to suggest what he do next, but since the last checkpoint, he already knew no portion of this test came with instructions.

He stepped into the darkness to find a dim path illuminated that led forward. Once he was all the way in, the door slammed shut behind him, causing him to spin around and come eye to eye with a hologram of an Exall.

The Exall grinned black fangs, glowing in the dark like a jellyfish in the night sea. Its gray skin sent chills up Kyle's back, and he had a brief flood of horrific memories from that day he watched his grandmother's murder.

His arms never trembled as he lined up a shot and blasted a round directly through the Exall's head. Its face exploded into hundreds of pixelated shards.

"I don't think so!" a voice shouted from behind, and Kyle spun back around to see another faux Exall charging him like a linebacker trying to sack a quarterback. Kyle pulled the trigger again and grinned as he watched another gray head explode into imaginary dust.

"Kyle?" a familiar voice called. His grandmother's voice. Kyle's head spun as he tried to process what he was hearing. Did they have a recording of her? Was this entire recruitment some elaborate way to reunite them? Was she still alive? "Kyle, I'm so proud of you. You're making our family proud by carrying on my life's work. Don't ever give up on this. The world needs you."

Her voice seemed to come from every corner of the dark room. Kyle returned to the dim path and continued forward, clueless as to how far he had to go before leaving this room of death.

"Kyle, I've missed you," she said.

It has to be a trap. That's all it is. It's not really her. You watched her die – this is part of the test.

As much as he assured himself of these facts, hearing her voice created a fresh pit in his chest, filled with the pain and sorrow that had been buried over the last four years.

He walked into a wall, his knee banging into it and shooting a small bolt of pain up his leg, but he hardly noticed. His mind was drawn to the sound of his grandmother's voice and sensed nothing else. He felt around in the dark, his hands eventually finding another doorknob that he twisted and pushed forward, opening into another dark room where his grandmother stood over a crackling fire pit, as if she were merely on a summer camping trip. She kept her focus on the flames, the orange glow illuminating a face that looked exactly as he remembered.

"Grandma?" Kyle called out, his legs frozen as his mind debated moving forward. His brain saw her as another hologram figure in this test, but his heart viewed her as real, *longed* for her to be real. "Grandma, is that you?"

"Ky," she said, looking up from the flames and meeting his gaze. "They told me I'd get to see you, but I didn't think it would be so soon."

Kyle took a step closer and saw a tear gliding down her cheek, his heart ignoring the fact that it was a pixelated tear.

HELLO! ARE YOU PAYING ATTENTION, KYLE? THIS IS STILL A TEST! his mind screamed. But no one was home.

"Come tell me about your stay here in D.C.," she said. "Have you gone to any of the museums yet?"

Kyle's throat swelled with a lump of shock as he took another step closer. He kept a tight grip around his rifle, but the weapon felt thousands of miles away.

"Have you talked to your dad?" she asked. "I just want him to know that I'm okay."

As he took one more step, standing within fifteen feet of his grandmother, the reality started to sprout back up in his mind. She was not real. Yes, she stood in front of him and spoke in the same voice he knew, but this wasn't real. This was a testing facility hundreds of feet below the Pentagon where no one would ever hear his screams if he were to be slaughtered by an alien species.

Kyle raised the rifle, fixing his aim on his grandmother's face. She looked to the gun, to his eyes, no concern on her face. "What are you doing, Ky?"

"You're not real." Saying this aloud made a warm tear streak from the corner of his eye.

"Of course I'm real. Come touch me, see for yourself. They saved me on that horrible day, and I can't begin to tell you how sorry I am for not letting the family know that I've been fine this whole time."

"I watched you die!"

"I didn't die, Ky. I had so much protection on that day, there was never a chance. It was all an act to make them think they got me, to protect you and your friends. I've been hiding here ever since because they're looking for me, Ky. And that's why you're here, to save us all. Use your special gift, Ky. Don't be afraid of it."

"I don't have a gift! I'll never be you."

"You're not expected to be me, you're expected to be *you*." Susan grinned as gently as ever, a tint of pride swimming in her eyes. "Now come give me a hug and let's talk this over." She opened her arms and Kyle took one more step closer, now within ten feet of his grandmother.

More tears streamed down his face as he realized what he needed to do, tightening his grip on the rifle, his index finger subconsciously sliding over the trigger. "I love you, grandma."

His voice wavered as these words came out, the rifle booming milliseconds after, Susan's holographic face exploding into more of the pixelated shards of light. Every ounce of tension that had risen from his toes to his brain vanished with that squeeze of the trigger, and he knew that regardless of what came next on this fucked-up test, he had the mental stability for life as a Crew member.

More lights illuminated the pathway, revealing a new door beyond where Susan had stood. Kyle wasted no time moving for it, needing salvation after what he had just endured. *Freedom. How long have I even been in here?*

The entire sequence of events from the start of the exam had felt like a solid hour, but only twenty minutes had passed in reality.

He pushed the door open and returned to the maze filled with bright lights, providing a fabricated outdoor sensation. His mind may have been playing tricks, but he thought he heard birds chirping much like they did in the Outside Room.

Colonel Griffins stood ahead of him, arms crossed behind his back with a stern expression smacked on his face. "That was impressive," he said flatly. "How are you feeling?"

"I'm okay. Why?"

"We've never put a recruit through that intense of a sequence before, at least not something so personal. This was a unique opportunity, as we had a lot of sound bites from Susan's work here and were able to form an authentic re-creation."

"I knew she was fake," Kyle replied, not acknowledging the initial confusion he had felt. "I knew it was all part of this test."

Colonel Griffins snickered, nodding his head. "If you insist. You have nine more checkpoints to complete, but we wanted to make sure you're mentally okay after that."

"I'm good. Let's finish this."

"That's what I like to hear." The colonel stepped aside and raised an arm to allow Kyle to pass. As Kyle strode by him, Griffins winked and nodded, clearly fighting the urge to grin. Kyle nodded and moved forward without another thought, his heart heavy with the memories of the fearless woman who had been preparing him his whole life for this very moment.

16

Chapter 16

"So why exactly did we get sent into the middle of nowhere for this mission?" Dante Rivers asked his partner, Ron Miley.

The two had trudged through the woods of northern Michigan while Kyle Wells rested in D.C. for the weekend after taking his initiation test. Night had fallen and the temperature dropped quickly, making it especially cool for a summer night. Dante knew very well why they were essentially off the grid for this mission, but had to say something as the terrain grew more uneven with each step, the cabin they were searching for seeming to become further with every minute that passed.

Dante and Ron had been part of the same training class at The Crew—class of 2010—and instantly became best friends when they were both fresh out of college, taking on this absurd organization who fought aliens in the night. They were both in their early thirties, now married with two kids each, essentially following in each other's life paths. Their wives and children had all become friends over the years and often kept each other company when the pair was sent out on a mission like this one.

Tonight they were dressed in complete combat attire, their

camouflage uniforms covering the full bodysuit of protective gear underneath.

"Colonel has lost his mind," Ron said, gasping for air as they climbed a small hill, his black bangs plastered to his forehead with sweat. Ron had splotches of dirt scattered across his face, thanks to tripping over a tree branch that was stuck in the ground shortly after they started their hike.

Dante had fallen onto his ass in laughter, grabbing his gut and rolling in the dirt, getting himself covered in grime as well. Both men looked like they might have just come out of a coal mine, speckles of dark matter covering their clothes and faces.

"Did anyone even question this decision?" Ron continued. "This could go horribly wrong."

"We'll be alright," Dante reassured. "It's two-on-one."

They moved through the trees, both men taller than six feet and built to crush bones with their bare hands. Someone might mistake them for a couple of Sasquatches if they didn't know any better.

"I'm not worried about us," Ron replied. "I'm worried about the rest of the world; this could spark something out of our control."

"Or it could not. You worry too much."

The two had grown to accept that they had polar opposite personalities, embracing it as a strength when they worked together, able to see perspectives from all angles.

"I only worry because it's a possibility. I've done my reading on this: never in the history of the Exalls or The Crew have we taken one of the peaceful Exalls. I don't know *why*, but I trust there's a good reason for it."

"We're making history. You should be proud."

"I'm not proud of *this*. We're kidnapping an innocent man."

"Don't call him innocent, and don't call him a man. He's – *it's* an Exall, and even if it has never personally harmed a human being, it's still associated with them. Don't pretend to not know what that thing's capable of doing to us."

"I know that—it just seems wrong, like we're picking a fight with the nerdy kid at school. He might not even know he's an Exall, and this could all be a waste of time."

"Not know and live in the middle of nowhere? Unlikely." Dante stopped suddenly, causing Ron to bump into him from behind. "There it is. Do you see it?" He raised a finger and pointed ahead through the trees where a faint glow of light appeared in the distance.

"About 300 yards out," Ron said, reaching over his shoulder to grab his rifle.

"Sounds right. Let me make sure he's alone." Dante pulled out his ETD and waited for the screen to load with their current area. It shone brightly, showing two flashing green dots that represented him and Ron, and a lone red dot on the other side of the screen. "It's just him."

They had been assigned a mission to capture the Exall and bring him back to the Pentagon. There were dozens of these peaceful aliens across the world who carried on with their lives as if they didn't know they were supposed to be raising hell for the humans on Earth.

Everyone had their conspiracy theories. Some believed the peaceful Exalls were the ones actually calling the shots for The Crew, that they were somehow the past leaders of the country brought back to life through a small infusion of Exall blood that allowed them to essentially be immortal.

Dante believed every theory he heard. Knowing the government was capable of hiding the existence of an alien species that walked among the population, was it that far-fetched to think that Kennedy had never died and was injected with the black blood to keep him alive? Was it so absurd to think that the Exalls had actually taken over and the peaceful ones were blackmailing the rest of the world with a threat to end humanity?

Dante pulled his rifle just as Ron had done, cocked it, and continued forward through the darkness, following the distant yellow light like a compass.

The night seemed to fall silent. Even the crickets stopped chirping as the two men crunched their way through sticks and leaves, weaving between a web of low-hanging branches. Ron trailed Dante and they stopped when they reached the perimeter of the property.

With the woods to their backs, they took their first step on even ground since beginning their trek from the car somewhere half a mile away.

"Are we really trying to take this guy back through all that mess?" Ron whispered.

Dante shook his head. "We'll tie him up, and one of us will go get the car."

"And *drive* through the trees? There's no road."

"It'll be easier to drive slow than to drag this monster half a mile."

While that was true, they only had a small SUV, which was not exactly equipped to drive through the woods.

"Let's just worry about that when we get there," Dante said. "One thing at a time."

The cabin blended in with the darkness, three windows revealing the soft glow from within, flickering like a fireplace. There was no moonlight, no ambient light from a nearby city, leaving them in complete blackness. They had arrived to town around lunch time, but it was now approaching midnight. Colonel Griffins insisted they make their move in the night, even though there was no chance of anyone spotting them in the middle of nowhere.

Dante proceeded onto the property. They had strict orders to not kill the Exall, but instead to detain him and bring him back to D.C. Still, Dante kept his rifle pointed ahead, ready for the worst should the Exall try anything suspicious. He didn't trust these gray bastards one bit, even the supposedly "peaceful" ones.

They continued toward the cabin, the light growing with each step and coming into clear focus that it was indeed from a fireplace. When they reached the front steps, Dante crouched, prompting Ron to follow suit as they moved with the stealth of two ninjas, their feet gliding over the ground to avoid making any sound. They were dressed in the darkest of camouflage, unable to see their own hands in front of their faces on this particular night.

The front entrance was a door centered between two windows with a thin curtain draped over them, not allowing a clear view into the cabin's entryway and living room. Dante climbed the first of three steps, his senses heightened as he felt the smooth wooden steps beneath his feet.

He reached the top landing. Now with a better view through the window, he saw nothing but an empty living room and kitchen, and a fireplace burning quietly along the back wall.

"I think we're clear," Dante whispered over his shoulder. "There's no one there."

"I don't like this," Ron shot back. "Why would he leave a fire burning and go to bed? If he's an Exall he wouldn't need any heat."

Dante appreciated the logic from his partner, but this wasn't the time to discuss semantics. They had to make a move quickly as they stood on the front deck of the wanted man's cabin.

"Let's just go in and get him. He might be asleep on a couch around the corner that we can't see. Are you ready?" Dante asked, not expecting an answer. He reached for the doorknob, wondering why anyone who lived in such a remote location would need to lock their doors at night. There weren't even animals in this part of the state that could wander in during your afternoon lunch.

To his delight, the knob kept turning until it clicked and the door gave way, gliding open to let a wave of warmth spill out. Dante thought of his mom yelling at him as a child to close the door when the heater was running, or goddammit, he'd pay for half of the gas bill.

The light from inside provided them enough to see each other, so Dante looked back and nodded to Ron, who nodded in return with a ghastly expression on his face.

Dante took the first step into the cabin and tightened his grip on the rifle. *Don't kill him, don't kill him,* he reminded himself. He prayed this would be easy, hoping the Exall would be sleeping where they could tie him up with no fight. But his instincts knew nothing was ever that easy with Exalls. And the creatures didn't *require* sleep.

They were both now entirely inside the entryway, the living room about thirty feet ahead where only the fire was visible from where they stood. The kitchen with its table, sink, and small counter was in front of the wall that divided it from the living room. A hallway ran left from the kitchen, likely to a bedroom and bathroom.

Dante looked around, noting the lack of decorations. The cabins he had been in—which were only a handful—usually had Southwestern art, or at the very least some sort of animal mounted above the mantle. But not this place. The walls were bare; nothing but wood in every direction. Not a single rug decorated the floor. There were no dishrags or pots and pans in the kitchen. It was as if the place had been abandoned years ago, some long-lost soul leaving it in the middle of the night with the fire still burning. A fire that would never go out.

It all swarmed Dante's already overloaded senses, and struck him as eerie, the hairs on his neck prickling. He didn't notice his hands give the slightest of trembles on the rifle, his legs turning into heavy logs that he had to drag for each step.

"Close the door," he whispered over his shoulder, paranoid thoughts present at every turn in his mind.

Ron obliged, gently closing the door to not make a sound. For a few seconds, maybe minutes, the two men stood in the entryway, unwilling to move forward, clearly wanting to turn around and make a run for the car half a mile away. They had only one prior encounter with an Exall, and even that instance was with a large group of Crew members leading an attack on the lone alien. This was a different ballgame with just Dante and Ron, no backup nearby.

"The peaceful ones shouldn't put up a fight – they might even come voluntarily," Colonel Griffins had told them. But Dante did not feel safe in this cabin, an unmistakably evil presence hanging in the air like a thick fog.

Ron stepped forward to join Dante at his side. They locked eyes and Ron nodded, taking the next step toward the living room, Dante now following behind. The next step Dante took caused a loud moan from the floorboards and all the blood to rush to his face. In the silent cabin, the simple creak felt like it had been amplified for the entire state of Michigan to hear. Ron continued forward, craning his neck to see around the wall that blocked the view into the living room. He lowered his rifle and shrugged, whispering, "No one's in there."

The entryway, living room, and kitchen were clear of the Exall, meaning he had to be in the bedroom or bathroom down the hallway. It also meant no one heard the obnoxious misstep Dante had taken.

Relieved, Dante took charge again and stepped into the hallway with confidence, looking left into a pit of darkness. The fire only provided enough light to see the first door in the hallway that stood ajar.

Ron pulled out a flashlight, but Dante quickly waved him off, shaking his head. They were close. The Exall was behind one of two doors, and they now had the advantage of containing the bastard within the confines of whichever room.

But why was the fire lit? he wondered. *Even though it wouldn't kill him, why risk having the whole place burn down just to keep the fire going overnight?*

"Cover me," Dante whispered, stepping into the hallway with his rifle leading the way. "Watch my back on this first door."

He glided toward the door and took a silent leap into the room, his rifle jerking left to right. Ron waited in the hallway, but nothing happened.

Dante flicked on the light switch to see it was the bathroom, again with no decorations or personal belongings scattered about the sink.

Do we have the right place? Dante asked himself. Surely The Crew never gave faulty intel for missions, but this particular cabin appeared as if it had never been lived in by so much as a mouse. Just because Exalls didn't require food to live or a bathroom to relieve themselves didn't mean the place should look untouched. Did the Exall just sit on the couch all day, staring at the walls? Staring at the fireplace?

Dante turned the bathroom light off and rejoined Ron in the hallway, both of their heads turning to the closed door they could now see at the end of the hall.

"He's in there," Ron said, just below a whisper.

Dante nodded. "Let's go in together and get him."

This was actually one of their favorite drills to practice: barging into a room and destroying everything in sight. Only this wasn't practice, and this time they couldn't kill the target.

Why? Dante pleaded with himself. *Just let me kill the gray piece of shit. They don't even belong on this planet.*

He thought Colonel Griffins was placing too much trust in the "peaceful" Exalls. Why wouldn't they fight back? Even an alien species wouldn't want to be arrested and taken away for doing nothing. They had abilities that made him quiver at the thought. *What if it controls my mind and makes me kill Ron? Or even kill myself? They can do anything without laying a finger on me.*

They remained silent as Dante reached out for the doorknob. He looked over his shoulder to confirm Ron was still ready, and when he nodded back, turned the knob as quietly as possible and pushed open the door.

It creaked, a long, drawn out groan as further darkness was revealed. Dante's heart thudded in his ears as he felt around the wall for a light switch, his fingers stumbling as his hands shook out of control. He knew whatever the light would reveal would change everything.

Why am I so scared? I've trained for this; I know what I'm doing.

His fingers found the switch and flipped it up.

"On your feet!" Dante barked, his free hand snapping back to his rifle.

The light revealed a bedroom no different than the rest of the house: bare walls and floors, an empty dresser and nightstand, and a perfectly made bed with not so much as a wrinkle on its solid blue comforter.

"What the fuck?" Ron asked, stepping in behind Dante. "Check the closet?"

The closet doors were on the wall to their left. Dante doubted their Exall friend was in there and strode right up to pull open the doors, revealing what he suspected.

"I don't get it," Ron said. "Where is he?"

"He had to have known we were coming and is hiding. I'm not sure what other explanation there is."

"How would he know?" Ron asked, voice cracking with fear.

"That doesn't matter. We just need to find him and finish this up."

A knock banged from the front door, causing the two men to jump as the sound echoed around the deserted cabin.

"Turn the light off," Ron snapped, and Dante obliged immediately. It had still been the only light on in the entire cabin. "It has to be him."

For a brief moment, Dante had a sick feeling that a whole gang of Exalls were waiting outside the cabin. That the one they had come for sent out a call for help and now there were at least a dozen of them waiting to take him and Ron away. But he shook off the thought as unlikely; these creatures didn't *need* help and could fend for themselves.

Another knock came, this time softer, like the person was

brushing their fist along the door instead of actually pounding it.

The looked at each other, puzzled.

"Let's go," Dante said, unsure why they were acting so scared with their rifles snug in their grip. If it came to it, they could blast any Exall making a threat on their lives. Sure, Griffins wanted the Exall returned alive, but he'd rather not have to clean up the mess of two dead Crew members. "Yeah, let's go," Dante said again, more to himself.

He took the first step out of the bedroom and felt Ron following behind.

Another knock never came as they tiptoed down the hallway, the sounds of their own beating hearts the loudest things they could hear. When they reached the end of the hall, they had a clear view of the living room, its fire still ablaze, and Dante peeked around the edge of the wall for a view of the front door.

"No one's there," he whispered, stepping completely into the living room. He crossed to the entryway and pulled open the door, wanting the confirmation for his own peace of mind.

"Are we just hearing things?" Ron asked in a nervous voice. "I mean, let's not kid ourselves – this is a bit scary, coming to an abandoned house."

"We're soldiers, Ron, we don't get scared," Dante said, knowing damn well they were both terrified.

A new knock came, this time from the bedroom they had just left, and Ron gasped, jumping into the living room.

Dante's heart nearly leapt out of his mouth, but he managed to keep his composure despite his vision drastically coming in and out of focus thanks to his throbbing adrenaline. "We need to go in that room and start shooting," he said, taking advantage of his adrenaline and bolting down the hallway. He lowered his shoulder into the door like a running back trying to plow his way through a defender.

The door swung open and banged against the wall as Dante started spraying bullets all across the bedroom, glass shattering from the windows as several rounds stuck into the cabin's wooden walls.

After firing off about three dozen rounds, Dante ceased, panting for breath and looking around the room in disappointment.

"What the fuck?!" he screamed to the ceiling. "Come out and fight us like a man, you piece of shit!"

Ron shuffled into the room, seeing the shards of wood on the floor, their corresponding chips in the walls scattered about like sprinkles on an ice cream cone. With the windows blown out, they stood and listened as the wind howled outside.

"It wasn't windy our entire walk up here," Ron commented, feeling like he needed to say *something* to ease the tension, but doing exactly the opposite. "Do you think the wind was making the knocking sound?"

It was a valid question, but one they both knew was false. No, the wind didn't knock on the front door, then run around to the other side of the house to knock on the bedroom window. It was a goddam Exall, and he was toying with them now, probably somewhere out in the woods laughing with all his gray friends as they watched the show with buckets of blood-covered popcorn.

The wind picked up, the intense rustling of the trees sounding more like a waterfall outside. Dante crossed the bedroom to the window for a better look, but refused to stick his head out. No Crew member was trained to be that stupid.

Ron trailed behind. "It sounds like a tornado out there."

"No shit. Were we expecting this weather?"

Every mission had a full-detailed report where the forecast was listed.

"No. We were told clear skies and no moon, just like it's been. I think the wind was making those sounds, listen to how strong it is. It could have blown over a trash can or something outside."

The wind howled like a rabid wolf, the cabin creaking as its structure fought to resist the gusts.

A hard *thump!* came from the kitchen, causing them to spin on their heels to look down the hallway.

"What was that?!" Ron gasped.

The sound was barely audible over the wind, but there was no mistaking its sharpness under the white noise.

Dante never saw it coming, only catching the glimmer of the blade reaching in from the open window before a squeezing pain erupted across his throat. Ron still had his back to him as he stared down the hallway. Dante opened his mouth to speak, but his throat swelled and clenched shut as if stuck in a bear trap. He thought drool was pouring out of his mouth, but he looked down to see scarlet droplets of blood splashing on the floor. His breathing slowed to desperate gasps for air as bright spots of lights flashed in his vision.

The rifle fell from his grip, clattering on the floor and drawing Ron's attention.

"Dante!" Ron shouted, dropping his own rifle and lunging toward his partner.

Dante collapsed to his knees, his hands clawing for his slashed open throat which blood spewed from like a fountain. He held himself on his knees for only a few seconds, all energy draining from his body, before tipping over to his side, head thumping on the ground with a hard thud.

"No! No! No!" Ron pleaded. "Goddammit, hang on, Dante."

Even with the world fading to darkness, Dante could still hear the panic in Ron's voice, knowing there was nothing either of them could do. Ron crouched over Dante, pulling off his jacket and attempting to wrap it around the oozing throat. He wanted to tell Ron to stop and turn around, but his throat would never allow another word to leave his lips.

The last thing Dante saw was the grinning Exall, standing over Ron with a bloody butterfly knife raised in the air. The Exall held up a gray finger to his lips, mocking Dante.

A warm tear streamed down his face as he witnessed what he believed to be the start of a new war.

17

Chapter 17

Kyle Wells never imagined he'd meet the president of the United States. During the week after he completed the test for his official designation as a Crew member, a panel of the highest-ranking members reviewed Kyle's test results, and discussed whether to accept him, or if he needed to return to the training program.

It was Friday, September 4th, and the previous evening Colonel Griffins had pulled Kyle into his office to let him know he had passed the test, leaving the final step of the process to meet with the president for final approval. Kyle tensed up at the thought, but was assured that every Crew member went through this same approval since Kennedy officially started the organization.

A president had never rejected an admission before, leaving it as more of an honorary event and symbolic swearing-in ceremony. The president would have an official contract that required both his and the new Crew member's signature.

Since Kyle was still a minor, one parent was required to sign the contract as well, and Travis volunteered to fly out.

Kyle sat in the back of a town car with Colonel Griffins, leaving the Pentagon en route to the White House.

"Nothing to be nervous about," Colonel Griffins assured Kyle, but he still trembled in anticipation.

Kyle kept to himself, gazing out the window as he tried to relax his thoughts. Not only was he meeting with the leader of the free world, he was also going to see his dad for the first time since leaving home. What would his dad think of this luxurious lifestyle? Did he still support Kyle's decision to move forward with life as a Crew member?

The car pulled up to a security checkpoint where a soldier poked his head into the car and nodded to Colonel Griffins in the back. A few seconds passed and they were waved forward.

"We get to enter from the back entrance," Griffins said as the car turned onto a pathway that circled the White House's South Lawn. Kyle's eyes bulged in amazement as the White House came into clear view after they broke out of the trees that covered the driveway. All his friends were back at home learning about the White House in school, and here he was about to experience it first hand as an employee of the United States government.

His mouth hung open and he forced himself to close it.

"Your dad should already be inside waiting for us. He landed about an hour ago and we had him brought straight here."

The car pulled up to the curb a few feet away from the back entrance where two Secret Service agents stood in suits with a bullet-proof vest covering their chests. The pathway to the door was covered by an elongated white tent. The only thing missing was a red carpet.

Their driver, who had remained silent the entire trip, jumped out of the car and ran around to open the door facing the curb.

Colonel Griffins slid out, followed by Kyle.

"Good morning, Colonel," one of the agents greeted, his stare forward, off into the distance while his eyes remained buried behind his sunglasses.

"Good morning, Collins. How's the family?"

"Doing great, sir, thank you for asking."

Collins spoke like a robot and refused eye contact with anyone.

I'm really here. This is the real Secret Service. They just stand here all day waiting for someone to try something.

"That's great to hear," the colonel said. "Are we cleared to enter?"

"All clear, sir." Collins nodded before Griffins and Kyle disappeared down the walkway and into the White House.

They entered the building, greeted by a massive chandelier and more agents. The floors glossed in crystal clarity as they passed through the entryway and took a left to climb a short flight of stairs to the main level. They stepped out of a side door and into the middle of a passing tour. All the tourists gawked at them for a brief second, then quickly looked away when they realized Kyle and Colonel Griffins weren't famous.

They waited for the group to clear out before starting down the long hallway where Travis waited, studying a portrait of President Kennedy.

"Mr. Wells," Colonel Griffins called out.

Travis spun around and started toward them, a wide grin on his face. "This place is so cool." He stuck out a hand for the colonel before wrapping Kyle in a tight bear-like embrace. "How have you been, son?"

"I'm good, Dad. Apparently ready to move on with this group."

"I knew you would be. My mom tried to do the same thing with me when I was a kid, but gave up after two summers. Never did explain to me what I did wrong, but oh well. Guess I'll have to live vicariously through you."

"I know this is quite the reunion for you two," Colonel Griffins said. "But we really need to get to the Oval Office. The president stays on a strict schedule, as you can imagine."

Travis raised his eyebrows. "The Oval Office? Well then, if you insist."

Colonel Griffins led them quickly down the main hallway that connected the east wing to the west wing. Portraits of past presidents decorated the walls the entire way, giving Kyle a brief outburst of gooseflesh as he thought about all of the history that had taken place in these very halls.

Kyle's palms started to slicken with sweat as they passed into another hallway, more guards nodding them along. Not even of voting age, he didn't care much for politics, finding most topics well above his understanding, but it was no surprise the current president sparked strong emotions from both sides of the spectrum. He was perhaps the most controversial figure in American history, and Kyle was a few seconds away from meeting him.

They stopped at a closed door where two more guards stood outside.

"Gentlemen," Griffins said. "We have a meeting with the president."

The man on the left checked his watch before turning and knocking on the door, waiting five seconds, then pushing it open enough to stick his head in. "Mr. President, your ten o'clock is here."

"Send them in," a raspy voice replied, and the agent pushed

the door all the way open.

The three of them stepped in, Kyle and Travis immediately gazing around the room in shock. *It really is shaped like an oval,* Kyle thought, noting the golden drapes that hung over the windows to match the gold-colored chairs and couch centered around a coffee table in the middle of the room. Flags decorated every corner of the room: American, military branches, presidential seal.

Sitting behind the iconic *Resolute* desk was President Donald Trump, his lips pursed as he watched the visitors enter the room. "Good morning, gentlemen," he said. "Please have a seat." He held out a hand to the three empty seats across from him. His desk was bare, with the exception of two phone sets and a single stack of papers.

The president looked just as he did on TV every day: navy blue suit, long red tie, spray-tanned skin, and his famous slicked combover the color of chicken broth.

"Good morning, Mr. President," Colonel Griffins said, shaking the president's hand across the desk.

"Good to see you, Colonel. Glad to know we're recruiting more for The Crew."

"Indeed. This is Kyle Wells and his father, Travis."

Kyle stepped up with confidence and grasped the president's hand, savoring the moment.

"Nice to meet you gentlemen," the president said. "Shall we get started?"

"Yes, sir," Kyle responded as they all settled into their seats, Kyle in the middle with his father to his left and Colonel Griffins on his right.

"Colonel Griffins tells me you're a bright star for The Crew," the president said in his slightly raspy voice, his lifelong

Queens accent ever present. "I'm told we've never had a minor officially sign on as a member. And he told me about your grandmother. A very amazing woman. A real patriot."

"Thank you, sir," Kyle replied with a grin. He saw his father out of the corner of his eye, also smiling at the compliment regarding his late mother.

"So tell me, Kyle, why do you want to do this?" the president asked.

"Well, sir, I didn't know at first, but after spending the last three months here, I've grown to love The Crew. I enjoy our work and am honored to follow in my grandmother's footsteps."

The president leaned back, arms crossed as he nodded. "They told me you watched your grandmother's death. Sad. I can't imagine. Do you want revenge?"

Kyle smirked at the question. Of course he thought about killing Brian and any of the other Exalls he had watched on the monitors that day. He thought about it at least five times a day.

"I won't be actively seeking revenge," Kyle said. "But if the opportunity presents itself, I won't look the other way, either."

"I see. You know, I'm against letting you join," the president said, sending a sinking pit into Kyle's gut. "I don't think a young man should be in any sort of combat until he's an adult. How bad would that look for me if something happened to you, especially two months before Election Day? A big mess, believe me. Not a fun phone call to make to sad parents."

The president paused as if gathering his next thoughts, but left his last statement to hang in the air between them.

He's not going to actually reject me, is he? Kyle wondered, panicking. *Why would they fly my dad out here to watch me be turned away?*

"They tell me I have no choice in the matter," the president continued. "But we know that's not true. I *am* the final choice. They tell me you're a tremendous young man, and I like what I've seen so far. If this is really what you want, then I'm not going to stand in your way. I'll push over the contract right now for you to sign."

The president glared down to the stack of papers, as if daring Kyle to try and snatch them from his desk.

"Yes, sir, it is absolutely what I want to do with the rest of my life."

The president turned to Colonel Griffins. "And you're sure about this?"

"Mr. President, I don't think The Crew has been so sure about a candidate since Kyle's grandmother. He didn't break any records during the exam, but he did pass it in one attempt, something accomplished by only two percent of those who take it. That alone puts Mr. Wells in an elite category. His potential is through the roof."

"Tremendous. Everyone loves a good story of accomplishment. It's what this country was built on. Very American. Let's sign some papers."

The president pulled in the stack of papers, flipped to the back page, signed his name, and then pushed the entire stack across the desk. "Can you go through the contract with them, Colonel? I'm not too familiar with these."

"Yes, sir."

Colonel Griffins scooted his chair closer to Kyle and leaned over as he and Travis flipped through the thirty page document.

"This first page just covers the basics like your salary, living situation, and things of that nature." Colonel Griffins spoke as if he had rehearsed this bit hundreds of times.

Kyle's eyes went down the page and did a double take as he looked at his salary of $275,000 on top of free living within the Pentagon until he turned eighteen. The Crew would also cover all of his meals in their cafeteria that really was more of a five-star restaurant. He'd be given a new government-issued cell phone. He would be chauffeured to any location he needed, and given access to a private jet in case he had to return home for a family emergency. Essentially anything that was necessary in life was covered, leaving his entire paycheck to go toward extracurricular activities.

I'm going to be a millionaire when I turn twenty-one. What the hell am I going to do with all that money?

Kyle suddenly grew uncomfortable with his dad by his side, reading over his shoulder. He suspected Travis never even made this much of a salary, but then again it didn't matter, as Susan had left him millions in her will.

Kyle signed the bottom of each page as Colonel Griffins led him through it. After the first page, it was mostly a bunch of disclosures to not share government secrets, as doing so was punishable by death. He had to agree to have a tracking device implanted in his body so The Crew could always know if he was safe or in danger. Don't harm civilians. Don't discuss anything about the job outside of Crew business. Don't mention anything about the underground world beneath the Pentagon to anyone. Et cetera. Et cetera. Et cetera.

Kyle had already known this, having it drilled in his mind by his grandmother during her last days, and reinforced by Travis following her death. This was clearly the biggest secret in the entire world, and they had managed to go several decades without a slip up. He wondered what would happen if an ex-Crew member lost their mind after a battle and decided to go on TV and tell the world the news. Of course that person would be executed, but would the world believe them? In these days of absurd headlines, probably not. But there was sure to be a group of people—even if small—who would pursue the matter until they found answers.

Then what? The world goes to war with an alien species that no one understands outside of The Crew?

The weight of bearing such a heavy secret both disturbed and excited Kyle. His biggest responsibility so far in his young life had been to complete his homework on time and make sure his room stayed clean. In the matter of four years, and accelerated over the past few months, he was now responsible for the livelihood of the entire human race. Kyle kept this thought at the front of his mind as he signed the bottom of each page, committing his life to The Crew. Between pages, he stole glances around the Oval Office, still in shock that he was inside the most famous office in the country.

And it felt right, like a long-lost destiny being fulfilled.

18

Chapter 18

Kyle was treated to a great surprise after he signed his contract to officially join The Crew. Colonel Griffins told him to enjoy the next two weeks off, and offered to book him a flight home if he wanted to spend the time back in Denver.

Kyle agreed and could hear his mother jumping and screaming for joy all the way across the country after he informed her that he would be home tonight.

All that was asked of Kyle was to remain in the tip-top shape he had worked so hard to achieve. He returned home with a clear mind and the burden of The Crew temporarily off his shoulders. His two weeks would be split between his mom and dad's houses, but he would still have the opportunity to see both of them each day.

It was strange returning home after so many months, seeing the way life carried on for both of his parents, but also how everything stayed the same. His mother kept her house spotless as always, even tidying up Kyle's bedroom, not a single item in his room being touched.

When Kyle first stepped into his old bedroom, an eerie

nostalgia settled over him as if he had walked into a dead person's room. The posters of Ariana Grande that lined his wall felt like a blast from the past. His desk had piles of sports cards and hand-written notes from Jessica, the kind with hearts above the letter "i" and written in some sort of glittery purple ink.

He had grown up in the last three months and didn't realize it until he arrived home. He was still 17 years old, but he no longer found interest in memorizing sports stats, keeping tabs on pop stars and staying up until three in the morning to play video games. Instead, his mind often wandered to the fantasy of killing Exalls, and as he crossed the room to sit on his bed, Kyle felt all the innocence of his youth leave his body like exorcised demons.

He lied down and cried a silent sob, tears streaming from his eyes to his pillow as he stared at the ceiling. He missed being a regular kid, only having to worry about homework and teachers instead of 7 A.M. drills and aliens. He rolled over and saw the gold trophy from his middle school basketball team that had won the championship. That moment in life felt like another lifetime ago. The celebration at the school had been the day that changed everything, but leading up to it, life had still been normal. His grandmother was alive, his parents were married, and he had all of his friends by his side. That evening changed all of their lives, creating a sacred bond between them that they would all take to the grave.

Kyle's mom entered the room and sat beside him, wiping the tears from his face. "What's wrong, Ky?" she asked in the gentle, comforting voice only mothers seemed capable of.

"I just miss my old life. This feels like someone else's bedroom even though I know it's mine. So much has changed."

"I know it has. You know, ever since you left, I've spent quite a few nights in here, lying right where you are, crying. I wasn't ready to let you go—I'm still not—but it's become a little easier. I think about you every day, and wish I could call you."

"I should have more free time now, and they just gave me a special cell phone that works underground."

"Thank God. I promise I won't bother you too much."

Kyle giggled, his emotions a trainwreck. "You don't need to worry about me, Mom. I'm safe there. I live underground like an ant. I'll be safe even if the world ends."

"I know that, but I'll still worry about you; it's out of my control."

Kyle looked back to the trophy, reminiscing on the day that had changed his life and led him to this moment.

"Why don't you go visit your friends?" his mom asked. "I told Mikey you were coming home for a bit. He and Jimmy are just waiting for the call."

"Yeah, I think I'll plan a night out with them. Can I?"

Even though he had lived on his own for three months, Kyle still felt he needed to ask permission from his mother.

She chuckled and nodded. "Of course."

They talked for a few more minutes, mainly about life in the Pentagon and the extreme training program, before Lori kissed him on the forehead and wished him a good night. Kyle slept deep his first night home in his own bed, wishing his grandmother would come visit him in his dreams.

* * *

The next day was a Saturday and Kyle sent a text message to Jimmy and Mikey first thing in the morning to arrange plans for that night. They were all set to meet at Uncle Tony's, their favorite pizzeria to grab a slice since middle school.

Kyle killed time during the day by raking the leaves in his mother's backyard and stuffing them into Halloween trash bags that looked like pumpkins and ghosts. There was still over a month until Halloween, but she insisted he put the leaves into them now as there wouldn't be enough later. It was refreshing for him to be out in nature. The Outside Room at the Pentagon did a phenomenal job of replicating an outdoor environment with its live animals and weather changes, but there was still the mental doubt that accompanied it by *knowing* you were still inside of a building.

He worked in the yard all morning, headphones in his ears as he charged through the day, anxious and excited to see his friends. Would they seem childish to him now, like his bedroom felt when he walked into it?

By the time six o'clock came around that evening, Kyle felt a churning in his stomach that he wasn't sure was nerves or excitement. He made the quick ten-minute drive across town, horrified at the prospect of his life changing any more. He hadn't talked to his friends since he left, and could only hope everything would feel normal upon their reunion.

When he pulled up to the restaurant, Kyle felt his inner teenage spirit crying through the depths of his soul, like a prisoner begging for release. Crew member or not, Kyle had changed a lot after the incident at his grandmother's house four years ago. Her funeral was followed by his parents' divorce a couple months later, a combination of events that put him into a dark place emotionally. So dark, he supposed, that he had yet to fully recover.

He recalled having suicidal thoughts one night, the melancholy of life too much to handle as he sat in his mother's house alone while she went out on a date. It never grew into a serious thought, but the fact that he wondered what it might feel like to swallow thirty pain pills was enough to disturb him into going outside for a run to clear his head.

Those thoughts plagued his mind from time to time, but mostly stayed in the dark corners where they belonged. He supposed everyone went through this at some point in their lives, where the will to live was overshadowed by the desire to roll over and croak.

In a nutshell, Kyle had been turned cold by the events that happened to him. So cold that he made deliberate efforts to fend off emotions that boiled up within. He had cried in his old bedroom the night before, but something about being home made him feel like it was okay. He hoped sitting around with his old friends would have the same effect in letting him be himself.

Kyle jumped out of his car and entered the pizzeria, his senses struck by the fresh dough baking somewhere in the back of the building. It was Saturday night and the place was crowded with families gathering for the dinner rush. He spotted Mikey and Jimmy sitting at a booth along the side wall and pushed his way through the crowd to meet them.

"Well, well," Mikey said. "Did you come here straight from the gym?"

Kyle looked down, still in the phase where it seemed everyone could see the growth in his body except for him. The countless hours in the Pentagon's gym had added up, but he didn't think he looked that much different.

"Funny," Kyle said, every worry disappearing by the second. Just *being* in this restaurant with his friends helped him feel like a normal teenager again.

"You might have to come out for the football team with me," Jimmy said, standing up and nearly hitting his head on the light hanging above their table. Jimmy had always been the tallest and most athletic of their group, and had now grown to six feet tall after a summer growth spurt. He hugged Kyle with a hard slap on the back before sitting down and letting Mikey do the same.

Mikey hadn't changed one bit aside from growing a couple inches and getting a pair of glasses. He kept his hair buzzed and his face in the books as always.

"How have you guys been? Tell me everything," Kyle said as they all settled into the booth.

"Smarty pants here is already getting ready for college," Jimmy said, shooting Mikey a grin across the table.

Mikey nodded. "I'm only talking with our new counselor about places I should apply. She thinks I can get into places like Yale or Stanford."

"He's only talking to our new counselor because she's hot," Jimmy interrupted, cackling at himself.

"Fuck you, I do not!" Mikey snapped.

"Please. We all do. There isn't a boy in school who hasn't been caught staring at her legs. See, she wears these short skirts every day when it's warm. It's impossible to not look. I think she flies somewhere to tan on the beach every weekend – I just don't understand how she can look so perfect."

And just like that everything was normal again, as if they had jumped right back into their lives, never skipping a beat. There was no such thing as Exalls or an underground civilization beneath the Pentagon. They were just three teenage boys living in the moment, drinking soda, eating pizza, and talking about girls and sports. Nothing else mattered.

Kyle sat back and listened for the next half hour as Mikey and Jimmy caught him up to speed with who was dating who, what teachers they liked this year, and how their lives had been over the summer. The fact that Kyle had nothing to contribute to the discussion was the gentle reminder he needed to know that his life indeed had moved on from high school. In two weeks he'd be back on a plane to Washington with no idea what his schedule would look like. Meanwhile his friends would be back in history class, dreaming of the next summer break.

Mikey finally shifted the conversation to Kyle. "How are *you* liking your new job?"

"It's going good," Kyle replied shyly, not wanting to go down this road. But they were his friends, and they had been by his side during the tragedy. He wasn't the only one scarred for life from what they had witnessed that day. "It's so busy. I wake up at six in the morning and don't get back to my room until seven or eight at night."

"Holy shit," Jimmy cried. "Six in the morning?! That's nuts."

"What do you do all day?" Mikey asked.

"So far it's been nothing but training. Time in the gym, shooting range, studying. I rarely leave the building."

"So you're really strong now?" Jimmy asked, leaning over the table to slurp the last of his soda.

"I wouldn't say really strong. Not like you. But I'm definitely stronger than before I left."

Kyle leaned back while he chewed his pizza and noticed Jimmy and Mikey exchange a suspicious look, looking away from Kyle, then immediately down to their plates as if avoiding eye contact.

"What's going on?" Kyle asked.

"You tell him, Mike," Jimmy said, stuffing more pizza into his mouth to avoid talking.

Mikey looked to his hands clasped beneath the table.

"We've been getting some strange messages," Mikey said.

"Messages? From who?" Kyle sprung forward, planting his elbows on the table.

Mikey tossed his hands in the air as he shrugged. "Brian?"

"Brian? Impossible."

Kyle knew it wasn't impossible after his first few months with the Crew. Brian *could* still be alive somewhere—as his regular self—but that didn't make it a likely scenario.

"That's what I thought at first. In fact, I ignored the text messages—thought it was a prank."

"Well, what did the messages say?" Kyle asked.

Mikey pulled his phone out of his pocket, and scrolled over the screen, flipping it around for Kyle to see.

Kyle grabbed it and started reading.

Help me, Mike. I'm trapped in this body and can't get out, was the first message. Mikey didn't reply.

The following day: *He leaves me alone for a couple minutes each day. Please help me get out!*

This prompted Mikey to ask: *Who is this?*

Twenty-four hours later the response came: *Brian*

Can you help?

Please get me out of here. I'm so scared.

I want to go home.

Mikey never sent a response, and the last sequence of text messages lingered on the screen like a bug splatter on a windshield. Kyle could only see the timestamps of the messages and not the actual date they were sent.

"When did you get these?" he asked.

"Earlier this week. What do you think of them?"

Kyle didn't know what to think. He was trained to fight Exalls, not study potential messages from old friends trapped within a body of one. He glared down to the phone, reading the sender's number as *Unknown*.

If it was a prankster, how would they know what happened to Brian? The only people who knew were sitting at this table, plus Kyle's parents. And the entire Crew, of course. Kyle wondered if the messages were sent from The Crew as a sort of test for him upon arriving home. Maybe they wanted to see if Mikey would even bother to say anything to test his sworn word of not discussing the matter any further.

Kyle rubbed his eyes out of frustration. He just wanted to come home and hang out with his family and friends. Why did this have to come up on his first night out?

I'm trapped in this body and can't get out.

This particular message hung in his mind. Trapped. Kyle didn't feel it was a prank, and the thought made him nauseous. He took a long sip of his soda before handing Mikey's phone back and slamming down his empty paper cup.

"Guys, I think it's real. Brian must still be alive."

19

Chapter 19

At the Pentagon, an unsettling mood spread throughout the entire Crew's underground offices. They were under attack and weren't prepared. Attacks were supposed to occur every three decades. It was supposed to be a time of peace, according to tradition, but now every member looked over their shoulder when leaving the building. Some even refused to leave the confines of their underground fort once they heard what happened to their two comrades in Michigan.

Colonel Griffins called an emergency meeting with the department leaders, having them cram into his office with the blinds shut, huddled around his desk.

"Three attacks, now," he said flatly. "Three attacks that we never saw coming. Three goddamn attacks with nothing to show on our tracking devices. What the *hell* is going on with those?!" He shot his question to their head of technology, Felicia Lewis, who slouched her shoulders and gazed to the ground. Colonel Griffins had made it clear that no one speak until he was done.

"No one in the public has suspected anything yet, we've got

that much going for us, but it won't last long at the rate we're going. We need the tracking devices to track again or this war may as well be declared over. How can we stop what we can't see coming?"

Even though he spoke in a low tone, an underlying rage still clung to every word that left his mouth. His face flushed a light shade of red as he clenched trembling fists. He didn't give a shit if they saw him this pissed off. Maybe it would get everything back in order. He rarely showed emotion, he was impossible to rattle, but today was a new day and it almost seemed as if no one had been doing their job over the past several weeks.

"We need new training on combatting the Exalls. The two we lost in Michigan were ambushed. A full investigation is being conducted and we'll be able to piece together what exactly happened. I want the scenario recreated and for every solider we have on this planet to go through a training for it."

Colonel Griffins paused, opened a drawer, and pulled out a flask to take a swig of whiskey, not offering it to anyone else. "A dark day is upon us, people. If we don't get our shit together right now, it's all over. Kiss it all goodbye. I suspect we'll see one more attack. Our friends started their party in Colorado and are moving east. I think they're coming here for the boy."

The head of research, Damien Kurtz, raised a finger to make a counterargument, but was promptly ignored by the colonel.

"I've been in this business a long time, and I've never seen anything like this. I've seen the ugliest from these assholes. I've even seen one of these gray fuckers vanish like dust through my fingers. But I have never seen the level of uncertainty that is plaguing our entire organization. I'm now getting daily calls from the White House wanting to know what the fuck is going on. We need drastic solutions. And quick.

If anyone has any brilliant ideas, they need to come forward now."

A momentary silence hung in the room as the department heads either looked at each other or looked around the office to avoid speaking.

"Sir," Damien said, a squeaky man with circle-framed glasses. "I think we need to reallocate all of our resources to these two who are moving east. I believe Michigan was a fluke, more self-defense by the Exall. These other two are the aggressors and causing death for innocent civilians."

"It's not death!" Colonel Griffins shouted, slamming his fist on the desk. "They're multiplying like fucking bunnies. This wouldn't be as bad if they were killing people, but they're not. We don't even know how many have been turned after the attack in Kansas City."

The room fell silent again, waiting for Colonel Griffins to have another outburst, but he spoke in a more relaxed tone.

"I don't care what any of the research says. We're dealing with uncharted territory. Throw out the playbook and start anew. They're attacking us, we can't track them, and no one besides me seems to realize just how terrible this situation can become. I need you all to lock yourselves in rooms with your teams today and report back to me with a status update. We need a plan going into tomorrow. It's only a matter of time until these two strike again. And, Ms. Lewis," Griffins turned his attention to their head of technology. She met his death stare with nervous eyes. "I don't want to see *your* face until our tracking devices work again. I don't care how long it takes."

"Yes, sir," she said softly.

"Anyone else have anything to say?" Griffins grumbled, impatience dripping from each word.

Everyone looked around to each other, but no one dared speak. The colonel had struck the fear he intended.

"Let's have a good day," he said, dismissing everyone with a wave of his hand toward the door.

They filed out of the office, leaving him alone at his desk. The weight of the recent attacks was starting to wear on him. As were the phone calls from the president and the scrolling headlines every week. Hopefully the two soldiers they lost at the cabin wouldn't reach any news stations. It was a remote enough location for no one else to have heard about except for The Crew. But those two men had families to grieve their losses, and it was impossible to know how those families would react. They usually stayed quiet, even after a sudden death, but every now and then someone opened their mouth and had to be handled by The Crew.

Griffins opened the drawer where he kept his flask and pistol, but rummaged for something else, sighing when he grabbed the box of cigarettes as if it liberated him. He hadn't smoked one in at least three years, but all the sudden his mind craved it. He popped the cigarette between his lips and lit it with a quick stroke of a match he kept taped to the box. The smoke filled his lungs in a long, relaxing draw before he picked up the phone to make his now daily call to the president, who demanded a solution to the latest attack on Crew members.

* * *

Over the next week, The Crew learned a lot more about the two Exalls who were traveling across the country. More importantly, they learned what had happened with all of those they had infected with their blood. Yes, they had been transformed into new Exalls, but none of the ones they found showed any signs of aggression typical in an Exall. Many of them seemed scared, afraid of their own shadows.

Colonel Griffins ordered a ground search in eastern Colorado and Kansas City, and everywhere in between. If the tracking devices wouldn't work, they had to take an old school approach to finding the Exalls. Griffins was sure to include this information in a memo that went out to the department heads, happy to create more urgency for Lewis and her team to get the technology fixed.

It had been a week and she still hadn't shown her face to the colonel, which both pleased and concerned him at the same time. Technology could take a day or several months to correct. Lewis had a team of twenty-five people, and word was that all of them were working around the clock, sleeping in the office, and pulling themselves through the days just to find a solution. If this group of some of the brightest minds in the world couldn't crack the code in a week, then The Crew's problems were about to grow much bigger than the scope of a few faulty tracking devices.

Every time Griffins let his mind roam, he thought about the mayhem that could unfold on Earth any day now. He could close his eyes and see the deserted world. Tall buildings demolished. Empty highways in the middle of rush hour. Playgrounds with no kids giggling and screaming as they ran around. All innocence in the world completely vanished.

The Exalls had the capability to do as they pleased. The Crew served as nothing more than a barrier to slow them down, but they could just as easily blow through them and rule the land. The Crew always operated in a defensive mode, unable to predict future actions from Exalls, and hoping to respond fast enough to each tragedy that popped up.

Griffins did have a handful of meetings with different department heads throughout the week. But no one offered suggestions on how to stop the onslaught of new attacks, and instead only provided newly learned information.

Through a simple investigation of asking people in the areas, it was believed the doctor and the boy were headed through Tennessee. They liked to stop at small town gas stations to either refuel or commandeer a new vehicle altogether. Helicopters patrolled the area for a majority of an entire day, but nothing ever came up. They knew how to hide, and more importantly, they still knew how keep themselves off the tracking devices.

A woman from the research team had drafted a report stating that the only way the Exalls could now avoid detection was if they had some new technology to wipe out the algorithms functioning within the tracking devices. The devices still detected the thermal energy Exalls put out, no matter how high or low their body temperatures were.

A team also followed the tracks of the two men in Michigan, putting together the story of what had happened. They figured out the timing of events, but remained puzzled as to why the men were in that specific room with the window blasted open, and why one would have stood by while the other was killed. Their deaths were seconds apart, and nothing in the story added up.

Colonel Griffins stayed late and arrived early every day. Each day started with his panicked thoughts and paranoia for the end of the world. Kyle was scheduled to arrive back in D.C. next week, and every instinct in his body told him that was when the next attack would come.

He wondered if the Exalls would actually be able to find a way into the Pentagon again, much like they had with Jonathon Browne a few years ago, infiltrating his body and controlling him to come in and shoot everyone else after hacking their system.

That was the most horrific event to ever take place within The Crew's hidden offices, but Colonel Griffins suspected it could just as easily happen again. He'd regroup with the security team to go over a revamped process regarding how Crew members entered and exited the building. A war was looming, and if no one else wanted to accept it, he'd be the only one ready when the time came to fight back.

20

Chapter 20

The doctor insisted they wear suits for their venture into downtown Richmond. Their last several weeks had been spent hiding in rural towns, finding abandoned barns and open fields to pass the time. The search had begun for them, the doctor said, but he never mentioned how he knew. The people who called themselves The Crew were on the hunt for Exalls, primarily the two who caused the horrific scene at the Country Jam in Kansas City.

"We're getting too close, and I don't want to blow our entire project right before the big day," he had told Brian earlier today. "We'll be taking a less aggressive approach to our recruitment, but will still have a blast doing it." He snickered, and Brian nodded nervously.

Brian was sick of Dr. Klemens, but felt magnetized to him. He had learned more about the monster living within himself, but had no clue where to begin in exorcising him from his mind. It was like having a seat in the back of a movie theater, but instead of enjoying a motion picture, he was forced to watch his life through the screen of his eyes. He *felt* the other presence in his mind, shoving Brian aside like someone squeezing onto the sliver of seat open next to you on the bus. His mind was suffocated and exhausted.

But every so often, he felt the pressure leave, as if it had floated off to pollute some other kid's brain. And it always came back. However, when it left, it didn't take its mystical powers with it. Brian felt those powers swarming through his body, like he could look at a building and set it on fire with his mind. He had once sat behind the wheel of a Lamborghini, and even though the car wasn't turned on, he could still feel its powerful presence. This sensation was exactly like that as he understood the powers he wielded, but was too shy to actually use.

He had done some experimenting over the years, moving objects with his mind, changing a traffic light from red to green, but didn't try anything of significance until he had willed a message from his mind to Mikey's cell phone. He still didn't understand how it worked, but when Mikey replied he heard the response in his head. In Mikey's voice. It had given him hope that he'd be able to escape the madness, but Mikey never answered his last couple of messages, so he assumed they were never received.

He had learned to keep his mind quiet around the doctor. Dr. Klemens had a full understanding of his powers and never shied away from using them in public. On this very trip, he started a fight between two cows who were minding their business. Started it and watched like a curious child until one had trampled the other in a bloody brawl. And he howled the laughter only a maniac could muster.

Brian tried to keep these memories from surfacing in his mind, but the doctor was such a lunatic that he felt obliged to have that constant, nagging reminder of what he was capable of doing. Brian would have to try another message to Mikey later, but for now they sat in a dimly lit five-star restaurant in Virginia.

"What are you planning?" Brian asked, looking around the restaurant packed with men in fancy suits and women in sparkling dresses.

"Planning? Look, kid, I don't plan. I just *do.* I already started the party when we arrived. Now we sit back and enjoy the show."

The doctor grinned, his flesh still its human color, but Brian could see the grayness lurking behind those dark eyes and artificial smile.

"What did you do?" Brian demanded in a low voice.

"Let's just say I faked a phone call to the chef. And when he stepped out back, I was there to greet him. He's one of us now." The doctor took a sip from his glass of the $1,000 wine he had ordered.

Brian looked around the restaurant, paranoid that someone was on to them. But why would a group of alien hunters even think of searching in a high-scale restaurant? Especially after their trek across the country had been nothing but small town diners and gas stations. They had stolen their suits from a mall in the middle of the night, the doctor getting in and out undetected.

"It shouldn't be much longer until the fireworks start," the doctor said with his coy smile. "Did you know if Exall blood is ingested through the stomach it will make the person incredibly sick before they transform into one of us?"

He stared wildly at Brian, who had no response.

"I haven't seen it for myself yet, but I do look forward to the show."

"What did you do?" Brian asked again, no longer wanting to eat from the basket of bread they shared on the table.

The doctor giggled. "Let's just say the chef will be sharing his new gift with everyone in this restaurant. It goes really well with steak, brings out the flavors and juices." He threw his head back and hooted.

They had been at the restaurant for half an hour already, and the doctor had said he forgot something in the car when they arrived. Brian pieced it all together and now glanced around the dining area in a brief moment of panic.

The doctor raised his wine glass in the air before tipping it back to chug the remains. He let out a loud belch that turned heads from those sitting nearby.

"Listen closely—it's starting," he said with a stupid grin. "A lady three tables over is complaining that her stomach hurts."

One of the abilities gained as an Exall was hyper-focused hearing. Brian let his mind wander through the clutter of conversation and zone in on the third table away from them, as if he were sitting at the table with the middle-age couple.

"What's wrong, Lisa?" a man's voice asked. "You look like a ghost."

The woman let out a couple of hiccups. "I don't know. I feel hot and my stomach is tight. I think I'm gonna-—"

Brian looked over to see the woman grasping her throat. From a distance she looked fine, minus the constant shuddering of her shoulders as she fought off vomit.

"Run to the bathroom," the man pleaded, but it was too late.

Lisa hurled all over the table with loud gagging sounds, yellowish liquid splashing onto her plate of steak and asparagus. Those sitting near her table gasped and recoiled away from their own tables. Chunks of vomit sprayed the man sitting across from her, his hands held out as he looked down his body to the fresh mess.

"Oh my God!" a younger man cried out, jumping up from his table at the opposite end of the restaurant, hands clenched over his gut. He flailed around like a fish out of water, before bursting vomit in a way that reminded Brian of the girl from *The Exorcist.*

More people shouted and stood from their seats, an awkward moment of silence as they looked from the woman to the man in complete disgust.

The doctor only stared across the table to Brian, his grin wide, and his teeth showing shades of decay. "And here we go," he said under his breath.

As if orchestrated, a handful of more people moaned as they either stood from the table and dashed toward the bathroom, or simply decided to upchuck all over their table.

A man burst into the dining room, waving his arms in the air. "People, please stop!" he pleaded. "If you feel sick, please step outside and away from our other guests enjoying dinner." The man, presumably the manager, kept his manners despite the sheer panic in his voice. Five people in total had vomited in the restaurant, and the rancid stench grew and spread like a slow-moving fog.

"Get the fuck out of the way!" another man bellowed, lowering his head and barreling through a group huddled behind their table. The people were too slow to react and watched in awe as the man charged at them, his face pale, lips pursed so tight they turned the color of snow.

The man watched his dinner fly from his lips and cover the entire group of people before he collapsed to the ground and writhed on the floor, clenching his abdomen.

"What the *hell* is going on?" a woman shrieked.

The manager, who had kept his distance from the various messes, stood frozen as he looked around the entirety of the restaurant as more and more guests followed suit. It was like watching a long line of dominoes fall, and by this point, those who *hadn't* vomited yet waited in grave anticipation for their turn.

"Everyone stay calm!" the manager shouted. "Let's file out of the restaurant until we figure out what's going on."

Chaos had officially erupted, the screaming and panic from the patrons overshadowing anything that came out of the manager's mouth.

"They're all mine!" the doctor cried out, clapping his hands like an excited child. "All of them!"

Brian had stood from his seat and didn't realize it. His hands gripped the back of his chair as he peered around, hoping some tumbling sick person wouldn't come knock him over. People were starting to run, whether it was to the bathroom or out the front door. Some who had vomited had fallen to the ground like the man they all watched, leaving them in the line of the stampede.

Over the next five minutes, it appeared as if everyone in the restaurant had either vomited or exited the building with queasy faces and arms wrapped around their stomachs. Everyone except for the doctor and the young boy with him.

No one paid any attention to the pair, however, too consumed with fighting to keep their dinner down.

The doctor stood up, tossed his napkin onto the table and hopped on his chair. "Everybody, STOP!" he shouted at the top of his lungs.

Those who remained in the restaurant, maybe twenty judging by a quick glance, stood as if called to attention by a drill sergeant. They gazed at the doctor as if possessed, taking slow, lifeless steps toward him.

"Come and gather around, my children," the doctor said, his grin widening, and no longer fake. It was obvious to Brian that he had become overtaken by sheer joy. He got kicks out of attacking innocent humans, but having power over all of these people elevated his excitement to a new level.

Some who had left the building returned, slipping and sliding on the pools of puke in the waiting area. The rotten stench clung to the air, but had no effect on Brian. His body was no longer wired to have a reaction to bad smells.

"Come, come!" the doctor said, elevating his arms like a preacher.

The manager started moving backwards, unable to break his stare from the man on the chair. He appeared to be the only one in the room unaffected, and Brian wondered if there were any cooks or staff hiding in the kitchen.

Within a minute the restaurant had filled back up with more than 50 people, all gathering around the table where Brian and the doctor stood.

"A new day is upon you all," the doctor said once he had everyone's attention. "Consider your old self dead and your new body resurrected with abilities beyond your imagination. You will do as we need to grow our army. You no longer need food, water, not even air. I demand you go somewhere reclusive and learn your new abilities. Once you understand your new potential, we'll be moving to Washington, D.C. where the fun will really begin."

The doctor threw his head back and howled like a werewolf,

a shrill sound that would have made the hairs stand on Brian's arms if he was able to have such a reaction. Then, the group of newly initiated Exalls started snickering. They looked around at each other and laughed like the doctor had told a wise joke.

Brian caught sight of the manager inching his way toward the back of the crowd, trying to slip out undetected, no longer concerned with his vomit-infested restaurant. The doctor saw him, too.

"You, sir!" the doctor barked. "Where do you think you're going?"

The manager, whose fine suit had been tarnished with splatters of puke, froze in place like a burglar getting a flashlight shined upon him. His wavy hair bounced like a slinky over his forehead that glimmered with sweat.

"Please," the manager gasped, holding his hands out in front of him to make a stop sign. "Just let me go."

"Let you go?" the doctor shot back, the new Exalls following the exchange back and forth like a tennis match. "You're going to join us."

The manager turned and sprinted like a baseball player trying to steal a base. He shoved one of the dazed Exalls out of the way before reaching the waiting area where he slipped on the vomit-covered tile floor, diving and sliding forward like a child on a Slip 'N Slide on a hot summer day. The man growled as he struggled to come to his feet, his hands clawing for a grip on the slick floor, feet kicking chunks in every direction like a tire stuck in mud.

"Get him," the doctor said calmly, winking at the crowd. "Bring him home to us."

A man in the back turned and dove on top of the manager, clobbering him on the head with a balled fist as he opened his mouth full of his new, black fangs. Brian hadn't noticed until now, but almost everyone's skin tone had deepened to a shade of gray, his included. It was as if the Exalls had a unified driving force that kept them bunched together as one unit.

Once they saw the man attacking the manager, everyone else started shouting and running toward the two wrestling on the ground, the floodgates of chaos officially open for business.

A dozen others piled on top of the manager like a bunch of football players diving on top of a fumbled ball, the manager shrieking for his life from the bottom. "Stop it! STOP!"

His screaming was cut off by the vicious growling of the Exalls.

"Well, he's ours now," the doctor said to Brian, the two of them now alone while everyone else clamored for a position in the scrum. "Between the diner, the concert, and here, we should be rolling into D.C. with at least 1,500 others—likely more. They won't be ready for that many of us. We can take over the country with that much power."

Brian watched as the scene died down, the new Exalls breaking apart and leaving the restaurant in droves until the place was completely empty. The manager lay on the ground, gashes across his face, blood oozing from his head, throat, and legs. Brian thought he was dead, but like any good Exall he rose to his feet, shot a grin across the room at the doctor, and ran out of the building as he had attempted to do as a human just minutes ago.

"Good things are coming for us, Brian," Dr. Klemens said, slinging an arm around Brian's shoulder as if they were friends. "Good things, indeed."

21

Chapter 21

Kyle had a rough rest of his stay in Colorado after hearing about Brian's text messages to Mikey. Sleep became impossible, his mind flooded with hundreds of morbid and terrifying thoughts.

"Do I tell The Crew about these messages?" Kyle asked himself in the spare room at his father's house. He wanted to talk to Travis about what he learned, but was still unsure how everything worked regarding the confidentiality enforced by The Crew. Travis was somewhat a Crew member thanks to his mother and initial testing, but that didn't mean he knew all of the happenings of the organization.

I have to tell them. This is absolutely Crew business, and I'm one of them now. They might not even know about this ability they have to send texts through their minds.

He assumed they did know, but there was always a chance the Exalls evolved some new ability overnight. And if they had, what did that mean for the future of the Crew? Griffins had assured him that the next major battle against their foes waited over two decades away, but Kyle suspected something bigger was at play. Everyone he had met within the Crew spoke like they had a dark secret hidden beneath the surface. Perhaps it was his imagination running wild after going through such a drastic change in his young life, but his instincts told him otherwise.

He couldn't help but feel his grandmother's presence in The Crew's underground headquarters, but as he sat in the room that once served as her home office, he sensed her even more. He still didn't understand how his dad thought it was a good idea to live in the house after what they had all witnessed, but thanks to some renovations, the interior appeared brand new, completely wiping out any hint of the life Susan had built.

Kyle wondered if the basement had undergone changes. Travis wasn't due home for another couple hours, so he made his way to the top of the staircase. Standing there in the kitchen, the back door behind him, Kyle felt the hairs on his arms and back stand at attention. Like everything else, the kitchen had been remodeled. The island counter where the two Exalls had stood behind was replaced by a new island fixated with a deep sink and stovetop. The once tile-flooring had been ripped out and laid over with a glossy hardwood. The old picture of The Last Supper that once hung over the stairwell had been removed, replaced by nothing but a fresh coat of paint.

Kyle stared down the steps that disappeared into a void of darkness, even in the middle of a sunny day. So many secrets were kept in the basement and beyond, but he now felt mentally equipped to face them. Would The Crew have thought to board up the secret panic room? He wasn't sure why they would go out of their way to do that, but wanted to see for himself.

He took the first step hesitantly, grabbing the handrail with a shaky grip. The last time he came down these steps was the day of the tragedy; he'd subconsciously refused to return to the basement since then. He still didn't *want* to go to the basement, but felt lured by it.

Kyle continued one step at a time, debating turning back up and running outside, but drawing deeper into the darkness. After what seemed like ten minutes of a dragged out internal debate, Kyle reached the basement landing and flicked on the light switch. He gasped and jumped, the painting of The Last Supper seeming to stare at him as it lay against the back wall like a piece of long-lost art. Kyle giggled, realizing how jumpy he had become.

The basement remained largely untouched, becoming more of a storage room for everything Travis had moved from upstairs. Boxes and tubs piled high as far as he could see, a lone pathway present from the bottom of the stairs to the miniature hallway that connected the laundry room, bathroom, and pantry. Susan's presence lingered as he passed the boxes of her life's mementos.

He reached the hallway and stepped into the pantry without another thought. He came down here to learn and didn't want to waste any more precious time being scared of the shadows that might jump out.

His hands flailed around on the pantry wall in search of the light switch, eventually finding it as his heart tried to leap out of his chest. He found the pantry had remained intact as he remembered, only with less food on the shelves.

Kyle's eyes jumped to the back corner, adrenaline now flooding his veins, as they landed on the old chest freezer. A couple of storage bins had been piled on top, perhaps a half-assed attempt by Travis to hide the freezer. But he knew what lied inside; he always would.

The silence in the basement seemed to thicken, creating a distant buzzing sound in the back of Kyle's mind that the brain produced for the sake of noise when none was present. His legs and arms trembled as he weaved through the standing shelves and started to slide the bins off the top of the freezer, dropping them on the ground with a light thud. He ran a hand over the top of the freezer, creating a white streak through the dust that had collected over the past few years. His fingers throbbed with anticipation as he flipped up the two latches and pulled open the cover, a gust of cold air slapping him across the face.

A couple of steaks and frozen pizzas lay across the bottom of the freezer, ice frosting the packages. Kyle removed these items, knowing anything would fall into the underground bunker below. With the freezer cleared, Kyle brushed aside some of the frost in search of the small button that released the freezer's floor. After a minute he was convinced it was gone, removed by The Crew so no one could ever accidentally stumble across what hid below, but he found it, both relief and panic filling him in an instant.

He looked around as if someone else was in the house. Maybe Colonel Griffins would barge through the backdoor and demand he stop. He laughed at himself again, knowing no such thing was going to happen. He was alone, and a Crew member. He had every right to be here. Not even Travis had the grounds to stop him.

This is property of the United States government, Kyle thought. *And that means me. This is official Crew business, Mr. Wells. Please back away from the freezer.*

Kyle tried to imagine talking to his father this way and let out another nervous chuckle. "That'll be the day."

He pushed the button and waited. Nothing happened for about thirty seconds, and just as he was reaching in to push it again, the freezer groaned to life as if waking from hibernation. Whatever cogs were inside ground together as the freezer's floor slowly slid open, revealing the bunker below.

The lights flickered on, blinding with obscene brightness. Kyle remembered how they each had to hang on the edge and fall down to the bunker, but he believed there had to be an easier way.

He glanced around the room, remembering he had once seen a ladder in this pantry, before recalling that it was stored in the laundry room across the hall.

Kyle closed the freezer lid and sprinted across the hallway where he tripped over a pile of clothes on the ground, but remained on his feet. He found the ladder tucked away in the corner and lugged it back to the pantry. Within a few seconds, he had snaked the ladder through the freezer opening and felt instant relief when it touched the ground far below. The top of the ladder reached just beyond the opening of the freezer's bottom, leaning sturdily against the inside wall where it scraped frost and ice.

The perfect size, he thought, climbing into the freezer and wiggling his legs until his feet found the top step of the ladder. He gave a quick nudge to ensure it was in place before climbing down.

It felt like he had stepped into another world as he looked up, seeing the pantry ceiling at least twenty feet above. Looking up gave him the chilling flashback to the last time he had done so, his grandmother's head peeking over just moments before she had closed the freezer and marched off to her death.

His gut twisted as the memories felt all too recent. He tried to clear his mind by absorbing the room. The wall of monitors remained in place, but they were all blank screens. Susan had maintained the hidden cameras around the property and Travis had no interest in continuing. A couple of shelves stood along the opposite wall, still fully stocked with canned foods and fruits. Kyle wondered how long those cans had been there, surely beyond their extended expiration dates.

The last time he had been in this secret room, Kyle wasn't exactly in an exploratory mood. He had only seen what stood out as the necessities: the food, the monitors, and a couple of rifles lined up against the wall.

Today he studied the room with more attention. A small filing cabinet stood next to the rack of rifles, a key in the lock. What looked like a nightstand stood next to that, a pile of paperbacks and magazines scattered across the top. Kyle couldn't imagine his grandmother coming down here for a comfortable place to read, but he also never knew she was living a secret life.

Kyle went through the books, seeing they were definitely Susan's by the collection of Danielle Steele and Nora Roberts novels. He put the books back and dug into the filing cabinet, thumbing through hundreds of folders that each contained various research on the Exalls. He recognized the forms as the same letterheads he had seen in D.C., every piece of correspondence stamped with the presidential seal at the top.

Kyle kept flipping until he stopped on a folder labeled with the word *family* in Susan's familiar handwriting. He pulled out this folder and sat on the floor as he read through its contents, a collection of handwritten notes:

May 7, 1998

Exalls have family members. They operate similar to us, with the elders looking over the young until they are raised into adults. Protecting family is the most sacred thing to them. They will kill to protect their family, and attack even more if someone harms their family. Many Exalls come to our planet knowing they might die and this is made clear to their families. Others come to research humanity and Earth with full intent on returning home to their families. When these Exalls are killed, revenge is immediately sought out against the murderer.

The Exalls believe in the eye-for-an-eye mentality. I killed one of their elder's grandchildren and now they will seek to kill mine through any means necessary. I've prepared my grandson for life as a Crew member; it's his only chance for survival. I just hope I'll be here as long as possible to keep an eye on him, and pray that I've done enough by the time I am taken from this world. Plans are already in place to have him entered into The Crew's protection as soon as possible.

Never underestimate the lengths they will go to seek revenge. There are no rules in their world, even though the peaceful Exalls claim there are. The fabric of our way of life is in constant danger, and letting our guards down for even one second can be the difference between life and death for all of humanity.

−S

Kyle scrunched his face. The notes had taken up two pages, but the stack had at least thirty more sheets of blank paper. He flipped through the pages, growing more puzzled with each blank page. Everything Susan had done was for a reason, and he didn't doubt for a second the empty pages were another part of some elaborate scheme. He held up a sheet to the light to see if perhaps there were watermarks on the paper.

None appeared, but he found the next clue on the second to last page. It was a handwritten list of subjects: *Exall culture, Combat techniques, weaponry, mid-1800's Exall research Kyle, Books, Movement patterns, Public Intelligence.*

The list was bullet-pointed, but his heart froze at the sight of his name.

It's a clue, he thought. *She knew I'd be here one day.*

The goosebumps returned to his arms and back as he realized Susan had made plans for him that stretched beyond her own life. Even in death, she was still working to conquer the Exalls.

The list of subjects matched the headings on some of the files in the cabinet, so Kyle quickly flipped through them until he found the one labeled *mid-1800's Exall research.* He opened the file and rummaged through its contents.

At first, he found nothing but pages of actual research, much of it written out like a textbook with never-ending paragraphs, and the occasional small photograph squeezed into the corner. The file had about forty pages of this same text, but Kyle came across the secret as he reached the end. The page was designed to look like the rest with big blocks of text, but this one in particular had a small line dividing one half of the page from the other, causing Kyle's eyes to jump to the second half where he read his name again, this time in typed fashion:

Kyle, it's impossible for me to know where you are in your career with the Exalls. You could be just starting, or you could be forty years into this life. All I do know is that you will one day find this message. I wish I was there to help you learn this new lifestyle. The biggest lesson I'd say you need to know is that the work never stops. Don't ever let your guard down. Even when we are in times of "peace" we are still vulnerable. Use the downtime of peace to learn as much as you can and advance your plans for keeping the world safe.

There is a secret door in this room and it leads to an even bigger secret. I've kept a live Exall in my hidden chambers since 1992. She's still in there, tied down to a table to never escape. You'll find more notes in the room about my findings, but this is the reason I've come to know so much. I call her "Sandra", and she's very kind. Sandra has been tied to my table for over two decades and has grown to understand she'll never be free. I took this matter into my own hands, and I know you'll do great in continuing my work.

Just go over to the left of the TV monitors and stand there for a few seconds, facing the wall. There is an eye recognition device setup that you can't see. I scanned your eye when you were a baby, but it will still work.

The special paragraphs ended, blending right back into a fresh block of text about an Exall attack in Europe, complete with a gory picture of a decapitated man outside of the Roman Colosseum.

Kyle snapped the file shut and returned it to the cabinet. He slammed the drawer closed as his heart rate picked up. He rose on wobbly legs as nerves wrecked his body, and crossed the room to the wall of monitors. The wall didn't show a trace of any sort of opening, but he planted his feet and bulged his eyes as much as he could, as if that helped the recognition device read it easier.

After twenty seconds, the lights in the bunker flickered along with the dozen screens, and a faint humming sound came from the walls as an opening slowly appeared.

How big is this place? Kyle thought as the humming stopped, revealing a four-foot tall black hole in the wall. Perhaps it was the terror running through his veins, but he thought he felt a presence ooze out of the dark opening.

A live Exall? For more almost thirty years?

Everything he had learned about their thirst for revenge made him wonder just how bad of an idea this was. The air coming from the darkness was cool against Kyle's face, but nothing chilled him to the core more than when he heard a woman's voice speak out, shaky and hoarse.

"Kyle?"

22

Chapter 22

A few miles west of Arlington provided the cover the doctor and Brian needed. They had left the restaurant shortly after the doctor's motivational speech to the Exalls' newest recruits, and he drove like a hellbent psychopath out of town.

"We'll have a few days to wait," he told Brian. "Until then, we need to hide like we've been doing all this time."

This led them to Fountainhead Regional Park, a space of 2,000 acres that surrounded the Occoquan Reservoir. While there was plenty of visitor activity near the reservoir, the surrounding woods provided enough cover away from hiking trails or camping sites.

Dr. Klemens drove them into the park like any other person entering through the wooden archway that welcomed its visitors. They were still in their stolen pickup truck, which helped them blend in—others with their tents, picnic baskets, and fishing poles sticking out the back of their trucks.

"Maybe we'll go hunting tonight," he said out of the side of his mouth.

Brian shook his head. "No more. I'm not going anywhere

with you until you tell me what's going on."

"I'm going to tell you everything tonight. Now that we're here, there's no turning back—not that you could, even if you wanted. "

That was the first verbal threat the doctor had made toward Brian. He'd had plenty of thoughts of running off in the middle of the night, but something within insisted he stay. Since undergoing his transformation, he didn't know if it was his own gut instinct, or the doctor forcing his thoughts through the mental hijacking he was capable of.

"Good," Brian said. "We've been hiding for four years now, and I'm sick of it. I hope you have a plan for us to get better."

The doctor threw his head back and howled. "Get better? This is the best we've ever been, don't you feel it? We never get sick, hungry, or tired. What else can you possibly want?"

Brian thought of his mother, alone and drowning in sorrow ever since he disappeared. Shortly after his transformation, he had kept a close eye on his house to check on his mom, finding she often arrived home from work and went straight to bed, judging by the fact the lights inside never turned on. He knew she was in there, crying and screaming for him to come back while he stood outside, a hopeless gray-skinned monster. He could have knocked on the door and he knew she'd welcome him in, gray skin and all.

But he didn't trust himself. The bursts of rage hit him as randomly as bird shit landing on your shoulder during a walk in the park. There was no buildup, no warning, just an internal flick of the switch and he became a crazed killing machine.

The doctor, on the other hand, embraced his inner lunatic, always switched on and ready to "convert" any innocent humans standing by. The scene at the bar in Colorado may have been the first group attack they carried out, but they had both taken a handful of individuals over their four years together.

"Just get me back to normal," Brian finally said. "I don't care what you decide, but *I* don't want to spend the rest of my life like this."

"There is no way back, young man," the doctor said. "I suggest for your sanity that you let go of that thought."

"Don't lie to me. We became this way; we can go back."

"It doesn't work like that, but if you want to hold on to that false hope, be my guest. Perhaps we can turn your disappointment into more anger."

"Why are you so angry? What did the world ever do to you that you need to kill innocent people?"

"I think you forget that I'm not a human, Brian. I'm not from this planet. I killed this doctor and drank his blood. Now he and I are one. I have his knowledge *and* my knowledge. The doctor and myself are quite the dynamic duo."

"I know you can help me."

"There's no way back. I infected your bloodstream when I was posing as the doctor, and it will be in you forever."

"What are we here for, then?" Brian demanded, deciding to change the topic.

The feeling struck Brian like a punch in the face. They were in the woods, and he now had the urge to find an animal and squeeze the life out of its throat, maybe even bite its head off.

"Stop it!" Brian screamed, the sensation of an invisible presence settling into his mind, pushing aside his own conscience. "Get out of me!"

"Relax, kid," the doctor said calmly. "It's just me. Don't resist. I need your mind in a dark place before I tell you what it is we're doing all the way on the east coast."

"Get the fuck out of my head!"

The presence inside his skull filled up to the point he thought his head might burst right open, spilling his brains on the ground to blend with the fallen leaves and sticks. He'd never had one, but imagined this is what a migraine felt like.

"Please let me go."

"I can't. You're too important to what we're trying to do. Do you remember shooting that old lady, Susan? Can you still feel the gun in your hand as you watched the bullet fly out and drill her in the back?"

"Fuck you!"

"We're all so proud of you. You sparked the change we needed, but there's just one more little step to take, although it may turn into a bigger mess. We're going to need you to appear as your human self and stay that way until I take back over."

"And I'm going to need you to stay out of my head."

"Well, I can't. If I could trust you to do this dirty work on your own, then I'd have no problem watching from the sidelines. But you'll never do it on your own."

"Do what, dammit? Just tell me."

The doctor flashed his wide grin, his teeth black as his skin had turned a shade gray. "Let's take this story back to the beginning. In 1988, the lovely Susan Wells murdered my son. We were exploring that day, not even looking to cause trouble. Spent the day at the National Museum of Natural History, figured that would be as good a place as any to learn about your culture. We had a great day together, lots of laughs and memories.

"When we left that evening, we were walking along the National Mall, discussing everything we learned that day. It was winter and the sun was already setting. It was apparently cold—not that we knew—but it left us alone outside. And that's when she attacked us.

"She shot at us from a distance, the first bullet caught my son square in the chest, and I started running. This was before we knew we were being tracked on those fancy devices they have. I had no idea we were being watched all day, Susan just waiting for a moment to get us alone to take us out."

The doctor shook his head, staring into the distance as he recounted the story, and looking more human than he ever had over the last four years. He had never shown emotions aside from his lunatic laughter toward violence, but Brian caught a glimpse of his pain.

"So you've been here since then trying to get revenge?" Brian asked. "But Susan is dead."

The thought of killing his best friend's grandmother while mentally sitting in the back row of his mind and watching it play out sent shivers up his back.

"It's bigger than her. She was the personal revenge, but there is so much more at play."

"If it was personal, why did you make me do it? Why didn't you do it yourself?"

His evil grin returned. "Oh, I did. Who do you think jumped into your mind and took over the wheel? That was me. And I enjoyed every second watching her die."

Brian shook his head. "So what are we doing here?"

"Don't act like you don't know. I know you've sent out calls for help to your friends—I can hear your thoughts, you know. Haven't you wondered why none of your messages get through to Kyle?"

Brian's jaw hung open as he processed the reality of having his private thoughts listened to by a mental stalker. All the times he had longed to go home, debated running away, and as mentioned, called out for help to whoever might listen. Every bad thing he had ever thought about the doctor had been overheard, or at least he assumed.

"I'm not sure what to say," Brian said, terrified to say or think anything.

"Nothing to say. I hear your thoughts, but I know your true intentions. You've had plenty of opportunities to run away during our time together, yet here you are, just outside the nation's capital, days away from the ultimate showdown."

"Showdown?"

"We're here for my species. This group of Crew people have gone on with their nonsense long enough. When we arrived on this planet, we had the intentions of learning your ways and adapting to blend in. Our home is gone and we live on a spacecraft looking for somewhere new to call home. Everything was meant to be peaceful, but a couple of our own got carried away, thought it'd be fun to torture humans for the sport of it. Those handful of us gave our entire species a bad name. Now, none of us can be trusted."

"But you're one of the most violent people I've ever known."

The doctor smiled, as if proud of this. "I wasn't always. Watching your son die can change you for the worse. There had been talks of the humans starting to kill us, even if we posed no threat. I didn't believe it, so his death is just as much my responsibility. We've tried abandoning this ugly world of yours. The human race is a disgusting bunch that we'd rather have nothing to do with, but there are no other nearby worlds with infrastructure in place, or large enough to fit us all. This planet would thrive if we can just eliminate all of the humans and have it to ourselves."

"You're still not telling me what this has to do with us being in the middle of nowhere."

"Two reasons: The Crew lives in Washington D.C., underneath the Pentagon building. We want to eliminate them all. There will be some clean-up work to do on the others who are out on missions, but nothing we can't handle. Once they're gone, who can stop us? Also, we're going to kill your friend, Kyle . . . *you're* going to kill Kyle."

"No," Brian said flatly, trying to close his mind off from the doctor. He would fight to not let anyone infiltrate his mind and control his body, and certainly not to kill his best friend.

"Yes," the doctor said with a wide grin. "Yes, yes, yes. And you'll enjoy it, and we can all live happily ever after it's done."

Brian sat on the ground, all feeling leaving his legs as his stomach sunk. More than ever he wanted to return to his former life. The events that led up to this moment played through his mind. From the moment he was attacked in the woods on their camping trip, to the hospital in Golden where he became infected with Exall blood without knowing it. It had all been an elaborate plan to bring them to this very moment. Did the Exalls have an ability to see the future? How else would they have known to align the situations perfectly to have him be the one to kill both Susan and Kyle?

He felt helpless knowing the doctor would slither into his mind and take control without even asking, using his body as a machine to go out and kill Kyle. Brian was shackled to his own body, unable to escape. Even if he tried, the doctor would just take control and make him return. A prisoner in his own body, Brian lay down on the ground, staring to the blue sky, praying for a way out of his lost life.

23

Chapter 23

Kyle stepped into the doorway, his body shaking as his throat tensed shut. The entry was pitch-black despite the adjoining panic room being lit with what felt like a million fluorescent lights. A musty smell oozed from the darkness like a cave, and Kyle wondered if the voice calling his name had been trapped in this room the entire time since Susan's death.

It had to have been. Who else would know about this? The message was clearly written to me.

Kyle sensed the uncovering of a major secret. Could you actually know your life was about to change within the coming minutes? He sure felt it creeping up his spine.

"Kyle?" the voice croaked, asking, yet expecting it to be no one else.

For a momentary flash, Kyle wondered if it was somehow his grandmother trapped in the dark room, but the voice didn't quite sound like hers.

She already told you its name is Sandra, he reminded himself. He thought he had been walking, but looked down to realize he hadn't moved more than one step from the room's entryway.

Forcefully, Kyle moved his legs forward, leaving the light behind, and pulling out his cellphone to use its flashlight. If he hadn't, he would have bumped into a wall as the pathway took a sharp right. The set up reminded him of the dark room from his final exam to join The Crew. He followed the path right where he took another ten steps before it made a left, and that's where a new light became visible, a soft orange-yellow glow that dimly illuminated what looked like a small laboratory.

Kyle froze again, seeing the table in the middle of the room with a woman tied down to it with thick ratchet straps, flat on her back, staring to the ceiling. Her head rolled over and revealed black eyes that looked like two rocks of coal, meeting his bulging stare.

"Kyle," she said confidently.

Everything in Kyle's body came to a halt with the exception of his racing heart trying to leap out of his body. His jaw wouldn't open to speak, his legs wouldn't move to run away, and his eyes refused to look away from the living Exall.

He remained fifteen feet away, studying every inch of her and the room. The Exall wore what looked like a hospital gown, her gray legs and arms bare. Four straps tied her down to the table, one over her ankles, knees, waist, and shoulders. The table was a black slab with a dozen drawers underneath. Black counters ran along the entire perimeter of the rectangular room. To Kyle's immediate left was a miniature stove with an oven below, next to a small refrigerator and sink. Rounding the corner stood a filing cabinet and other desktop organizers with folders and binders filling them. A dormant computer waited in the furthest corner, untouched for at least four years. To Kyle's right the countertops were bare, but he noticed they had more drawers underneath. Somewhere above him, birds sang tunes from the trees while the sun shined over the Earth, unaware of an alien creature held captive twenty feet underground.

The Exall never looked away from Kyle, but seemed content giving Kyle a moment to soak in his surroundings. The fact that she wasn't trying to break free and lunge toward him, or even say anything else, made him feel a little more at ease, the tension slowly leaving his tight throat.

"Who are you?" he asked in a shaky voice.

Her black eyes remained on him, and even though they appeared as pits of death, a certain gentleness carried across the room.

"If you're in here, then you know my name is Sandra."

Kyle took another step closer. "I know that, but *why* are you in here? Like this? Is that your real name?"

"We don't have names where I'm from. Your grandmother named me Sandra after a childhood friend. The straps are so I can't leave. I don't plan on leaving here, but that doesn't mean it's under my control."

One more step closer, and Kyle was now a short lunge away from being able to touch this alien. Everything he had just learned in training rushed through his mind about how to combat an Exall, and how he must always be alert. Could the handwritten note actually be from this Exall and not Susan? Was this some sort of trap she had laid out where Kyle would never be found underground?

This is your grandmother's underground hideout, he reminded himself, despite feeling 3,000 miles away from Larkwood, Colorado.

"You knew my grandma?" he asked, one smaller step closer and deciding to stop now that he was within arm's reach of "Sandra" the Exall.

Sandra grinned, her face like rubber as it made no wrinkles, her lips parting to show the black fangs that Kyle had only seen up close in textbooks. "Knew her? We were the best of friends. She used to come down here every day and we'd share stories. I know all about you, and she knew all about my lost family."

"Lost?"

"You call it murdered. My family was all lost in an attack by The Crew. This was many years ago, but I played dead when they started firing their special guns at us. She was with five other Crew members, but they all left once they thought we were all dead, except for Susan. It was like she knew to come check on me."

Kyle decided this couldn't be a trap. Why would an Exall go through all this small talk when he was already hypnotized by her mere presence? And the story sounded exactly like something his grandmother would do.

"What does any of that have to do with you being here?"

"Well, I have an ability to read spirits. I think you have people like that here on Earth as well – I forget what they're called, though. But as soon as Susan came over to me, I sensed the strength and beauty in her spirit. I knew right away she was one of the better ones on this planet, even if she was a part of The Crew. She tied me up and that's when I started talking to her. We learned about each other, and she told me she was looking for a way to end the war against us. That's when she brought me here to her house."

"When was this?"

"I don't know how your time works, but she told me you had been born only a few weeks earlier."

"You've been down here for seventeen years?!" Kyle gasped, unable to hide his shock.

"If you say so. We don't measure time because there is no end for us, unless we are lost, of course."

"What have you been doing the last four years?"

"If that's how long Susan has been gone, then I've been doing exactly this, looking at the ceiling and waiting for you. She told me it could be anywhere from five to fifty years for you to find me, and I told her I would wait."

"So what did my grandma do with you down here?"

Sandra looked into the distance as if reminiscing on her life's fondest memories. Did she even realize she was being held captive against her will? Kyle wondered if she had developed an intense case of Stockholm syndrome toward Susan. It was certainly possible after being held down here for so long, and she even seemed to miss Susan.

"We wanted to change our worlds," Sandra said. Kyle took another step closer and truly examined the Exall's body. He had never even heard of a female Exall in his courses at the Pentagon, and he still wasn't sure if that's what Sandra was. She had long black hair that pooled underneath her head, but she had no breasts. He thought at first that maybe the straps had kept them flat, but as he was now close enough, noticed her chest was as flat as his. Yet, she still had softer facial features like a woman.

Sandra must have read his mind or had a keen sense for body language.

"Your grandmother looked at me the same way when we first met," she said. "Yes, I'm really a female. Did you know your grandmother was the first female member of the Crew?"

"Yes. Everyone knows her name."

"Well, I'm the first female Exall to come down to Earth."

"Why?" Kyle asked, not sure what else to say.

"For us, the females run everything on our spacecraft to make sure we keep moving. We navigate it, but also keep the peace among each other. You see, there is a lot of panic between the Exalls. Everyone has an idea on how we can find a new planet to live on. We are the rulers. What we say goes in any dispute."

"How many of you are there?"

"I couldn't tell you now, but before I came here I'd say about forty thousand of us."

"Forty thousand?! How big is this spacecraft?"

"Slightly smaller than the planet Mercury."

"Planet? I was picturing something much smaller, but it's your own little world."

"Yes, and it's a lovely place, but it's not a home."

"So why did you come here?"

"I demanded it. I insisted that I could provide a fresh perspective for our research, and I forced my way onto our exploratory team."

"I guess I don't understand what you and my grandma did down here all the time."

"All we did was learn about each other. We traded stories about our lives and about the worlds we're from. Susan told me she was working on a secret project to find a planet safe for us to inhabit. She wanted to help us and said if your planet were to take on another species that would be the end of it—it can't sustain any more life than it already has."

"Did she find somewhere?"

"She found Mars, but said there was too much activity. It could work, but apparently the humans have found ways to get little robots to Mars. She said it would be catastrophic if a different living species were ever discovered."

"Why do you come back every thirty years?"

"We've studied this planet and the humans on it. We've seen the way humans treat the planet and each other. It's only a matter of time before the humans kill themselves, and then we can peacefully transition our life to this beautiful place you call Earth."

"How do you know English?"

Sandra grinned as if she had heard this question before. "We've been on this planet for hundreds of years. We have a very high capacity for retaining knowledge, and language is one of those things. We can speak every language on this planet."

"What is your actual language when you speak with each other, though?"

"When we're in private we speak to each other in our native tongue. We don't have a name for it, as we never understood there could be different languages until we arrived here on Earth."

Kyle nodded, intimidated by the Exall's vast knowledge of Earth. "I'm sorry, but I'm not sure why you're waiting for me or what I'm supposed to do with you. Did my grandma give you any sort of an idea?"

"Susan has many files about our discussions; they're underneath this table and the other counters. All she ever told me was that you would do the right thing. I don't know what that means, but I trust her. She had a sense for things, even knew that her death was coming, and wished me farewell."

"She *knew* she was going to die?" Kyle took one final step and now hovered over Sandra, staring down into the black pits of her eyes.

Sandra nodded. "I wouldn't say she *knew*, but she definitely had a sense it was possible. She told me she might have to sacrifice her life to save her family, primarily you. She thought very highly of you, not just as her grandson, but as a future key to The Crew and all of her research."

"Do you mind if I take a look around?" Kyle asked, feeling more like a guest in this secret laboratory. "I just don't know what I'm supposed to do, and not even sure if this is real or of I'm dreaming."

"This is real, Kyle. Just as real as Susan tried to kill me, then saved me after learning who I was."

Kyle nodded before crouching down to pull open the drawers and start reading through thousands of files from nearly two decades of documented research about Sandra and the Exalls. Judging by the amount of drawers he assumed were full of papers, Kyle would need a lot more than the week he had left in Denver to read through everything.

Am I supposed to tell the Colonel about this? Does he already know?

The thought rushed Kyle's mind, overwhelmed by keeping such a heavy secret, one that went beyond simply keeping his mouth shut about the existence of Exalls and The Crew.

This was a live alien being held prisoner underneath his grandmother's house. The exposure of this could revolutionize The Crew's research moving forward, but he didn't know if it was his place to let this secret out quite yet.

Kyle sat on the ground and flipped open the first file to start reading, in hopes of finding the answer he needed.

24

Chapter 24

Colonel Griffins pored over the new day's briefing, a tremor slowly working its way from his stomach to his chest. He knew this day would come, but not so soon. The boy had just officially joined The Crew and was still on his post-graduation vacation.

Small progress had been made on the tracking devices. More Exalls sprouted up on the map when turning one on, but there were still hundreds unaccounted for across the world. During these times of peace, The Crew was normally able to keep tabs on every Exall since their population on Earth had shrunk to under 1,000.

As of the recent updates to the software, only half of those could be located. They'd never discovered a trend in the past where more than half of their peaceful population left, so everyone believed the tracking devices remained lumps of faulty equipment.

The Crew had to resort to a more . . . traditional method for finding the doctor and his young companion: stalking. They had Crew members going into every bar and gas station that ran along the path from Denver to Kansas City to Washington,

D.C. The colonel knew they were coming, but he didn't want to alert anyone without proof.

It had become obvious after the attacks at the country music festival that the time had arrived for the Exalls to make a move on The Crew, more specifically on Kyle Wells. Susan had put that writing on the wall, leaving behind all sorts of hints and clues on what to look for. Griffins always questioned how she seemed to have a sense for what the Exalls were up to; it sometimes felt as if she had an insider feeding her information.

Colonel Griffins pulled out one of the last notes Susan had left him, reading it for the thirtieth time this week to make sure everything was as it seemed.

Not all remaining Exalls are peaceful.

They will make uncharacteristic attacks.

These new kind of attacks will have the goal of infecting as many humans as possible, growing their population of violence-crazed individuals.

The Exalls are coming for me and my grandson. They know I have the capability to bring them down, and will fight to the death to hurt me and Kyle.

If any of these events happens, prepare to defend the city.

Colonel Griffins checked his watch to find the time was just past eleven at night, and sighed at the thought of having to sleep in one of the dormitories for the third straight night. The days were starting to take their toll on him, making him drag himself out of bed in the mornings because all he wanted was more sleep. But knowing what was coming in the next couple of weeks meant sleep would have to wait, or else the entire world might be put to rest.

He dreaded the phone call he had to make, but it was time to make arrangements for the pending attacks likely headed directly for the Pentagon.

Colonel Griffins pulled open his drawer and took a quick swig from his flask before picking up the phone, his fingers running on autopilot as they dialed Kyle's number.

The phone rang and rang, and Colonel Griffins was about to slam the handpiece down when a teenage voice answered, "Hello?"

"Kyle Wells, it's the colonel. How are things going out there?"

"They're going fine." The boy sounded exhausted.

"Were you napping, son? It's only three o'clock your time."

"I haven't got much sleep the last couple of days, Colonel."

The colonel held the phone between his shoulder and ear as he flipped open his laptop to pull up the tracking software. He zoomed into Denver and found Kyle at Susan's old house, just to be sure.

"What's keeping you up at night?" He figured it was just teenage drama. Maybe Kyle ran into an old crush from high school and couldn't sleep, the way teenagers obsessed over those they dreamed of dating.

Kyle cleared his throat and a loud ruffle came from the phone as he adjusted himself. "Colonel, have you ever been to my grandma's basement?"

"A couple of times, yes."

"I mean have you really *been* into it. All the way?"

Colonel Griffins was too tired for questions. "Yes, yes, I've been down there. Is there something you need to tell me?"

A long pause.

"Kyle?"

"I think you need to come here. There's something you need to see."

"I surely can't go there right now. I was actually calling you to let you know we need you back in D.C. first thing in the morning."

"I can't leave yet, Colonel."

"What the hell do you mean you can't leave?!" Colonel Griffins stood from his seat and slammed a free hand on top of his desk as he spoke. "I need you back in D.C. immediately, and that's an order."

"Sir, I don't think you understand."

The colonel's head itched with fatigue and he felt his tipping point fast approaching if this teenage boy continued to refuse to come back to work.

"Whatever you have, you need to bring with you. We are on the verge of a crisis here and you're needed. In fact, forget about tomorrow morning, we'll get you on a flight tonight."

"Colonel, whatever is going on, I might have the answers here. It's not something I can bring back to Washington with me. But if you come look, you might find a way to make that happen."

"This isn't a discussion, Wells. Get your ass on the next flight to D.C. and we can discuss whatever you need in my office."

Colonel Griffins slammed the phone down, hanging up on Kyle, who was surely taken aback by the sudden burst of rage. They had just finished their last war four years ago, and it didn't end well, with Susan losing her life. The past few years had been peaceful, but ever since the attacks at the Colorado bar, everything seemed to be falling apart, his sanity included.

Why are the Exalls attacking us again? Why don't our trackers work? Why does no one seem to know what's going on these days?

Colonel Griffins found himself asking these same questions dozens of times each day. There was a time when The Crew seemed to always be one step ahead of the Exalls. But lately, everything had been a reaction to their savage attacks on human life. Attacks inching closer to Washington. Many within the Crew grew wary of what a showdown would look like. It was no secret the Crew no longer held an intelligence advantage. The two members who were killed in Michigan during their private raid sent a fresh wave of worry throughout the organization.

If two of the finest Crew members couldn't contain one Exall in isolation, what could that mean for the supposed army the Exalls were building as they moved east? No one liked discussing the possibilities, but Colonel Griffins certainly thought about them every day, all day long. The day was coming, he sensed, where he'd have to make the unfortunate trip to the Oval Office to discuss Plan D with the president.

Griffins always suspected the day would come. The Crew simply couldn't keep up with the way the Exalls advanced every thirty years when they returned. Eventually the aliens would reach a break-even point and pass them. He imagined this time would come well after he was a pile of bones in the ground, not in the middle of 2020 with a teenager as their freshest recruit.

Kyle was supposed to be groomed over the next two decades, The Crew filling his head with all the knowledge of hundreds of years of research on the Exalls. Only once he had that knowledge would he be fully equipped to go out into the world and destroy Exalls just as his grandmother had.

Dr. Klemens had chucked the rulebook out the window, and knew by doing so, The Crew was vulnerable. Preparations for battle typically took five years to solidify, including new combat training for all soldiers who would go out into the field and put their lives on the line.

Now, there was no preparation, and the leadership argued with each other about every little thing. Everyone had an opinion on what to do next as the Crew scrambled to stay afloat despite the glaring doomsday that lie ahead.

Griffins sent a text message to the head of intelligence, Brandon Grady, to come to his office. Within two minutes, Grady knocked on the door and let himself into the room.

"Close the door and have a seat," Griffins said, the whiskey he had sipped earlier now settling in and making him the slightest bit of relaxed.

"Something wrong, sir?" Grady asked as he made his way into his seat.

"Something is always wrong, you know that. I wanted to ask you about our plans for an attack here in D.C. We know they're coming east, and we know they want Wells. There's no denying any of that at this point. My concern is that they will not be subtle with their intentions, and we can't afford chaos in the streets. This is the nation's capital, for fuck's sake. If there is an attack by the Exalls in this city, the news will be to Hong Kong within five minutes."

Grady nodded as he listened, as if he knew all of this already.

"We've had teams going at it around the clock in Colorado, Kansas City, and Louisville. We can confirm that at least 250 people were infected across all three attacks—very likely more. We still don't know where they're all hiding. Just about everyone in that Louisville restaurant was attacked, but not one person can be found. It's like they disappeared off the map."

"Any word on the trackers?"

"The technology team is saying the trackers are fine now, but there are still hundreds of Exalls unaccounted for, so they're going back to the drawing board to see if they can find a way to get the devices to read even lower thermal outputs without having to redesign the entire device."

"Jesus Christ. We don't have time for starting from scratch."

"I know that, sir. They know that, too. But there really is no choice at the moment. If they don't find a way by starting over, then we are stuck with the devices we have and can only hope the Exalls don't discover they can no longer be tracked."

"Of course they know it already. Why do you think they're coming this way so aggressively? We can't read a damn thing about where this doctor and kid are. Do we have a tail on them yet?"

"No, sir. We thought we found them, but it was a false alarm."

"I want them shot on sight. I don't care who comes across them, just shoot them and get it over with."

"I'll get the word out immediately." Grady whipped a cell phone out of his jacket's inside pocket and started typing on his screen.

"Do you know anything about Susan Wells' bunker? Anything special about it?"

Grady scrunched his face as he ran through the mental files in his mind. "No. All bunkers should be built the same except for the president's. Hers might even be a bit outdated, considering when it was made. Why do you ask?"

"Just curious. That's all I needed for today. If you can get that word out and keep doing what you're doing, we just have to take this one day at a time."

"Thank you, sir, let me know if you need anything else."

Grady let himself out of the room and left Griffins to lean back in his chair and stare to the ceiling. The colonel knew

Susan liked to keep a lot of secrets to herself.
What could have Kyle found in that basement?

Chapter 25

Kyle felt his brain on the verge of physically splitting down the center. He had rushed out of the secret lab to receive the call from Colonel Griffins. When his phone had buzzed in his pocket, he was standing over the greatest secret in the country. Sandra didn't say anything as Kyle left the room, shouting that he'd be right back.

He probably shouldn't have answered the call, his mind in a state of shock. But the colonel didn't seem to suspect anything, and he clearly didn't know about the secret Exall.

Kyle had started reading through the documents Susan left behind. Most of the information came directly from Sandra instead of Susan's observations. Susan was working on finding a cure for any infection received by a human through Exall blood. Notes and charts stuffed the file with different combinations of potential chemicals to counteract the blood, but the experiment appeared incomplete, the notes abruptly stopping in late 2008.

Nothing suggested what Kyle was supposed to do with all of this information. Sandra had told him that Susan knew he would do the 'right' thing, but what did that mean?

His natural instinct to keep secrets kicked in, but this wasn't so much a secret as it was a discovery. Nowhere did it say he shouldn't tell anyone about what he found. Susan had left him personalized notes, knowing he would uncover this. If she meant for it to remain hidden from The Crew, then wouldn't she have mentioned that?

The right thing to do was tell Colonel Griffins. Kyle was too new to The Crew to take this on alone. Maybe the right thing to do depended on *when* Kyle found the secret. If he discovered this twenty years later, as a seasoned Crew member, it might be a different scenario. But as of today, this was way above his head and pay grade.

The colonel wouldn't listen, however, and demanded Kyle return to D.C. immediately, hanging up the call before he could respond. Kyle knew better than to disobey an order, and rushed back into the laboratory.

"I need to leave," he told Sandra, stuffing papers back into files and returning them to their cabinet drawers.

"You just got here," she replied, turning her head to watch as Kyle paced frantically around the room. "When are you coming back?"

"I don't know, but hopefully soon. They just called me and said I need to get back to Washington."

"They did that to Susan quite a bit. Seemed like she was always having to drop everything and fly to some other city. But she always came back."

"I'll be back, I promise. And I'm probably going to bring someone else with me."

"Don't let them kill me," Sandra said flatly, almost uninterested in the conversation. "I know lots of your kind only want to kill us. I don't mean any trouble for you, and I'm willing to help however you need."

"No one is going to kill you."

Kyle didn't know this for certain, and had a fresh wave of doubt about telling the colonel. His internal clock ticked, despite not knowing the actual time. He had come into the basement shortly after noon, and a quick check of his cell phone showed that it was already three o'clock.

"I really need to go. I'll see you again very soon."

Kyle ran out of the lab and down the twisted hallway to the panic room. He arranged the ladder and climbed out of the freezer, returning to the pantry, quiet and undisturbed, slamming the freezer door shut, mind racing.

A real Exall, living under us the whole time.

The thought sent a chill up his back, all the hairs on his body stiffening. He desperately wanted to ask his father if he knew, but didn't want to frighten him in case he didn't. Kyle owned this secret until he returned to the Pentagon and told Colonel Griffins in person.

Kyle turned off all the lights in the basement before sprinting upstairs, through the kitchen and into his bedroom.

"The quicker I get to D.C., the quicker I come back here with the colonel," he said to himself, throwing his suitcase on the bed and stuffing clothes into it with no sort of organization.

He pulled out his cellphone and called his dad.

"Where are you?" Kyle asked as soon as Travis answered.

"Just finishing up at the gym. Is everything okay?"

"I don't know. I just got called back to D.C. I need to leave now."

"Well, shit. Do you need a ride to the airport?"

"Yes, please."

"Okay, I'll be right there. Ten minutes."

As soon as he hung up with Travis, Kyle called his mom.

"Mom, I'm leaving right now."

"Leaving? I thought you had another week?" Her voice instantly broke at the news.

"I know, but they called me and said I need to get back immediately. I should be able to come back soon."

"What are they making you go back for?"

"I don't know, but it sounded important."

"Goddammit," she snarled. "I'm stuck at work or I'd stop over to say bye. Will you let me know when you get to D.C.?"

"Of course."

"Okay, have a safe trip. I love you."

"I love you, too."

Kyle hung up and tossed his phone onto the bed, sitting down at the empty desk next to the room's only window that overlooked the front yard, oblivious that it was the final conversation he'd ever have with his mother.

The secret grew like a brain tumor, pushing against his skull, begging to be let out.

Kyle craned his neck to look out the window and saw his dad's convertible Audi crawl up the driveway, the engine a steady hum in the quiet neighborhood. His stomach plummeted at the sight, not knowing for sure when he'd come back to visit his new friend stashed underground like a prisoner. He hoped whatever the colonel needed him for would distract his mind enough. If not, he just might lose all of his sanity.

The backdoor creaked open as Travis entered. *I should have just stayed down there,* Kyle thought. *Stayed there until they came to find me, if the tracking device even works that well underground.*

He knew they would check the bunker, but if no one knew about the secret lab, he could have hidden there forever.

Stop talking about hiding. Cowards hide. There's not even anything to hide from.

"Kyle?" Travis asked from the bedroom doorway, startling his son. "I've been calling your name. Is everything okay? You look a bit off."

"I'm fine, just a little nervous."

"About going back?"

"Yeah. The colonel sounded pretty fired up. I'm not sure if he's mad at me or just mad at the world."

"I'm sure he's not mad at you. Don't take it so personally. You're in the military now, even if it's a secret military."

"It doesn't feel anything like what I'd imagined the military was like. I'm bottom of the totem pole and can get a ride in my own private town car whenever I like. I don't think new recruits to the Army are getting that same treatment."

"True. Are you ready to get going, then?"

"Yes." Kyle grabbed his bags and slung one over each shoulder, his legs wobbly. It seemed like lunacy to walk away from a living, breathing Exall. How would he sleep at night knowing his dad lived in this house completely oblivious to the truth?

You won't need to sleep, because you're going to tell the colonel as soon as you see him. Then you'll both be back here on a return flight tonight.

Kyle giggled nervously, earning a side-eye stare from his father. He focused on clearing his mind as they left the room, unable to deny the presence below his feet as they glided across the hardwood floor.

He followed Travis out the backdoor where the Audi's trunk

was already open and waiting for Kyle's bags.

Kyle felt his dad watching him, and focused on appearing as normal as possible. He tossed his bags in the trunk and slammed the door shut, fighting the urge to stare at the house, as if Sandra was going to blast out of the walls and demand to go with Kyle.

They both sat down in the car, Travis turning on the engine and backing out of the driveway. As they pulled onto the road, Kyle caught the glimpse of the house he wanted. It stood quietly, innocent, the oak tree in the front yard smothering its shade in every direction. This was the same house he came to every day after school, doing his homework at the kitchen table while Susan prepared dinner. Sometimes she went down to the pantry to get food, and now Kyle wondered if she did a little more on these seemingly innocent trips downstairs.

They drove away, leaving the house behind, and with it, a world of secrets.

Chapter 26

Kyle woke up on the plane five hours later, landing in Washington shortly after 10 P.M. The town car would be waiting outside.

Kyle had stopped by one of the airport shops in Denver to buy a packet of melatonin. His mind was out of control, like a pinball bouncing off the bumpers, and the only solution for him to have a relaxing flight was to drug himself to sleep. He took the pills right when the boarding process started, knowing they would kick in by the time he settled into his seat. He had grabbed a window seat toward the back and was snoring before the flight attendant had a chance to show him how to properly put on a seat belt.

When he woke, he jumped out of his seat, startled. It was some of the deepest sleep he had ever experienced, and he was surprised to see he nearly missed his row of passengers getting up to leave. He quickly sent his mother a text message letting her know he had arrived safely.

For those brief moments after waking up, the thought of Sandra living under his grandmother's house had been the furthest thing from his mind. He had to remind himself that a live alien was occupying the same house as his father. When he remembered, Kyle grabbed his bag and sped down the aisle that had just about been cleared.

His head remained cloudy from the sleep, like he was in a dream, as he sped-walked through the concourse toward the baggage claim to get his checked bag. The carousel was already spinning, and much to his delight, his solid green bag was waiting for him. Kyle wasted no time, the fogginess in his brain giving way to the urgency that had plagued him before he got on the plane.

He had to get to the colonel's office immediately. This news was too big to wait overnight, and if he had to call him at home to tell him that, then that's what he'd do.

With bags in hand, he worked his way through the concourse toward the arrivals area. A soft breeze welcomed him as he stepped outside, a needed relief after the stuffy airplane. The night was quiet with the exception of taxis and cars creeping through the area.

Kyle scanned the area until he found a town car with a suited man standing on the curb. He recognized the man as one of The Crew's drivers—Jason, maybe?—and started for him.

"Good evening, Mr. Wells," Jason said. Kyle read his badge and confirmed his name. Jason was probably the same age as Travis, and greeted Kyle with a grin before pulling open the backseat door and taking the luggage out of Kyle's hands. "Are we just going to the Pentagon?"

Kyle didn't realize he had a say, considering Colonel Griffins demanded his immediate return. What was a teenage boy to say? Let's stop at a strip club first?

"Yes, the Pentagon please."

Kyle waited in the car while Jason tossed the luggage in the trunk before circling back to the driver's seat. Every town car The Crew used came equipped with a glass divider to separate the front from the back. The divider was normally in place, but Kyle was pleased to find that tonight it was wide open, giving him a clear view of the road ahead. They drove off and started to exit the airport.

"Busy night for you?" Kyle asked, unsure if it was okay to speak to the drivers who never seemed to show any emotion. Jason seemed a bit different tonight, though.

"Not busy at all," Jason replied. "Weeknights this late are typically very slow. An occasional airport run from time to time, otherwise I hang out at the office and read a book to pass the time."

"Do you know of anything going on at the office? I was supposed to be home for another week, but they called me back tonight. Sounded urgent."

"I've not heard anything, but it's not that uncommon, either. There could be an important meeting in the morning. Especially for those of you in the field. If any bit of information comes up that is critical to saving lives, they will call all hands on deck to get everyone on the same page."

Kyle slouched. Called across the country for a meeting? *I should have just stayed in the basement and taken my chances. I'm sure a live Exall would be more exciting than a meeting.*

After the flight and extended, drug-induced nap, Sandra felt millions of miles away. It seemed impossible that Kyle was just speaking with an Exall five hours earlier. Now he was back in D.C., where they'd expect him to continue his new normal.

Kyle gazed out the window to the dark night, the bright buildings of the capital city miles away in the distance. They reached the freeway and accelerated to a higher speed, the street lights passing in a blur. Jason had soft jazz playing on the radio, and for the late hour something about it felt just right, relaxing Kyle's frantic thoughts. The distance from Colorado helped him push Sandra out of his mind, as her presence wasn't throbbing beneath his feet like a dirty secret.

Raindrops started to fall, splashing quietly on the windshield before gradually showering the entire car and road ahead.

"We're expecting some good rain over the next couple of days," Jason commented as he flicked on the wipers. "This is your first autumn here, right?"

"Yeah."

"Autumn can get tons of rain—we actually broke the city's record for most rainfall just last year. Looking like this year will give it another try."

Kyle looked out the window, remembering how as a kid he'd follow the journey of one lone drop of water as it clung to the window and either streamed slowly to the bottom or hung on for dear life as the wind tried to blow it off.

Gazing out the dark tint in the middle of a rainy night made it impossible to see anything aside from the occasional passing streetlight. But the headlights of a pickup truck that zoomed by at lightning speed made Kyle stiffen in his seat, recoiling away from the window. Jason didn't make a sound, but Kyle felt the car swerve slightly.

"Did you see that?" Kyle asked.

"Hold on." Jason sounded distant and occupied. "He's not leaving us."

Kyle craned his neck over the center console for a better view and saw the truck a few feet ahead of them, matching an identical speed to the town car.

"Is it a drunk driver?" Kyle asked.

"Could be."

Jason pushed a button that was a red exclamation mark on the touchscreen panel, and let off the accelerator to slow down the vehicle. The truck, who drove in the shoulder, slowed down immediately, letting the town car pass.

Jason sped up the car again, his eyes glued to the mirrors instead of the freeway. "Shit!" he cried. "There are two pistols in the glove box. Can you get them out for us?"

Kyle's heart thumped quicker at the mention of pistols. Why on earth would they need a pistol on the freeway? Adrenaline flowing, he unclicked his seatbelt and lunged over the center console, arms outstretched as they flailed for the glove compartment. The dim light glowed enough to reveal the two pistols resting atop a small collection of papers. He handed one to Jason, who immediately cocked it and lay it on his lap.

"What's going on?" Kyle asked, returning to the backseat with the other gun in hand.

"You're right, it might just be a drunk driver, but I'm not sure."

"What do you mean?"

"I'm just being cautious."

Kyle turned to look out the back window, the truck's headlights glowing like bright, devilish eyes in the night. One hundred feet separated them and the truck, but the distance shrunk by the second as the truck accelerated to deadly speeds for a second time.

The truck matched and maintained the speed of the town car, its front bumper lined up perfectly with the town car's rear bumper.

"Hold on!" Jason screamed, looking over his shoulder to

switch lanes to the right, but it was too late.

The truck veered into them, metal crunching against metal, knocking it off balance and sending Jason and Kyle into a wobbly three-sixty spin. Kyle hung on to the door as the world blurred in front of them through the windshield. Jason seemed to hold a scream the entire time, much like a child shrieking during an entire roller coaster ride.

They spun in what felt like a dozen circles before the car came to a rest, facing the wrong way on the freeway. Kyle's whole body pulsed with adrenaline, even his vision throbbing in and out of focus. They both looked around for the truck, not seeing it until bright headlights flashed from the passenger side of the car.

"Get down!" Jason barked.

The truck's engine roared like a beast as the sound of screeching rubber and its smoke filled the air. It rammed into the side of the car, breaking the passenger side windows and growling louder as it pushed the car toward the short concrete wall that served as the freeway's median.

Kyle remained tucked in his corner, safely away from the truck, but feeling the heat of the pending collision with the median. Rain droplets splashed inside the car as he watched, bug-eyed, as the truck burnt more rubber and kept push-ing. Through the missing windows he could clearly read the "DODGE" letters on the truck's chrome grill. Its passenger-side headlight had shattered, but the other one remained shining bright, staring at Kyle like a watchful eye.

The truck struggled to push them at first, but caught trac-tion—or the town car *lost* traction, he'd never know—and sent them flying toward the median. It felt like the wheels may have come off the ground, but neither he or Jason had time to process what was happening as they flew toward the wall, the metal screeching against the concrete that had no interest in giving an inch. Kyle's head slammed against the window, not shattering as the bulk of the impact occurred to the body of the car. He immediately reached for the warm trickle of blood oozing through his hair and down his head.

The headlights vanished as the truck sped away, leaving them in complete silence with the exception of the soft rapping sound of rain drops hitting the car's roof.

"Kyle! Mr. Wells!" Jason's voice called, distant in Kyle's mind.

Kyle stared out the window, seeing other cars pull over, people running to them and yelling. But the noise fell on deaf ears. Kyle felt isolated in the world, stranded on his own island. Sandra was nowhere near his thoughts, neither was Colonel Griffins or the Pentagon or The Crew. All he could envision was the Exalls they had encountered during their trip to the mountains four years ago. The same Exalls who had tailed them as they drove out of town in search of a hospital from Brian. They had followed them in the same manner the truck had tonight. The same Exalls who had crashed their SUV into Kyle's middle school, killing classmates and teachers, and scarring the community forever.

He didn't need any proof to know who had tried to kill them on the middle of the freeway. *They want me. Why didn't they just kill me in the mountains? Why go through all the trouble of following us home and raising hell for my family and friends?*

"Grandma," Kyle said through a lumped throat. "Come save me."

He leaned his head back and fainted.

27

Chapter 27

The next thirty minutes passed in a foggy haze for Kyle. He came in and out of consciousness, seeing images of his grandmother when he went under, and blurry, gray clouds through a car window when his eyes opened. He heard multiple voices and felt his head get moved around, poked and prodded by wandering fingers as the bleeding was stopped from the back of his head.

"He's going to be just fine," a slurred voice said.

"We need him more than ever," another voice said, perhaps Colonel Griffins, but Kyle's mind was too loopy to know for sure.

The voices came from near his feet while his head remained against a back wall looking out a window. *Am I in an ambulance? Am I dead?*

He'd heard stories of people who had experienced death, citing a floating sensation as they hovered above their own body for a bird's eye of view of their current state. There was no floating, and he couldn't see anything besides the streaking water running across the window. Just like it had before the truck attacked them on the freeway.

The skies gave way to a deeper darkness, dim orange lights passing by every so often, and Kyle realized they were back at the Pentagon, driving through the underground garage.

Maybe a special ambulance used by The Crew.

The voices reduced to soft whispers just quiet enough for Kyle to not hear them. As he came more into consciousness, Kyle felt how stiff his neck was and had a brief panic attack of paralysis. He wiggled his toes and fingers to make sure everything was connected, and fought to turn his neck so much as a centimeter, which it did much to his relief.

The vehicle came to a stop, and doors immediately opened and closed. Kyle kept his gaze out the window until the door it belonged to swung open, letting in a rush of cool air, and revealing the face of Colonel Griffins with two other soldiers standing by his side.

"Kyle," Colonel Griffins grumbled. "Glad to see you're awake. How are you feeling?"

Feels like I got trampled by a stampede of hungry hippos, Kyle thought.

"I'm okay. Can I still walk?"

"Yes," the colonel snapped, as if expecting this question. "You're completely fine. You'll have some mild soreness and a mild concussion. We can get all the aches massaged out tonight, and the concussion won't affect you so long as you don't bonk your head again. We need you ready for tomorrow."

Concussion? The word cut into Kyle like a knife.

"What happened?" Kyle asked, his head suddenly spinning now that he knew his brain was injured.

"Exall attack," the colonel said bluntly. "Let's get you out of this van and I can explain everything."

The colonel nodded to the two soldiers, one man and one woman, standing by his side. Kyle was indeed on a stretcher, and they rolled him out of the van, dropping the wheels on the ground and rolling him toward the Crew's main entrance.

Kyle caught a glimpse of the vehicle he had ridden in, a large black van that reminded him of the kind in movies that police used during a stakeout.

The group of them charged into the office, pushing Kyle through the doorways. His neck already felt looser, but still too stiff to look around freely. Out of the corner of his eyes, Kyle saw fellow Crew members gawking at him as they ran down the hallway with him on the gurney.

Colonel Griffins shouted. "I need every Crew member in the D.C. area to come into this office right now. Call everyone on your teams, and tell them to get their asses here right away!"

They marched forward, to the back where the colonel's office awaited.

"We need to run him through a quick CT scan, Colonel," the male soldier said.

Colonel Griffins grunted. "Fine. Take him quickly and bring him right back to my office."

The colonel trailed off to his office, and the two soldiers took a hard right and started moving faster. Kyle watched the ceiling and lights pass in a bright blur. Kyle remembered there was an infirmary on the seventh floor below them, and assumed this was where they were going.

The two soldiers didn't say anything, moving quickly as if they had done this same routine hundreds of times. The ground shifted and Kyle felt blood rush to his head as they started down a slanted ramp. They barged through one more door into a room that had even brighter lights, making Kyle recoil, his arm shooting up to shield his eyes.

"Mr. Wells," the female soldier said in a harsh voice. "We've done preliminary tests while you were asleep. Your reflexes and pupils reacted correctly, but we still suspect you have a mild concussion. This CT scan is to ensure your brain is not bleeding or severely bruised."

Without further explanation, they both grabbed Kyle from each side and hoisted him upward, moving him to another bed that would slide into the machine scanning his brain. This was the first moment Kyle realized his clothes had been removed, stripped down to his underwear, a heavy black blanket covering his body. The transfer from the stretcher allowed his head to bob back an inch, loosening his neck muscles a little more.

"Where's my stuff?" he asked, realizing his wallet, bags, and tracking device were no longer with him.

"Colonel Griffins has all of your things," the woman said, this time her voice softer and caring.

"Where is Jason? Is he okay?"

"Jason is fine. He got a couple scratches and bruises, but he was able to walk away from the accident on his own. He's with our intelligence team, telling them everything that happened."

Kyle was satisfied with this response, and couldn't have said anything more as the machine started humming and his body started sliding away into the depths of the CT scan.

"Stay still, this'll just be a few seconds," the man assured him.

Kyle's head slid into a confined place, the scanner humming above his face as it took a reading of his brain. He lay there for about thirty seconds, wondering why The Crew had one of these machines in their underground offices. Surely it wasn't needed too often.

They might have run Exalls through this to see inside their bodies. The thought caused an instant spread of goosebumps across his back, the idea of lying on the same machine as them making him queasy.

His body slowly pulled out from the scanner, the soldiers waiting on each side again.

"I think I can walk on my own," Kyle said.

"We can't let you do that yet," the woman replied. "Colonel's orders. He doesn't want you doing anything until you have all of the soreness rubbed out."

"Do we have a massage therapist or something?"

"We have everything," she replied with a grin.

They lifted and returned him to the stretcher. His body was already feeling better, but if they insisted on pampering him with a massage, then so be it. He had almost died in a violent car crash, after all.

They wheeled him back up the ramp with the same urgency, jogging through the office as the man pushed the stretcher and the woman matched his pace by his side. When they arrived to the colonel's office they were both gasping for air, and put their hands on their hips as they caught their breath.

"Thank you both," Colonel Griffins said. Kyle wanted to turn his head to see the colonel, but feared they might attack him for straining any of his muscles. Instead, he kept his eyes to the ceiling, seeing a woman in a chair out of the corner of his eye.

The two soldiers left and closed the door behind them.

"Wells," the colonel grumbled. "This is Ms. Fletcher. She's the head of our technology department, but is also a certified physical therapist."

The woman stood up, joints popping, and her warm, smiling

face appeared in Kyle's vision. She studied him from behind a pair of round glasses, her light brown ponytail hanging limply to the side as she looked down to him.

"Hi, Kyle," she said. "You can call me Fletch, like everyone else around here. Would you mind rolling over on your stomach?" She grabbed an arm and helped him rotate. "The colonel tells me your neck is stiff. Is there anywhere else that is sore?" She asked this as she ran fingers over the surface of his neck.

"Not really; it's just my neck and upper back."

"Understood. I'll massage your whole back, but will focus on the upper area. You can go ahead, Colonel, don't mind me."

Colonel Griffins cleared his throat and began speaking just as Fletch sunk her fingers deep into Kyle's flesh, applying an intense pressure on his neck. Kyle fought every urge to let out a grunt that felt more like a reflex than anything.

"We have a major issue, Kyle," the colonel said in a softer voice. "I wouldn't have called you back here if it wasn't urgent. In fact, every Crew member across the country is headed this way as we speak."

Kyle wanted to ask why, but kept his lips clenched to not let out a scream from the excruciating pain Fletch was applying to his back. It felt like she was trying to push her way through his skin to rip out his spine. His eyes welled with tears as the colonel continued.

"They're coming to attack us, but all they want is you."

"*Me?*" Kyle managed to ask in a tone that sounded like a cry for help.

"I'm afraid so. The Exalls were terrified of your grandmother, and we suspect they've kept an eye on you since her passing. Now they're worried because you're her direct bloodline. All of the attacks these last few weeks have been them recruiting new Exalls while making their way across the country. They're here, and that's who tried to kill you on the freeway."

Kyle's mind spun. *Maybe now isn't the right time to tell him about Sandra.*

Fletch ran her forearm over Kyle's back, and seemed to put all of her body weight into it. Kyle thought his eyes might pop right out of their sockets if she managed to push any harder. There was a brief moment of relief as she stood to adjust her position over him.

"What do you want me to do?" he asked quickly, before Fletch clamped down on his back for more punishment.

"That's what I wanted to let you know. We have a plan, but it involves using you as bait. It's not what it sounds like, though. Simply having you present with us is all the bait we need—it's not like we're going to dangle you in front of their eyes. You'll be fully armed and suited with protection. And you'll be behind our entire team of soldiers."

Kyle felt the pressure on his back lighten. "When?" he asked.

"Tomorrow." The colonel checked his watch. "Well, today. We don't have much time. In fact, we're out of time. They already tried to kill you tonight. If your head would have struck the window at just the right – or wrong – angle, we wouldn't be having this conversation. We don't know if they know you're alive, but we assume they do. They seem to know everything lately, and are always a step ahead of us. Do you remember your friend Brian?"

"Of course."

"Well, you might have to kill him. I just want to put that out there so you're not surprised. He is very much part of this group of Exalls trying to hunt you."

Kyle thought back to the text messages that Mikey received on his phone from Brian. Brian was still alive, even if having no control of his body. His conscience still floated, crying for help to return to normal.

"Brian isn't dead—he texted my other friend, Mikey." Kyle let the words fly out of his mouth and strained his eyes to meet the colonel.

"What do you mean he 'texted' your friend?"

"When I was home, Mikey showed me. It was a chain of messages from a blocked number, saying it was Brian trapped and trying to get out."

Fletch stepped back and shook her hands. "All set. Anything else you need from me, Colonel?"

"Functioning ETD's would be good. Thanks for your help."

Kyle sat up and put his shirt back on, his clothes piled neatly on the corner of the colonel's desk. His entire body completely relaxed, like he was floating on an inflatable bed in a swimming pool. The pain had been worth it, seeing how he now felt drunk with relaxation.

Fletch packed up her duffel bag and quickly left the office, likely not wanting to hear where this conversation was headed.

"Look, Kyle, I already know where you're going with this; you want to save your friend. I'm afraid it's too late. We can only save those who have been partially infected by Exall blood. He was infected four years ago, and has since been on the run with this doctor. There's zero chance his blood level is less than ninety percent Exall blood."

"Why not try?"

"We have tried. The blood is too toxic and kills anything we try to infuse it with, human blood included."

Kyle scrunched his face, wishing there was a way out of this entire situation, but knowing it would never happen.

"Look, you should probably head to sleep," the colonel continued. "Tomorrow is a big day for all of us. Security will be heightened all night, so we'll be safe here. Tomorrow we have to take action before it's too late."

Kyle didn't know how he'd sleep while scheduled to be live Exall bait the next day. It also became clear that a conversation about Sandra would have to wait. Aside from putting more on the colonel's plate, it didn't sound like there were any resources to even send to Denver at the moment. Whether he told him now, or later, they would still have to wait until this battle with the Exalls passed before doing anything.

"Thank you, Colonel."

Kyle stood, his body feeling light as a feather, and held out a hand to shake.

"Thank *you*, young man. Let's rest tonight, and tomorrow we can go out there and make your grandmother proud."

They shook hands and Kyle departed for his room, knowing sleep would be an impossible task.

28

Chapter 28

The heavy rain continued well into the night and deep into the woods. The doctor cackled during the entire drive back, many times looking up to the truck's ceiling and howling like someone had just told him the world's greatest joke.

Brian sat in the passenger seat, his hands with a death grip on the door's handle ever since they had arrived to the airport over an hour ago, waiting for Kyle's arrival. He had tried slipping out of the trance the doctor held over him, desperately wanting to send another message, this time to Kyle's phone. Only this time he was blocked, trapped within his own mind and unable to do anything but watch the terror unfold.

He remained silent while they sped away in the dark night, the streets slick and shiny with rain.

When they approached the woods where they were hiding, the doctor said, "We have company."

Brian didn't know what that meant, and didn't ask. The doctor didn't sound worried, perhaps even a bit excited, but it had become impossible to know what madness was riling him up recently.

They reached the open space where they had parked their truck earlier, tucked behind a thick stand of trees. There were another dozen cars and trucks jammed together in the lot, and Brian's mind immediately sunk into a state of complete panic.

Every day that passed, going back four years when he had undergone this transformation, he suspected was one day closer to his inevitable death. He was on the run from a secret military whose only job was to kill those like him. Going closer to Washington where they were headquartered seemed like the worst idea in the world, but here he was, out of his own control, as the doctor hijacked his mind and made him his involuntary sidekick.

They parked and the doctor hopped out of the truck with a childish grin stuck on his face. "Tonight has already been so intense, and it's only getting better."

Brian followed suit, dragging his feet through the dirt and freezing at the sound of distant howling.

The doctor sensed his concern and explained, "Our people have arrived. I told them when and where to meet, and here they are. Do you hear that sound they're making? That's the sound of fulfilling our destiny."

He threw his head back and howled to join the chorus, reminding Brian of a werewolf on the eve of a full moon.

"Let's go," the doctor growled, starting into the woods, rocks and sticks crunching beneath every step like old bones.

Their campsite was a quarter mile into the trees, where a fifty-foot radius opened up on flat land. They had a small tent, and Brian used it each night to try and sleep while the doctor wandered the woods like a Sasquatch.

They jogged through the trees, their vision unaffected by the darkness of night as they could see as clearly as if the sun were at high noon. The howling grew louder, and the soft orange glow of a fire splashed across the trees in a haunting strobe.

"I'm here, ladies and gentlemen," the doctor shouted as they stepped onto the flatland. At least 500 Exalls were huddled around multiple campfires, their gray faces tight with intensity, but their expressions relaxed at the sight of Dr. Klemens.

Their huddle tightened, each Exall seeming to take another step closer to the fire, rubbing shoulders with each other as they gazed in unison at the doctor walking toward them, his hands held high, grin widening with each step.

"My good friend and I have already started tonight's festivities. Tomorrow we FEAST!"

The crowd cheered, screaming, howling. Brian looked around, sure the noise in the silent night would draw the attention of a park ranger who would have the misfortune of tumbling into this mess with no chance of escaping.

Just another recruit, Brian thought.

"More of us are coming," the doctor said. "A *lot* more. When we gather in the morning, there will be 1,500 of us, and once we have that, we'll make our move."

They howled again, like a pack of hyenas, and Brian wondered if they even knew what they were going to do in the morning. Dr. Klemens had been vague with every one of his statements. The Exalls were likely just brainwashed, programmed like robots to cheer for any words that left the doctor's mouth.

Just then, an idea struck Brian, and he stepped forward, sliding in front of the doctor, all Exall eyes now glued to him.

"Are you all ready to kill?!" he shouted.

The Exalls looked around, unsure how to react, then howled.

"Can you taste the human blood in your mouths?!" Brian shouted again.

The Exalls responded with more excitement, and Brian felt the doctor grinning proudly behind him.

"Tomorrow we're going to snap their necks and feast until there are none left!"

The Exalls lost all means of control as they jumped, whistled, and screamed to the night sky.

Brian had only wanted to see if they would respond to him. If they would, he'd have a chance to prevent whatever doom waited on the other side of dawn.

The doctor's hand fell on Brian's shoulder and squeezed it briefly.

"Let's settle down, everyone. Save your energy for tomorrow," the doctor said. "The night is yours to do as you please. If you want to relax here, please do. If you want to go recruit some more people for our big day, go right ahead. Just be back here by 7 A.M. sharp. That's when the rest will be here."

They gave one more cheer for the doctor, and some dispersed away from the fire. Others sat down in the dirt, settling into their positions for the rest of the night.

Brian wondered where the other 1,000 Exalls were coming from. Were they just marching down the street, walking here like a group of zombies following the scent of blood? Or were they all driving trucks like he and the doctor had on their trip across the country?

Brian wanted to sleep, but knew he'd never be able to. He also toyed with the thought of slipping away from the group. Perhaps there were enough Exalls where he could take off without the doctor noticing, assuming he still wasn't in his mind like a leach refusing to let go. If he could make it to the truck undetected, he just might be able to make it all the way to Kyle, warn him about what was coming, and either get killed by a swarm of Crew people, or disappear into the night.

The only problem was that the doctor never seemed to leave. Brian looked and found him mingling with his new Exalls, laughing, clapping hands on their backs as they swapped stories about traveling across the country as an alien species.

Oh, you killed people at a gas station, too? Haha! How original, because that's what we did on our way. Those silly country bumpkins and their pickup trucks make it so easy for us in the middle of nowhere!

Brian had the confidence built up, only needing an opportunity to turn and make a mad dash for freedom. He watched the doctor from across the open space, much like a hawk tracking its prey from hundreds of feet in the sky.

At one point, the doctor let his gaze wander across the gathering and met Brian's intense eyes. He winked at him, as if daring him to try something.

He can't possibly know what I'm trying to do, Brian thought. But deep down he knew the doctor could probably hear any thought that popped into his head as clearly as if Brian were standing on top of a nearby tree and shouting it.

A prisoner in my own head, he reminded himself. And the doctor nodded as if he agreed.

He wished he could die, but wasn't even sure of how to kill himself. He didn't bleed like a human, didn't even feel pain. During one of their earlier days together, the doctor was proud to demonstrate to Brian just how strong their new bodies were. Giggling, of course, he had pulled out a scalpel from his work bag, and slashed a quick gash across his leg. The black tarry blood had oozed out and formed a pool on the ground like a car leaking oil. The doctor howled when he saw the sheer terror on Brian's face. He handed the scalpel to Brian, who promptly chucked it away and took off running for his tent.

Later that night, Brian experimented, first by biting down on his lip as hard as he could. He felt nothing, as if he had bitten into a thick cut of raw sirloin. He then scratched at his own flesh on his arms and legs, again feeling nothing, and not seeing so much as the little red and white streaks that accompanied a claw mark. He progressed later that night, as the tug of fear wore off, and grabbed a switch blade they had found in one of their first stolen trucks. He cautiously cut at the flabby skin of his calf, not wanting to stab at it like a serial killer, but rather use the precision of a heart surgeon. A line of blood appeared, but no pain accompanied it. When he cut himself, his flesh started to turn the gray color that was common for Exalls, and this was when reality started to settle in his mind. It was the first time he accepted what he had become, and wondered what abilities he had beyond a resistance to pain. He raised the switchblade and stabbed himself in the thigh, bracing for a burst of screeching pain, but nothing ever came.

It may have been the first and only time Brian smiled as an Exall, fear washed away by a new sense of invincibility. Who wouldn't want to live forever, after all?

Brian had lost sight of this feeling, the maniacal doctor distracting him from all the beauty that life as an Exall had to offer. *Why have I been so ungrateful?* he wondered, finding the doctor in the crowd and shooting him a grin. *I was given this chance for a reason, and all I want to do is piss it away to save my friend who will kill me when he gets the chance.*

A new confidence now bubbled up within Brian. A confidence that he could leave a legacy as one of the deadliest Exalls to have roamed the planet. A confidence that engrained the belief that he would kill Kyle before Kyle killed him.

Don't worry, Doc, I'm not going anywhere besides where I'm needed. Send me in first. I'm not afraid of the little Crew people and their bullets.

Brian threw his head back and howled to the night sky, his human soul buried under layers of madness, resuming its screams for salvation that no one would ever hear.

29

Chapter 29

The night passed just as Kyle expected: tossing and turning while he checked the time on his cell phone every two minutes. Calling it the longest night of his life was an understatement. Even the night after watching his grandmother get slaughtered by an alien species didn't prove this difficult to fall into a deep REM cycle. Tonight, however, Kyle's mind was too occupied to relax. He thought back to moments as a child when Susan ran him through homemade obstacle courses in her backyard. Or the other times she kept him at the kitchen table after completing his homework to work on what she called "more advanced" problems. It all led to this moment that she knew would come. According to Colonel Griffins, Susan had always been ahead of her time, and this proved no different. How could she ever have known that he would pass the rigorous exam offered by the Crew?

Around three in the morning, Kyle had pulled out his tracking device—Susan's tracking device—and fueled his growing sense of doom. Whatever was happening with the devices' malfunction grew worse with each passing day. When he had moved to Washington, they were already losing steam, revealing less Exalls than The Crew knew existed. By this never-ending night, the device in his hand showed an entire handful of Exalls spread across the world, not a single one within the United States.

But they're out there, he thought, looking at the blank screen. Somewhere within a five mile radius was the Exall who just tried to kill him and Jason on the freeway. Somewhere on the blank map was at least one Exall upset that he survived, plotting their next move to wipe Kyle off the face of the Earth. *And somewhere there's an Exall strapped to a table underground.*

Sandra occupied his early morning thoughts for a few minutes, but nothing could overshadow the twisting knot in his gut that sensed death in the air. The tracking devices were as good as offline, leaving the entire Crew vulnerable to any attack once they stepped outside the Pentagon.

Once five o'clock rolled around, the sun made its first appearance over the horizon, not that Kyle knew. He'd managed a whole night without sleep and now had to function as a hooked worm to lure the Exalls to The Crew. His brain itched with fatigue while his eyes puffed in their sockets.

The thought of taking on such a grand task while mentally running on fumes made him want to tip over on his bed and cry. He tried, in fact, to do just that, but no tears could be generated, just raw, trembling fear.

Accepting his fate, Kyle rose from bed and dressed as slowly as he could, slipping into his official Crew combat uniform for the first time since trying it on for size. The material was thin and stretchy, black to blend in with the night if need be, but also made of a special fiber to deflect bullets and blades. The protection it provided only worked from a distance—a gunshot from close range would still cause lethal damage. Yet, if he was that close to an Exall, he was expected to engage in the hand-to-hand combat that had been a focal part of the training program.

Brian, he thought, the idea of having to kill his friend left intentionally distant in his mind until this moment. *It's not really Brian; it only looks like him. And sounds like him. And moves like him. And sends text messages to Mikey.*

Once dressed, he made his way to the cafeteria. He never drank coffee, scared of the way people seemed addicted to the caffeine and pretended it was normal, but this morning he had no choice. He'd drink all the coffee in the building if he had to, because once he got further along in the day, his body would demand sleep. And since he didn't know when he might be in his room next, it was best to prepare for the worst.

The cafeteria was nearly deserted at this time of the morning, only a couple other people standing in line at the counter, three others at a table in the far corner, sipping their coffee and nibbling on muffins as if everything were okay in the world.

Kyle went straight for the coffee bar that already had pots brewing. He grabbed a foam cup and filled it to the rim, taking a cautious sip as steam oozed from the surface.

The flavor hit his tongue and made him gag, and he immediately remembered he needed to add milk and sugar so it wouldn't taste like dirt. He did this, not knowing which sugar was best, and clueless as to how much milk was required. He poured until the coffee turned light brown, mixed it, and took another sip more bearable for his taste buds.

He stayed by the bar, gulping down the first cup and beginning a second. With a fresh cup in hand, Kyle swiped a banana from the counter and found a spot in a side booth, trying to look and feel as normal as he could manage. The other table of Crew members had left, leaving him alone in the entire cafeteria. The thought shook him, and his paranoia kicked in.

What if an Exall barged in here right now? How much time would I have before someone showed up to help?

He checked his cell phone to find only 40 minutes had passed since he decided to get out of bed and attempt the day ahead. If he returned to his room, an hour of sleep awaited before he was required in the colonel's office.

He finished off the second cup of coffee, the caffeine no match for his mind's desperation for a quick hour of shuteye. Kyle bolted out of the cafeteria, never so anxious to return to his room where the stiff mattress and pillow awaited him like tempting fluffy clouds to grace his exhausted body.

On the journey to his room he only passed one person, many still asleep or getting ready in their rooms. When he reached his hallway, Kyle rushed to his door, lunging into it as he slid the key into the lock and twisted in one smooth motion. He dove for his bed, slamming the door shut behind him, and let the flood of relief pour over his mind and body.

The room spun around him as he stared to the ceiling, his brain fighting to shut itself down. When his cell phone buzzed in his pocket, Kyle let out a childish whimper, begging God to just let him sleep. He pulled out his phone and immediately jolted at the sight of the message flashing on his screen, like someone had tossed a bucket of ice water on his head.

His hands shook as he opened a text message from Brian.

Kyle, I'm still alive in my body. When we meet today, please don't kill me. I KNOW I can make it out of this, I just need your help.

Kyle stared at the message for the next five minutes, trying to dissect every word, looking for some sort of hidden message, and deciding Brian wouldn't have the time to craft a hidden message with his limited resources. What he said is what he meant.

He got through to me, Kyle thought, a tired grin crossing his face. *He knows I'm with The Crew, too, and can help.*

He jumped off his bed, riding the momentary wave of adrenaline, and left for Colonel Griffins's office an hour early.

30

Chapter 30

"It's time!" the doctor shouted to the crowd of 1,500 Exalls gathered around. They had been trickling in all night, sharing stories of their new lives on the run, bragging to the doctor about the new recruits they were able to snag. It seemed whenever a new Exall introduced themselves to Dr. Klemens, it became an instant battle of egos. They wanted to impress him, yet he didn't want to be outdone by someone who had just become gray within the past few weeks.

"Everything is in motion," he continued, the crowd falling silent as he spoke in a devious tone. "You all know the plan and where you need to be for us to execute it. There will be gunfire, and there will be death. Some of you will not be back here when this is all over. I want to thank you now for your sacrifice." Dozens in the group nodded their head as if this fact didn't bother them one bit. "For the sake of our species and for our future on this planet, we must capture the Wells boy. Do not kill him—I want him alive. Once we have him, open up fire on The Crew. I don't want you to stop shooting until you either die, or there is no one left to shoot. Is that clear?"

They howled: a chilling, lunatic sound. The sun made its first appearance of the morning, a golden, fiery glow kissing the tops of the trees, clearing the light morning fog that had settled over their meeting grounds.

Brian stood in the back, his soul being ripped into several pieces as he watched from within. Part of him wanted to howl with the rest of them—in fact, he did—while the other part, his human side, longed to turn around and sprint away. Running off to live in a remote city far from Washington sounded much better than what was going to happen in a few hours.

He had what he thought were dreams the night before, but he hadn't slept. It was more like a vision, a hallucination. He figured the doctor had somehow implanted the visions in his mind—nothing else seemed a rational explanation.

Whenever he closed his eyes he saw Kyle, dead on the ground, blood oozing from his skull. The setting was unknown. They were in the middle of what seemed like a park, but there were no benches, pathways, or people around to know for sure, just a wide expanse of grass as far as the eye could see. The vision disturbed the shred of humanity that clung to life within Brian's body. Kyle was his best friend – he always looked out for him, and would never do a thing to harm him. Brian felt the same, but he no longer called the shots. Was the doctor twisted enough to show him a preview of what was to come?

Within his deepest fibers, he knew today ended with either himself or Kyle dead, possibly even both. He wanted neither, but was shackled to his own body that now ran like a car remote-controlled by the lunatic doctor. He only hoped that he'd be set free should he survive the day. Free from Hudson Klemens. Free from the Exalls. Free to return to the life he once had as an innocent teenager. He was supposed to be starting his senior year, a life full of college plans and figuring out who to ask to prom. Not killing innocent people because an otherworldly monster had taken control of his mind and body.

Death awaited and there was nothing he could do about it. Within twenty-four hours, Kyle would be dead – Brian was certain of it. The doctor wouldn't allow any other situation to unfold. Brian had done his best and sent a message to Kyle's phone through the will of his new, powerful mind. Hopefully it reached him.

Conversation had broken out across the group of Exalls, but faded into whispers. Brian, who had hidden in the back, looked up to see the Exalls waddling their way to the center of the open space they had already turned into an outdoor meeting area. He couldn't see over the crowd and pushed his way toward the front.

The doctor had both hands raised in the air, a cocky grin on his face. He remained silent, yet managed to gather the entire group of Exalls, as if they were hypnotized. The Exalls subtly rocked from side to side as they waited.

The world fell silent, and somewhere in the distance a crow cawed to provide the only audible sound. With the entire crowd's attention, the doctor spoke in a confident, booming voice.

"Ladies and gentlemen, I thought it might be a few hours for everything to be ready, but the time is now. For years, as humans, you've endured lives of stress and pent-up aggression. Even those of you who think you lived happy lives, you surely have some dark corners in your little souls. Today I ask you to tap into the darkness and unleash the rage. If we don't succeed, our entire population will be wiped off the planet within a couple of days. It's important you make every decision with total confidence. If we succeed, the world is ours. Are there any questions?"

The silence remained as the Exalls looked mindlessly around at each other. Brian had slunk back into the crowd, not wanting to be seen.

"You'll attack any and all members of The Crew. They are the only ones in the world who have access to the special ammunition that can kill us. Eliminate anyone else who gets in your way. Police officers, and even regular military have no way of stopping us. Their bullets will pass through your skin without any pain. The Crew can still be harmed by regular bullets, but they will be heavily armored. Stealth is key once you come into close proximity to a Crew member. If you get the opportunity to disarm them before engaging, I highly suggest you do so. Without their special guns, they're just regular humans you can pulverize. And make sure you do so with a smile."

The doctor widened his grin, looking like a mental asylum escapee covered in gray chalk.

"Now head back to your vehicles, grab your weapons if you haven't already, and let's head for the Pentagon. They should no longer be able to tell that we are coming, so this will be a complete ambush."

The doctor reared his head back and puffed out his chest, his face to the bright blue sky above as he howled.

The rest of the Exalls joined the chorus for a brief, sonic moment of unity. The howling died down and everyone dispersed from the meeting area, working their way through the woods to return to their cars and trucks. Everyone but Brian. He wanted to turn and walk, but his feet remained stuck in the dirt, unable to so much as wiggle his toes.

A few minutes passed for the hundreds of Exalls to clear out, but when they did, it was just the doctor smiling at Brian who hadn't moved the entire time.

"If you try to contact your friend again, I will personally kill him while you watch, and then you'll be joining him right after. Are we clear?"

Brian fought with all his might to move his feet, but failed, an invisible shackle strapped around each ankle.

"Yes," he replied, defeated. There was no point in lying to someone who was already in your head.

"Good. Either way is fine with me, I'd just prefer to not put myself in the line of fire. But I will do so to prove my point."

The doctor walked past Brian and patted him on the head like an obedient dog. The tension around Brian's ankles released and he tumbled forward, arms swinging to catch his balance.

"Let's go," the doctor called over his shoulder. "I'll give you a lift."

Brian hung his head and watched as his legs followed the doctor against his will.

31

Chapter 31

Kyle panted for breath as he reached the Colonel's office, having just run across the complex. He knocked rapidly and urgently, debated barging in, but knew he had no right to do so.

"I'm coming, I'm coming – relax," the colonel grumbled from inside. Seconds later the lock unlatched and his familiar bushy eyebrows appeared through the crack in the doorway. "Wells? What are you doing here already?" His eyes examined Kyle, trying to piece together why the teenage phenom was already dressed for the day ahead.

"I need to talk to you," Kyle said, still huffing and puffing, beads of sweat forming on his forehead.

"Come in."

Colonel Griffins pulled the door open and stepped aside, closing it once Kyle was situated in the seat at his desk. He crossed the room in slow motion, his mind and body exhausted from the last week of events.

"Colonel, I got a text message from Brian," Kyle said before Griffins had even sat down.

"From Brian?"

Kyle nodded, eyes bulging, heart racing at the anticipation of what would happen with this information. The thought of Sandra also pushed to the front of his mind, pulsing like a distant heartbeat buried underground.

"That doesn't make any sense, he's—"

"An Exall, yes. And it does make sense. He's been sending these messages to my friends, and now I got one. The messages always come from a blocked number."

"If they have cell phones, then we should be able to track them. Our ETD's are basically worthless at this point—they found a way to go undetected."

Colonel Griffins scrunched his face while he stared at his desk. Kyle dropped his cell phone into his vision, snapping the old man out of his trance.

"I don't want it," Kyle said. "If I get another message I'm not sure how I'll handle it. I just need to focus on today; I can't have any of these mind games right now."

Griffins nodded and grabbed the phone, studying it like an ancient artifact. "I agree. We'll make sure you have a radio before we head out there; we still need to have a line of communication to you."

"What's going to happen today?" Kyle asked.

A knock rapped on the door, interrupting them.

"Come in!" Griffins growled.

A familiar face popped in, but not one Kyle knew on a first name basis. The man had a buzz cut, glasses perched on a pointy nose, and brown eyes swimming with terror.

"Captain Ramírez," Griffins said. "What's the problem?"

"Sir, they're on the way."

"Who's on the way?"

"The Exalls, sir."

"Here?"

"Yes, sir."

"Bullshit! Why would they come *here*? They have no chance."

"That's what we thought as well, at first. Figured it was maybe a decoy, but it appears they are headed right for the Pentagon."

"How are you tracking them?"

"We have people tailing a couple of them. They disappeared into the woods in Virginia last night, and drove out a few minutes ago with a lot of other cars following. We're not certain all of the cars are filled with Exalls, but we suspect it. They're all driving in a single-file line, headed this way."

Griffins's phone rang and he snapped it off the hook in a quick, jerky motion.

"Grady, tell me something good," he said.

Griffins nodded as he listened, his face stonier than ever.

"Stop them," Griffins said bluntly. "By any means."

He slammed the phone down, shaking his head. "It's time for us to head out there."

Griffins stood from his desk, turned to the closet behind him, and swung open the doors to reveal a rack of rifles. He rummaged through the bottom and pulled out a bulletproof vest, sliding into it as easily as he might a windbreaker. He snatched a rifle and stormed out of the office. "Follow me," he grumbled over his shoulder.

There were no secrets when working for The Crew, especially when it regarded the safety of its members. Word would have already spread about the phone call Griffins had just received, and all the Crew members in the bullpen gawked at him, many pulling pistols out of their desk drawers and ensuring they were loaded.

"Colonel Griffins!" a woman from one of the desks shouted as she stood up, pistol in a wavering hand. "They can't actually get in here, right?"

"Of course not. We're going to secure the exterior right now and will meet them head-on. No one is getting into this office. Once I leave, I'm calling for quarantine until the threat has been neutralized. You all need to stay here, and stay safe."

Griffins continued forward, his rifle perched over his shoulder, Kyle and Captain Ramírez following behind like scared mice. He charged through the office and into the main lobby, not looking to whoever sat behind the reception desk as he pushed open the door to the garage.

A black SUV awaited them, exhaust puttering faint gray clouds into the air, the rear passenger door open with a driver standing nearby, a bulletproof vest strapped over his black suit.

"Good morning, Colonel," he greeted, nodding to Kyle and Ramírez as they all piled into the back of the vehicle.

Apparently the arrangements had already been made, as the driver didn't ask where they were going, and started driving as soon as he sat down. It was normally a slow drive through the garage and up the spiral road to ground level, but today tires screeched at every subtle turn, nearly scraping the concrete walls that surrounded them.

Colonel Griffins scrolled on his cell phone during the ride up, not once breaking eye contact with his screen. Kyle wondered where his phone had gone, likely still in the colonel's office with its secret message from Brian.

Once sunlight broke through the darkness of the garage,

the colonel looked up and slid his phone back into his pocket. "Take us to the front gate please," he said in a hurried tone. Kyle had never seen the colonel in a flustered mood—and still wouldn't consider this one—but he definitely seemed a bit more anxious than usual.

The driver zoomed across the lot toward the Pentagon's main gated entrance where a soldier paced back and forth, rifle embraced in two bulging arms.

Colonel Griffins hopped out of the SUV when they reached the gate and stomped directly over to the soldier. Kyle followed their conversation through the window, but couldn't make out anything as their voices were distorted. The soldier nodded to Griffins before the colonel patted him on the shoulder and returned to the SUV, plopping down as he pulled out his cell phone, keeping his gaze to the ground as he waited for someone on the other end to answer.

"It's Griffins," he finally said. "Where are they?" Griffins nodded as he raised his head, his eyes dancing around the idle vehicle. "Okay, block the freeway, we'll be right there."

Griffins hung up and looked to the driver. "We need to go to I-395, just after the I-95 interchange."

"Yes, sir," the driver said, and blazed out of the parking lot with the same urgency he had left the garage.

Griffins was already dialing his phone again by the time they reached the main road. "It's Griffins. I need all hands on deck. I-95 northbound. We're going to cut them off right now. Roads will be closed in less than five minutes."

The colonel hung up and slipped his phone back into his pocket, shaking his head.

Kyle slouched in his seat, anxious from hearing the words Griffins had spoken. *Closing the freeways? Cutting* them *off?*

How many of them *are there? Is Brian with them?*

"We should be there in about fifteen minutes," Griffins said in a relaxed voice, as if they were driving to a movie theater for a quiet afternoon indoors.

Ramírez, who hadn't spoken a word since they left the offices, cleared his throat and asked, "How many are there?"

"Hundreds," Griffins mumbled, clearly not wanting his own words to be true. "They're driving as a caravan, en route for the Pentagon, but we'll cut them off before they can even get close."

Ramírez sunk back and let his shoulders slump as he stared at twiddling fingers.

"Nothing to worry about. I've been in this situation once before. When we arrive with 500 of our own soldiers, we'll have them all extinguished quickly. I give it two minutes until they're all dead on the freeway."

The colonel's tone shifted from angst to near giddiness.

Kyle's palms turned slick with sweat, and felt beads of moisture forming around his head, oozing down his neck and back.

"Wells," Griffins said, making direct eye contact with Kyle. "You ready for this?"

"Yes, sir." Kyle had to force the words out of his mouth, his throat swollen with fear.

Yes, he had been trained for this exact scenario, and jumping out of a truck to start shooting Exalls would come naturally once he started, but mentally he was far from ready. He was supposed to be starting his final year of high school, lounging around the halls as unofficial kings, enjoying a light schedule full of gym and art classes. Kyle wanted desperately to be with his friends, as far away from the nation's capital as possible.

Instead, he'd look death straight in the eye in a few minutes, and God willing, would wake up tomorrow.

The SUV turned onto the freeway when Kyle realized he was the only one without a bulletproof vest, and asked the colonel if there were any extras.

"We have everything you need in the trunk. Vest, rifles, grenades, you name it. We'll get you suited up when we get there."

How could he be so nonchalant about what was waiting down the freeway? Couldn't they be attacked at any moment during the drive, just like when he had arrived at the airport last night? Kyle was exposed and vulnerable to whatever might happen in the next few minutes, and Colonel Griffins didn't show an ounce of concern.

Griffins leaned forward, his heavy brow furrowed as he stared at Kyle, Ramírez essentially absent as he slunk into the corner of his seat. "When we spoke on the phone last night, you sounded like you had something important to say. Was everything okay?"

Really? Kyle thought. This *is the moment you want to have this discussion?*

Kyle had been so focused on his own mortality that he forgot all about Sandra locked in the basement thousands of miles away. His tongue turned dry at the thought of having this conversation, subconsciously expecting it to come much later, perhaps over a celebratory dinner after wiping out the Exalls.

"Everything was fine . . . there was just something I think you needed to know."

Griffins raised his eyebrows, pushing half a dozen wrinkles into his forehead. "And that is?"

"Did my grandma ever tell you about a secret she kept in her basement?"

Griffins leaned back and looked to the ceiling as he thought back to the several decades he had known Susan Wells. "She had many secrets, but I'm not sure which one you're hinting at."

Kyle's eyes dashed to Ramírez and saw him staring to the ground, disengaged from the conversation.

"About the Exall," Kyle said in a tone just above a whisper, as if his throat needed to be cleared.

"Exall?"

Shit, Kyle thought. *He really doesn't know.*

"I really don't know if now is the best time to discuss this, Colonel."

"We have five more minutes; tell me what you can."

Kyle took a deep breath before speaking, seeing Ramírez drop his head to the ground from the corner of his eye. "There is a living Exall in her basement. I found a secret door in her panic room and followed it into a lab where she has an Exall named Sandra tied down to a table."

He spoke these words quickly, as if they were exploding from his lips to escape.

Colonel Griffins smirked, keeping his gaze on Kyle's troubled face.

"I always suspected it," he said, not an ounce of surprise in his voice. He shook his head. "Oh, Susan, you never fail to amaze me."

"I thought you might have a much different reaction," Kyle admitted.

Griffins nodded, his smirk remaining. "A few years ago, yes. But your grandmother has left a trail of information that's been slowly unraveled since her death. I had a hunch this revelation might come, although I didn't expect it to happen during my lifetime. We had lots of conversations—her and I—about keeping an Exall over a long duration of time. Normally when we capture one, they're already dead or they vanish into dust. I've seen that firsthand."

The SUV slowed down, and Kyle looked out the front windshield to wide open freeway ahead. Not a single car in sight. Colonel Griffins didn't pay any mind and kept his full attention on Kyle. Ramírez looked up from his corner, but remained very much invisible.

"Susan always talked about capturing a young one, but they were so rare to come across to begin with. She thought that would be our best chance since they might not know how to make themselves vanish yet. I don't know *how* she knew this, but I never doubted her for one second. Did you speak with the Exall?"

Kyle nodded. "I did. Her name is Sandra and she told me all about her time with my grandma. But she doesn't understand the concept of time—at least our time. She doesn't know anything about age or how long she's been locked down there."

"She was nice to you? No violent urges?"

"Nothing that she showed, but again, she is strapped down to a table and can barely move her head around to see."

"Fascinating. Susan had to have left notes about her findings. There's no way she just left a ticking bomb like this behind for us to try and figure out on our own."

"Oh, there are plenty of notes, drawers full of them. But I didn't have time to look through all of it; that's when you called me to leave."

The SUV came to a complete stop, but Colonel Griffins didn't seem to care.

"I want to get on the next flight to Denver with you—after we handle today, of course—and you and I can work on this as a special side project. I have thousands of questions and I suspect Susan's notes have the answers."

The colonel glanced over at Ramírez, who had now appeared alert with his head perched and his gaze out the window. Ramírez surely heard everything being discussed, but played it off as if he were in his own world. No Crew member could stay oblivious to their surroundings no matter how hard they tried.

The SUV had stopped in front of a barricade of orange cones lining the width of the freeway on both sides of the median.

"This is our stop," the colonel said. "We'll have to continue this conversation later. Let's go take care of our business."

Griffins nodded to Kyle and Ramírez before opening his door, the two of them following. The morning grew warmer and more humid by the second, the sun beating down on them mercilessly as the caravan of Exalls continued to approach them from five miles away.

32

Chapter 32

Colonel Griffins immediately ordered Kyle to the back of the SUV where the trunk door had popped open, revealing a stockpile of rifles, pistols, ammunition, and vests. Kyle rummaged through everything until he found a vest and helmet his size, and a rifle to his liking, immediately loading it with the special choker bullets that sucked the life out of Exalls. His hands shook, reality again creeping up his esophagus in small, terrorizing tremors.

Brian shot my grandma. Whether he was in charge of his body or not, he was still the one who pulled the trigger. Whoever or whatever was controlling him will only keep doing it until they can't.

The thought of killing his best friend had tried to poison his thoughts at random times. But he always managed to fight off the idea, pushing it aside as improbable, a long shot scenario of events that might actually happen.

Once Kyle slipped into his vest and had his loaded rifle perched by his side, Colonel Griffins joined him. "Wells, I have something for you." The colonel reached a thick hand inside his vest and pulled out a palm-sized, rectangular card, tattered around the edges. He handed it over. "This was your grandmother's."

Kyle grabbed the card and studied an image of Saint Michael choking a demon on the front, and a short prayer on the back.

"He's the patron saint of protection. Susan kept it under her vest every time she went into battle. And it never failed her."

Until Brian shot her in the back.

Kyle felt an instant connection with the prayer card, as if it had Susan's grit and determination smeared across it. Grabbing it settled his nerves and ceased the trembling in his hands. While a simple piece of paper wouldn't stop a bullet, it throbbed like an ancient relic in his hand, promising that everything would end okay.

More soldiers had arrived, pouring out of SUVs and tankers alike, filling the open space in front of the road blocks. There were at least one hundred soldiers conversing, carrying on with the day as normal, while more vehicles pulled up with Crew members.

Colonel Griffins felt the volume of the chatter growing and acknowledged the swelling population of Crew members crammed together. "Good luck, today. I know you're going to do great."

"Thank you, Colonel."

Griffins nodded and left, pushing his way through the crowd to the front. He put two fingers between his lips and whistled a shrill, piercing sound that earned everyone's attention. The chatter fell silent as all eyes turned their attention.

"Good morning," Griffins said, elevating his voice. "The Exalls are five minutes away. We've recently learned that they've become even more advanced than our last encounter four years ago. We're also not sure why they are interested in attacking us so soon. There has long been a pattern they return every thirty years. It appears that a few never left and have infected hundreds of innocent lives to amass an army. I don't know what their motive is today, nor do I care. The interstate is closed in both directions to provide us with isolation. There is no risk in harming civilians so long as we keep this contained within the barriers currently in place.

"Use any and all means necessary to wipe out this population of Exalls. We're not interested in capturing today, simply exterminating. Thank you for your service, today and every day. Now who's ready?"

More Crew members were still working their way into the mass huddle, but collectively let out a thunderous cheer. Men and women, young and old, all stood together on this morning for a united cause. Kyle noticed every Crew member carried themselves with pride and joy, a palpable dedication to their role in keeping the world and humanity safe. The Crew took care of its members, so they only needed to stress about solving the mystery of the Exalls. Today, however, they were all killing machines, leaning on their years of training for this exact moment. There wasn't an ounce of doubt or fear present in this growing group of Crew members, and it rubbed off on Kyle.

He was not alone. If the Exalls were coming for him, they'd have a hell of a fight capturing him. Confidence radiated through the group, and Kyle noticed many of the soldiers smiling at each other, even laughing, as if they looked forward to this day like a special holiday. He wondered if his grandmother would be here today if she were still alive. He closed his eyes, trying to take a step back mentally, and imagined Susan Wells in this group of Crew members, likely next to Colonel Griffins getting everyone riled up.

The thought brought a smile to Kyle. He may have only been a Crew member for a few months, but his life had been one long preparation for this moment. He tightened his grip on his pistol and joined the rest of the group starting to disperse into their positions.

"Two minutes!" Colonel Griffins shouted, his voice drowned out by the rising chatter.

No more nerves crept into Kyle's gut as he looked up to see the glimmering of dozens of vehicles approaching in the distance.

"Everyone get behind a vehicle!" Colonel Griffins shouted, taking his own advice and jogging behind a tanker the size of a diesel truck. All of the soldiers followed the command and spread across the open space behind the tankers, SUVs, and trucks.

Kyle ran through the training that would forever remain stuck in his mind like a wine stain on a white shirt. He recognized the triangular formation the other soldiers had lined up, and immediately joined them, finding his spot in the back of a triangle where the newest members belonged, leaving the more experienced troops on the front line.

They waited, everyone facing forward in anxious anticipation. Colonel Griffins stood in the centermost triangle, craning his neck around the tanker for a view of the approaching Exalls. The soldiers were spread the entire width of the highway, yet everyone still had a clear view of the colonel.

What had been a loud chatter moments ago gave way to deadly silence. The world felt deserted, even the white noise of traffic absent from the freeway.

"They're coming on foot!" Colonel Griffins barked. "Let's

march forward!"

Without hesitation all the soldiers marched through the small gaps between vehicles, bottlenecking before reforming in their proper formations on the other side of the orange cones. Kyle saw a growing blob of people marching toward them. Crew members all stood shoulder to shoulder, rifles gripped in front of them.

"On my command!" Griffins shouted.

Everyone lowered their rifles and cocked them, an authoritative clicking sound nearly in sync. The group of Exalls grew closer, their hundreds of footsteps clopping and clicking on the asphalt. They were roughly three hundred yards away and advancing quickly.

"Forward!" Griffins shouted, prompting all Crew soldiers to start their way toward the Exalls. Kyle looked over his shoulder to see the separation between themselves and the tanks. *Shouldn't the tanks be the ones moving forward and blasting away the gray people?* Surely they were no match for a United States military vehicle.

Kyle could see all of the Exalls holding weapons of their own. Even as they approached each other, Kyle's confidence grew. The Exalls had no formation, likely no strategy aside from spraying bullets and hoping for the best. They weren't equipped to match the Crew and would all be roadkill before brunch was served. The Exalls were spread evenly across the freeway, standing in what looked like three long rows.

One blast from the tank can wipe out half of them, Kyle thought, wondering why so many soldiers were even needed at this point.

The Exalls stopped in their tracks, entering a staredown with the Crew as they stood patiently with their own guns.

They were one hundred yards away when Colonel Griffins commanded that the Crew stop as well.

They watched hundreds of Exalls all swaying in unison like leaves on a tree, their gray skin visible under the sun that grew hotter by the minute. Kyle, like his fellow soldiers, had been focused to the point he didn't notice the streaks of sweat pouring down his back. Matters as such proved minor nuances when your life was on the line. They all stood in silence as they waited for the next command. Kyle glanced over to see Colonel Griffins studying the Exalls, trying to figure out the next best move. It was a real-life chess match, only a false move here would result in death.

They were close enough to start shooting, but Colonel Griffins held off on giving the command as he stared with tense eyes toward the alien species across the way. No one else seemed to be watching the colonel, only looking through their scopes with fingers tight on the triggers.

The Exalls parted down the middle of their grouping, each of them shuffling aside to make a path. The Crew watched, ready, but clearly unsure of what their foes were doing. The Exalls had spaced apart what looked like ten feet, yet they all remained facing The Crew.

A horn blared, the kind that belonged to a diesel truck, and within seconds the truck it belonged to roared through the gap, its motor rumbling the world around them as it gained speed.

"Everybody get back!" Colonel Griffins shouted, pivoting to run and return behind the tanks.

The rest of The Crew followed suit in this brief moment of panic, yet everyone still remained calm and collected as they sprinted like runners at a track meet.

"Fire the tanks!" Griffins screamed, a pleading tone buried

underneath his usual confidence.

The two tanks had lined up sideways, one on each side of the highway's median, their tracks perpendicular with the direction traffic flowed. Their main guns were already pointed in the direction of the oncoming semi-truck. Each tank had a soldier on top manning machine guns, and they wasted no more time before opening fire.

The machine guns blasted in chaotic succession right before both tanks erupted in unison. The ground shook for a brief moment, before ramping up to what felt like an earthquake.

The semi-truck ruptured into a ball of flames, a wave of heat blasting across The Crew. Scraps of metal soared through the air, transforming into lethal missiles and causing everyone to duck and cover. The semi flipped onto its side and slid across the freeway, sparks shooting up in every direction as the sound of metal screeching against pavement sent a piercing scream into the quiet day. It had gained too much speed to be completely stopped, ramming into the tank where all of The Crew members hid behind, and rocking it in its tracks.

Smoke clouded the air, reducing visibility to a mere three feet as many Crew members started coughing after breathing in the particles.

"Go, go, go!" Colonel Griffins yelled from somewhere in the smoke. Footsteps ran away, but some also approached, gun fire ringing both near and far. "It's a trap! Take cover!"

The colonel's voice held on by a thread, clearly on the verge of a heavy coughing attack. Kyle sucked in short gasps of air, feeling the smoke in his lungs, but able to resist coughing out his brains. His eyes welled while his hands subconsciously prepared his rifle.

Those who had left the cover of the tanks were heard screaming from the other side, but their words came out muffled and distant, Kyle's head still ringing from the explosion of the tanks and the resulting eruption of the semi-truck.

He regained control and jogged out from behind the tank, viewing the battlefield ahead. Hundreds of gray people engaged with hundreds of Crew members, more still charging onto the scene from both directions. Most Exalls had guns of their own, but a few carried crow bars, machetes, and knives. They all had crazed looks on their faces: nostrils flared, eyes bulging, black fanglike teeth revealed from psychotic grins.

Kyle froze, unable to join his fellow Crew members or turn around and return to safety. The sight of a war unfolding in the middle of the road jammed the circuits for every instinct in his body. Soldiers and Exalls alike were lying face down on the interstate, blood oozing from wounds, red from the humans, black from the Exalls, some beside each other and blending together to make the color of a dark red wine.

The semi-truck lay on its side, a fire raging across its entire length, black smoke pouring into the sky like a bonfire. If the truck had been a distraction like Colonel Griffins thought, then it worked. It prevented many Crew soldiers from seeing and breathing, resulting in broken formations and a general collapse of their strategy.

The few Exalls with close-range weapons were doing plenty of damage and still appeared unharmed. One drew closer to Kyle, swinging a machete through the air, slashing Crew soldiers across their throats with perfectly landed blows above their protective vests. Kyle watched as one soldier was attacked thirty feet in front of him, dropping their rifle as their hands flailed for their throat, blood shooting out from gloved fingers like a burst pipe. The soldier collapsed to the ground, a gurgling that sounded like a pot of boiling potato soup escaping their throat.

The Exall who caused the damage looked from his victim to Kyle, a mad grin spreading across his face as he started toward him. Kyle fumbled his rifle, trying to get his finger on the trigger, but unable to do so as his arms trembled beyond his control. The Exall stepped closer, maybe fifteen feet away, when its head exploded with black liquid flying from it and landing on the asphalt with an audible *gloop!*

Seeing this woke up Kyle. He sprinted to the other side of the tank where Colonel Griffins had been earlier, but now he was no longer in sight. There were only a couple dozen of Crew soldiers still hiding behind the tanks, either catching their breath or regaining their bearings. The semi-truck that rocked the tank had apparently hit with enough force to send two soldiers flying several yards back. They lay on the ground, one dead, the other with his tibia splintering out of his pants like a broken tree branch, blood pouring from the wound like lava down a volcano.

Gunfire continued on the other side of the tank, mixed with the unmistakable sounds of bodies thudding to the ground. Kyle's heart jumped like a manic kangaroo, his vision pulsing in and out of focus as the reality settled in that he might be one of the few survivors remaining.

Needing to know, Kyle leaned his back on the tank and slid around the corner for a view of what lay ahead. There were indeed more bodies—both gray and human—than what he had seen just a minute ago. The scene matched what he saw in war films: dead bodies on the ground while others fought in the distance. The battle had moved away from The Crew's tanks that had stopped firing for no obvious reason. Kyle assumed those who manned the tanks had been either captured or killed.

Heat still radiated from the burning truck, the flames starting to shrink, but the smoke remaining thick. Not wanting to cower any more, Kyle stepped out from behind the tank and started forward.

He stepped over dead body after dead body, tiptoeing through a maze of death, the heat from the smoldering truck singeing the hairs on the back of his neck. Up ahead were about fifteen Crew soldiers crouched behind the concrete median that separated the freeway. They continued to engage in a shootout with a group of Exalls huddled together, their weapons firing at the median, blasting chunks of concrete into the air.

The smoke created a haze that spread across the entirety of the I-95 battlefield, making it impossible for Kyle to see who was still shooting from the Crew side. Colonel Griffins wasn't in sight, either dead or alive.

"Oh, shit," Kyle whispered as he swung his rifle upward. One of the Exalls had broken away from their group and started walking toward Kyle at a pace of strolling through the park on a Sunday afternoon.

Kyle lined up a shot, watching the Exall through his scope still one hundred feet away, but hesitated pulling the trigger. Through the scope he saw the Exall's skin wasn't gray, but light like his own. Dirty blond hair with a youthful face. A teenager's face, with even a few blemishes and a crooked smile . He looked up and met Kyle's stare.

"Brian?"

33

Chapter 33

In that brief moment, the two boys at a standstill, eyes locked, Kyle forgot about his grandmother, the colonel, Sandra, his entire life. He had expected Brian here today, but didn't once think he'd actually see his old friend.

No one moved, as if they were in an old spaghetti Western showdown. *This town's not big enough for the two of us*, Kyle thought. *This* world *is not big enough for the two of us.* His rifle remained cocked and aimed straight ahead, but Brian had no weapon, just his bare hands protruding from the end of raggedy sleeves.

"Kyle," he said, still not moving or breaking his deadlocked stare. "Did you get my messages?"

One course that Kyle had enjoyed thoroughly was Exall Psychology, a class that focused on what made the Exalls tick, and more importantly, how to engage in a discussion with them should the occasion arise. Exalls were not negotiators. They had a goal and exhausted all options to achieve it. If an Exall engaged in conversation, they likely had a plan to either work their hypnosis over the other person, or at the very least play mind games. Having a history with Brian complicated matters, but Kyle kept his training at his mind's forefront.

"I saw the messages you sent to Mikey," Kyle said, subconsciously tightening his grip on the rifle. "Let me help you."

Brian's face remained expressionless, his blank stare trying to burn into Kyle's soul, but failing.

"You can make this simple and come with me," Brian said. "We can run away from this place and never look back. Get me away from that doctor – all he does is use me as a pawn in his games."

"You know I can't go with you. Even if I did, the whole Crew would be after me. They'll kill you."

"That wouldn't be the worst thing. I'm basically spending my life in a prison right now."

"That's why you need to come with me. We can reverse this."

Kyle knew a reversal was possible, but not likely in Brian's case. Those procedures had to take place shortly after an infection. Brian had been wandering for nearly half of a decade.

Just shoot him before it's too late, Kyle's better conscience pleaded. *You know what this is all for. Get yourself out of this situation.*

He looked beyond Brian where Exalls and Crew soldiers continued fighting, blasting at each other from across the freeway. No one paid them any attention, as if they were alone in their own private battle.

"Why me?" Kyle asked. Exalls rarely expected questions to be asked toward them, a strategy used to try and fluster them.

"I don't know, Ky. I'm just doing what I'm told."

Nothing about Brian seemed to be that of an Exall. If Kyle hadn't known his friend was infected, he may have fallen for his trap.

Brian took a step closer and Kyle raised his rifle to line up squarely with his chest. "Don't do it, Brian. Don't make me."

"I don't wanna fight. I just want my life back."

Everything sounded too scripted for Kyle's liking. Yes, it was his best friend's voice and body, but none of it *felt* real.

Brian took another step, daring Kyle to make a move he dreaded.

"Brian!" he shouted. "Stop it! Let's just go our own ways."

Brian's flat expression gave way to a crooked smirk. His pale face started melting into a gray tone, his eyes turning darker by the second.

"You're coming with me," Brian growled, and charged forward, his arms flailing like a toddler still learning how to run. Drool flew from his mouth where his teeth started turning black and fanglike.

Kyle, swarmed by a world of confidence thanks to his lifelong training, held his ground, feet buried into their positions, shoulders squared up to maximize his accuracy. Eight feet away, Brian leapt through the air for Kyle, his face wild like a possessed zombie. Kyle pulled the trigger and watched the life vanish from Brian's face before he fell to the ground in a heavy thud of bones hitting asphalt.

Black blood immediately squirted from Brian's chest. He was already dead—the special choker bullets instantly removed all oxygen from an Exall's body. As he lay on the ground, Brian's skin faded back to its normal color from the gray tone it had just morphed into. The blackness left his eyes, and the underlying evil that swam beneath his surface disappeared like a spirit leaving a body, allowing his teenage innocence to return.

His body lay a couple feet in front of Kyle, prompting him to stick out a foot to nudge his friend's body, receiving the limp, lifeless response he expected.

I killed him, he thought, his brain still trying to process what happened, his heart drumming on the verge of an explosion. Tears welled in his eyes. *I killed the monster that killed my grandma. But I also killed my best friend.*

Kyle had no intention of pulling the trigger unless Brian forced his hand. If he had turned and walked away, Kyle would have left him in peace until their next inevitable meeting. But how many times would the cycle continue? Emotions crept up, but he had to sweep them aside as soon as they arrived, interrupted by the gunfire still continuing across the way. From the looks of it, the battle was almost over. Only a couple of Exalls remained, while a dozen Crew soldiers readied to make their move for final kills.

"I didn't think you had the balls to kill your friend," a voice said from behind.

Kyle spun around, rifle swinging through the air as he saw an Exall standing behind him, along with Colonel Griffins with his wrists bound together with a rope, duct tape wrapped around his mouth and neck.

The colonel's face was flushed beet red, beads of sweat around his forehead, dripping to a stop on his thick eyebrows.

The Exall looked at Kyle's rifle while he spoke, as if having a conversation with the firearm. "Don't you dare shoot that gun at me, Kyle," he said in a rather calm voice. "If you do, the colonel dies."

The colonel's eyes locked onto Kyle's, desperation on the surface of what was normally unhinged confidence.

"What do you want from me?" Kyle shouted. "You're not even supposed to be here for another twenty-five years."

The Exall giggled. "Oh, Kyle, Kyle, you are precious. I'm not one of these gray monsters born in the sky coming down here for a little tourist time. I took over this doctor's body four years ago and have accumulated all of his knowledge and strength. Earth is my home, and I can't live peacefully knowing there are people actively trying to kill me and all of my new friends."

"We're not trying—we did. Look around."

He chuckled.

"I don't care about these people. They were hired help to try and eliminate your little Crew. I'd say they did an honorable job, wouldn't you? I've counted over 400 Crew members dead with one colonel about to join them. And can you believe it, Griffins, I saw about fifteen of your soldiers run away. Fifteen people who could have killed me and saved you from this exact predicament. Instead they turned their backs and sprinted as fast as they can."

The Exall tousled Griffins's hair like a little child, giggling as he did so.

"What do you want from me?" Kyle asked again.

"You," the Exall said with a smirk. "You pose the greatest threat. I spent so many nights outside of your house, just watching you."

That comment spread chills down Kyle's spine. There had been a few nights where he *felt* like he was being watched, but with the trauma of events at Susan's house, chalked it up as a new paranoia he'd have the rest of his life.

"The others tried stopping me, so I ate them. All three of them who came to my house, right down to the bone. Now I have the strength of four Exalls, plus a charming doctor."

"If you kill me, they'll just come for you. There are thousands of us around the planet, and looks like only you left."

The Exall threw his head back and howled. "I'm not going

to kill you, Kyle. I'm going to convert you. If I can turn my biggest threat into my biggest weapon, then nothing will stop us. How would you like to rule the world with me? We can take over one city at a time, turning the world mad one day at a time."

"Fuck you," Kyle said, squeezing the trigger on his rifle, a flash and boom flying out of the muzzle.

The Exall's left hand shot up simultaneously, his forefinger and thumb pinching the bullet inches in front of his face. He grinned, studied the bullet, and flicked it aside like a booger.

"Stop the games, little boy. I was expecting someone a bit more threatening than yourself. Is that the best you can do? Shooting me to make me shut up? I'll stop talking when *I* want to stop."

Kyle froze, unable to believe what he just saw.

"I said I have the power of four Exalls in one body. Why bother shooting me? It'll only make me angry."

The Exall's black eyes peered into Kyle, his teeth transforming into black fangs, saliva dripping from their sharp tips.

"Get down!" a voice barked from the other side of the tank.

A grenade soared through the air, landing precisely at the Exall's feet. The alien looked down at it, grinning, before looking back up at Kyle. A soldier burst from the side of the tank, charging for Colonel Griffins, lunging toward and tackling him, putting as much distance possible between him and the grenade.

Kyle leapt away from the scene, hands over his neck, as the grenade exploded shards of metal across the road. He landed face down, just missing a dead body a few feet away. Colonel Griffins appeared okay, being helped up by the soldier who sacrificed his body to save him.

The Exall was nowhere to be seen. Kyle jumped to his feet, whipping his head around in every direction, expecting the gray bastard to jump out and try to take him away.

"Where did he go?" Kyle gasped. His rifle lay on the ground several feet away, out of immediate reach.

The soldier paid him no attention as he tended to Colonel Griffins, unstrapping the duct tape. Kyle kept rotating in place, craning his neck for a view around the tank, but unwilling to move himself, terrified of what might wait on the other side. It turned into a fucked up version of hide-and-seek.

"Wells," Colonel Griffins grumbled, his voice hoarse, throat obviously full of mucus. "Are you okay?"

A grenade just blew up in front of him—he had been the closest at the time—and he had yet to check himself for any injuries. The flow of adrenaline would have immediately numbed any pain, but he looked up and down his body to see no more than a few shards of metal wedged into his protective vest. His hands had small cuts, but nothing that required immediate attention.

"I'm fine. Where did he go?"

"I told you they can do this," Griffins said. "Some of them just vanish."

"What do we do?"

"Nothing we can do about it. Just have to stay prepared. How do you both feel mentally?"

"I'm okay, Colonel," the soldier said.

"I'm fine," Kyle replied.

"Okay, good. If either of you feel like you're losing control of your mind at any point, you need to tell me immediately. We can't take any chances and have a repeat of the Browne incident."

Colonel Griffins retrieved his phone and placed a call for assistance in cleaning up the freeway. The few hundred feet beyond the tanks looked like a war zone, blood and bodies peppered across the pavement as far as they could see.

"We have a long road ahead of us," Colonel Griffins said after he hung up the phone. "Today was a goddamn disaster." He shuffled his boots away from the tanks, toward the battlefield that was I-95. His fingers balled into a fist over his lips as he studied the canvas of death on the road, shaking his head.

In all, more than 500 corpses lay strewn on the ground. They waited for twenty minutes for a fresh crew to arrive to clean up the scene. No one said a word, the other soldier wandering off to a nearby gathering spot where the few surviving soldiers grouped to mourn the loss of their Crew mates.

Kyle had the fortune of not yet growing close to anyone within The Crew, with the exception of Colonel Griffins. The dead bodies might have been familiar faces, but none he could even place a name to. Aside, of course, from his best friend, Brian Carsner.

When the next collection of trucks and SUVs arrived, the tanks left with a handful of the other vehicles that had arrived earlier. The dozen or so remaining soldiers piled into three different vehicles, Colonel Griffins and Kyle included. They drove away, leaving the cleaning crew alone for what would surely be the next several hours.

Kyle gazed out the window, grateful to still be breathing, praying for those souls lost, and wondering what lay ahead for the Crew and the rest of the country.

34

Chapter 34

They were back at the Pentagon within a half hour. Colonel Griffins had apologized to the truck full of six soldiers. He spoke softly, disappointment dripping from each word, an obvious disgust clinging to each sentence. Despite the hundreds of moving parts within the Crew, many dedicated to recognizing a pending attack by the Exalls, Griffins assumed full responsibility. He admitted they took too long to react, and that meeting the Exalls in the woods would have been a better plan instead of letting it approach the bustling city. A main interstate was closed, and they had to lie to the public about the reason why.

"Sir, we have a problem," the driver called from the front, stopping the van at the armed gate to enter the parking garage. Griffins craned his neck to see out the front windshield, eyes bulging as he whispered, "Jesus Christ."

Everyone was fighting for a view, seeing the solider who had been manning the entry all morning face down on the pavement, blood caked around his head.

"It was a decoy," Griffins cried. "Jesus Christ, we've had no control over this because the goddamn trackers don't work. Fuck! Get us inside right now. We have to see how much damage is done."

The tires squealed as the van blasted through the arm gate and bolted through the parking lot before entering the garage. Within two minutes, which consisted of everyone reloading their guns, they unloaded from the truck, an invisible sickness plaguing each soldier, like they had all just left a buffet and caught food poisoning. They had only left the Pentagon two hours earlier, and now they were back, the Exalls thought to be defeated, but a clear doubt hanging above them.

No one was at the front desk to greet them, but Griffins didn't hesitate to enter the sixth floor, walking in a daze. He pulled open the door into the main offices and froze. "Mother of God."

Kyle and the others followed, stopping at the sight of more dead bodies. The office was silent, not a living soul present. At least thirty Crew members had been slaughtered, facedown on their desks, precise bullet wounds in the back of their heads. Blood splattered the walls and computer screens like abstract art. The lights were off, and the strong stench of gunpowder suggested this massacre had taken place within the last hour.

He kicked a small trash bin from the desk at his side, sending it sailing across the office as papers and a banana peel fell out. "We're done for."

Griffins raised his pistol in front of him, giving a quick look over his shoulder to ensure the rest of the team was also prepared.

"They're still here. I know it," Griffins said. Numerous guns clicked in a matter of seconds as they cocked them and prepared for the next battle in this never ending nightmare.

"This is our home. For some of us, literally. Shoot anything that moves."

"Yes, sir," the soldier who had saved him said, pushing his way to the front of their group. Kyle had learned on the drive back that his name was Anderson Ortiz, a Crew veteran of fifteen years. Ortiz took a deep inhale before shouting across the room. "If you are a Crew member, reveal yourself right now. If you do not, you will be shot on sight."

He paused a moment, waiting for a response, receiving nothing but chilling silence. He looked back to Colonel Griffins who nodded in approval.

"Let's move," Ortiz said, starting forward, the rest following behind.

"Wells, stay back with me," Griffins said as Kyle took a step to follow the soldiers. Kyle spun around, eyebrows raised.

"Are you sure, sir?"

"Yes. We can't have you in the line of danger at the moment. Not after what you told me about Susan's basement. I've had my suspicions about why she knew so much about the Exalls, and I think she passed it on to you. We'll need to run a few tests."

"Tests? What is it you think she did?"

A shot rang out and Kyle jolted his head up to look ahead. An Exall grinned from the opposite wall, just beside Griffins's office door. He held a pistol and lowered it as the group of soldiers fired twelve rounds into him, sending him instantly to the ground.

Kyle looked to Colonel Griffins and the world came to an immediate halt. A river of blood flowed from the colonel's throat, a small hole just below his Adam's apple, three inches above where his vest provided coverage.

"Colonel," Kyle gasped, stepping toward him with an arm extended. Griffins looked down to his blood-covered fingers that had patted the hole in his throat, looking from his hand to Kyle with his eyes popping out of their sockets. He fell to his knees with a hollow thud, and Kyle swooped behind to ease his collapse by grabbing him under the arms. "Someone help!" he screamed, but it didn't matter. There was no saving Griffins, the blood making a dark stream down the colonel's camouflage uniform.

Kyle felt the last bit of fight within the colonel, his body shuddering as it clung to its final seconds. The tension gave way to a limp, deadweight body, his head slung forward, and Kyle leaned him backwards so he wouldn't have to lie face down in a pool of his own blood.

"Oh my God," Kyle cried, fresh tears rolling down his cheeks. He looked up through blurry vision as the soldiers who had shot the murderous Exall rushed across the office, their boots clapping and echoing in the silent, deserted building, the odor of gunpowder growing stronger with each passing second.

"Colonel Griffins is down!" one soldier shouted into a radio. "I repeat, Colonel Griffins is down! Send help to the main office, sixth floor, right now!"

They gathered around, one soldier throwing his jacket to the ground and removing his t-shirt, pressing it on the colonel's throat wound. The shirt was gray, but darkened within seconds. The soldier pushed down on the colonel's chest in an attempt to begin CPR, but when he pushed, more blood squirted, soaking through the shirt and pooling at the sides of his neck.

"Gah!" the soldier gasped when he saw this unfold, giving up on the CPR and placing two fingers on Griffins's jugular to check for a pulse. "C'mon, c'mon, don't fucking die on us."

This moment lasted for about thirty seconds, but felt like five minutes as they all huddled around the soldier, waiting for him to look up and deliver the news.

"He's gone. That fucking Exall piece of shit!" The soldier jumped to his feet and sprinted across the office to where they had shot the Exall. Kyle couldn't see the alien's corpse, blocked from rows of desks where it lay on the ground. "Motherfucker!" the soldier shouted, pulling out a pistol, and firing six more rounds into the already dead Exall.

The other soldier who had called on the radio continued calling, but received no response. "I think we're alone, gentlemen. No one's answering, and there is *always* someone manning the dispatch. Is anyone here?" He called out, his question echoing right back to the group of them standing around Colonel Griffins. "Where the hell is everyone?" His voice quivered in a way that suggested he knew the disturbing truth. They all did. Everyone on the main floor had been murdered, so it wasn't a stretch of the imagination to assume that everyone else in the building was dead. But to what extent? Did the Exalls only kill Crew members? There were other departments of the government that filled the Pentagon's ground level floors and above. Those others had no idea of the existence of Exalls, let alone how to fight them in a battle. The Exalls might have eliminated the entire Department of Defense, leaving the country vulnerable to both alien and foreign attacks.

"There's only one way to find out," another soldier said, raising his rifle into a shooting position, nodding ahead. "We have to sweep the building."

The soldiers nodded in agreement, Kyle wishing he could shrink into a fly on the wall and buzz his way out of the building. If they killed Colonel Griffins so easily, they'd have no issue wiping out a small group of Crew members. Hundreds already lay dead on the freeway thirty minutes west.

"Goodbye, Colonel," Kyle said, removing his helmet and nodding toward the stunned, ghastly face. The others followed suit, saluting the colonel as they took a step closer to him.

"I think our best bet will be to move as a circle," Ortiz said. "That way every angle is covered. Let's start from the very bottom and move our way up."

He led the way toward the elevator across the office, not far from the colonel's office. They formed a natural circle as they walked, Kyle thankful to be on the backside of it, sandwiched between two giants whose arms seemed bigger than his torso. He didn't know if these soldiers would go as far to protect his life—they might not even know the value he had to offer The Crew—a value that he wasn't quite sure of himself. But he trusted them just the same. Special or not, these men were potentially the last survivors of the D.C.-area Crew. The attack on Griffins caught them by surprise, but now they were ready for anything that might jump out from the shadows.

They reached the elevator and Kyle caught a glance of the dead Exall. It lay flat on its back, arms splayed to the side like it was enjoying a comfortable sleep in a king-sized bed to itself. Its tarry blood oozed from the several bullet wounds, gray smoke steaming from them like a pot of boiling water.

"He killed my two friends," one of the soldiers next to Kyle said, holding up dog tags with the names of Dante Rivers and Ron Miley. "I'm sure you heard of the two Crew members we lost on a mission in Michigan not too long ago. Dante was my best friend." He shook his head as the elevator chimed and the doors parted.

"Yes, I remember," Kyle said flatly, having partly forgotten, but now having his own best friend on his mind. Brian's desperation for freedom had risen to the surface, his soul trying to leap out of his eyeballs in a final mad dash before the lights went out. Kyle would forever have the image burned into his memory: a gray version of Brian, lunging toward him, his own finger pulling the trigger, Brian's head flinging back as black liquid splattered from his skull. Kyle had thought, in some distant part of his conscience, that he heard Brian calling out for help. Screaming and shouting from the depths of the spirit buried under the gray skin. Surely the screams he heard belonged to his conscience or imagination, and that was what he'd tell himself for the rest of his life.

35

Chapter 35

The comprehensive sweep of the Pentagon included all of its private and public floors. They didn't encounter much in terms of killing Exalls: only two, to be precise. The first was on sublevel six where they had started, found in an office humping the corpse of a male Crew soldier. He thrust his hips in an awkward, jerky motion, only grinning over his shoulder when the group of soldiers walked in before promptly firing nine rounds into his head and back. The second had been a crippled one on sublevel four, a quick shot to the chest to put it out of its misery.

They didn't find anything beyond dead bodies in every room. There wasn't one survivor in their offices. As they passed through the abandoned halls, bloody footsteps following their every move, Kyle wondered what would become of The Crew now that it had no leader or any soldiers.

There were plenty of other Crew members around the world, so it's wasn't like the entire department had been wiped off the map. They still had members who would surely relocate to Washington to help them rebuild. There had been plenty of instances in the past where a large amount of Crew members had their lives taken. Though none were as less positive as this incident, they always regrouped and came back stronger and smarter to counter their Exall foes.

Even this group of twelve soldiers wasted no time in gathering their emotions and continuing on with their business. When dealing with Exalls, there was no real time off. A good Crew member understood they were on the clock for twenty-four hours each and every day. One second with your guard down—much like Colonel Griffins just experienced—could cost your life.

Beside the images of Brian that plagued his mind, Kyle would be forever haunted by the scene of Colonel Griffins taking a slug to the throat and the resulting gurgling sound as he choked on his own blood. He had stood only two feet from the colonel and was lucky to be alive, wondering if the bullet was really meant for him. He fought off these thoughts as the team made its way through the building, praying he wouldn't end up with a similar fate.

When they completed their sweep of the fourth sublevel, they had to exit the office and walk across the parking garage to catch a different elevator to the rest of the building. Sublevels three through one were all parking lots, giving the appearance to those above that there was nothing further below. The tension within the group grew as it rode the elevator. A moment of truth awaited on the underground's third level. They'd either find life continuing as normal for those who lived in oblivion to the Exalls, or find what could very well be the end of civilization in the United States. If the Exalls carried their attacks to this level, there was no saying the damage done to the entire nation.

The elevator chimed as the doors parted. Everything in the garage appeared as normal: no dead bodies, no blood spills, no gray people. They marched forward, boots clapping in near unison, rifles cradled, pistols drawn. They reached the elevator in seconds, riding it up to the ground level where more offices awaited.

"Jesus Christ," one of them groaned when the doors parted. They remained in their circular formation, so Kyle had to crane his neck to get a view inside the office. He couldn't see much through the wavering soldiers, but caught glimpses of an already familiar scene of death and blood on the floor.

They moved into the office, feet shuffling through a place they were not familiar with.

"Is anyone in here alive?" Ortiz called out.

They continued forward and Kyle saw a man sitting at a cubicle, face down on his desk, neck twisted so his glossy eyes stared at them in the hallway, his throat slit in the shape of a smiley face.

"What department is on this floor?" one soldier asked.

"The Missile Defense Agency," Ortiz snapped back immediately.

A phone rang somewhere in the office, prompting many of the soldiers to jump.

"Is it safe to assume the entire building is like this?" the soldier next to Kyle asked.

"I think it is, but we have to check to be sure. If there's even one person who survived, we need to speak with them. " Ortiz continued forward where another elevator waited to take them to the rest of the Pentagon.

The same story unfolded on the Pentagon's five floors above ground. Not a sole survivor revealed themselves as the remnants of The Crew worked their way through. Kyle figured if there was a survivor, they were too scared to show themselves to anyone passing through the doors. There surely had to be *one* person who made it out alive.

The moment that had sent chills up Kyle's back was when they completed the internal sweep and moved outside to the back entrance of the building. Dead soldiers lay on the ground, their firearms missing, guts spilled on the pavement.

For the Exalls to complete a clean gutting of the entire Pentagon, they would have needed hundreds—if not thousands—of infected gray people to infest the building, killing everyone in sight without a discussion. They had yet to see any bullet holes or wounds aside from Colonel Griffins. Surely a handful of Exalls with their fists wouldn't have been able to pull off what they did without someone fighting back. It was a well-planned sneak attack.

The attacks happened in the blink of an eye. There were at least 12,000 people working in the Pentagon at any given moment, yet miraculously not a single person had a moment's notice to realize they were under attack and call the police, another department, or even their own family. 12,000 people was a low estimate—there were probably closer to 16,000 at the time of the attacks.

The group of Crew soldiers only swept main offices, forgoing the checking of every individual conference room and closet door. There could be survivors somewhere in the building, but it seemed more like a poisonous smoke bomb had gone off, suffocating every person no matter where they were.

Even a group of, say, 1,000 Exalls couldn't massacre 16,000 people on their own. Something was not adding up, and they all knew it, a sense of doom settling over them like a dark cloud.

If 16,000 people didn't stand a chance, why would their little squad of twelve think they were anything special?

"How did this happen?" one of the soldiers asked.

"I have no idea," Ortiz snapped.

"How is there not *one* person alive? Impossible."

The fear grew palpable in their voices, yet Kyle felt an odd calm. If the Exalls were going to attack them, what were they waiting for? They had just spent two hours walking through the entire building, floor after floor of dead bodies.

"We missed them," Kyle said. "They killed everyone and left. There's no one waiting for us—they're gone."

The soldiers lowered their weapons as if Kyle's words were a trusted prophecy. If the wonderkid said they were gone, then they were gone, no reason to doubt it.

"We need to get word to the White House," Ortiz said. "I don't know what else we can do."

"Has no one in D.C. tried contacting the Pentagon?" another asked. "How can they have gone two hours without knowing what happened here?"

After a pause the answer was obvious, but no one said it aloud.

"I think we need to get back to The Crew offices," Ortiz said with a new urgency. "We don't have much time."

On cue, a rumbling like thunder vibrated in the clear blue sky, the ground trembling beneath their feet.

"Run!" Ortiz screamed, pivoting and bolting toward the Pentagon's entrance.

Everyone followed suit, Kyle trailing behind and looking up to the deafening, thunderous noise of Air Force jets zooming above. Ten of them flew by in a V-formation, rumbling the world below.

"Get the fuck inside!" the last soldier cried out.

Kyle dashed and lunged through the door, following the trail of soldiers sprinting through the halls toward the elevator.

"Hurry! Hurry!"

The ground vibrated, and Kyle's first thought was that an earthquake was beginning. So why on Earth would they want to go further down into the ground?

* * *

They jammed into the elevator, the door closing with a banal chime before it started its descent to the second underground level where they'd have to scurry across the parking lot to catch the other elevator to return to their secret office.

"What's going on?" Kyle asked as they all panted like thirsty dogs.

"No time to explain. We need to keep moving."

The elevator doors parted and they immediately ran, the ground no longer vibrating. Their boots sounded like a stampede of wild stallions galloping through the dim garage as they reached the other elevators. Ortiz stood with his arms over his head as he caught his breath waiting for the elevator to arrive. He laughed nervously when it opened and took relaxed steps inside.

"We made it," he said as they started their descent. "Holy shit, we made it."

They were now gasping for air, having just gone from the Pentagon's back door to their underground lair within two minutes, surely a record time.

"Tell me what's going on," Kyle demanded. It was clear that everyone was in on the secret besides him.

Anderson held up a finger as his lungs still begged for fresh oxygen. A few seconds passed and he said, "Plan D. . . Doomsday."

Kyle fuzzily recalled learning about Plan D during his training. It was briefly discussed and dismissed as a last resort, essentially only to be used if it was deemed the country was already doomed by an alien invasion so massive that The Crew couldn't contain it.

"What does it mean?" Kyle asked, knowing, but needing to hear it spoken aloud by someone else.

"Over the next twenty-four hours, our country will be wiped out until it's a pile of rubble. The only people who have a chance at living through this are any Crew members able to get underground, and the president and his family."

"I don't get why we can't just kill the Exalls."

"Because they've already won," the leading soldier said calmly. "We either wipe out ourselves or they'll do it for us. If we do nothing, they will burn this country to the ground, and then the rest of the world. We can either eliminate our entire population, or sit by and watch as the entire world becomes infected with Exall blood. It's a sick decision that can only be made by the president. If he feels our only hope for saving the human race is to start over with a handful of people, then he has no choice."

The soldiers sat in silence, nodding to themselves as they processed this reality. Kyle thought he felt the ground shake, but chalked it up to his imagination. They were too far below ground to feel anything. *Please let Mom and Dad be hiding in the bunker. They might just make it out alive.*

"So what happens next?" Kyle asked. All he wanted to do was call his parents and tell them he loved them. To find shelter. Hide in the panic room. But his cell phone was still on the colonel's desk.

"Today we just need to try and relax, whatever that means to each and every one of you. Natural sleep will be impossible, so maybe head to the First Aid office and grab some sleeping pills. Trust that you are safe down here. The bombs deployed are designed to explode twenty feet into the ground. We're ninety feet down."

Susan's secret room was definitely more than twenty feet below ground. Kyle jumped up and ran away. "I gotta go."

No one tried stopping him as he dashed across the office, toward the back where the colonel's office remained unattended, the dead Exall on the ground in front of it. He barged in and swiped the phone from his desk, a flood of relief sweeping over him as he dialed his mother.

It rang once and cut to silence. He dialed again, getting the same result, his face flushing with rage. He dialed his dad, Mikey, and Jimmy, all to no avail. It always rang once before cutting away to silence.

"Oh my God, no. Please God, no," Kyle cried, eyes ballooning with liquid. He opened Facebook to try sending a message through the app, but the gray circle just spun in circles as it tried to load, the rest of the screen remaining a blank white. "Oh, fuck." His fingers glided as they opened a web browser, trying to load all of his favorite websites, getting nothing but more blank screens in return.

Kyle threw his phone to the ground, its case splattering in an explosion of plastic, and sprinted down the hallway toward the staircase that led to the game room. There were still no other Crew members, not that he expected any, but the sound of his heavy breathing bounced around the walls in a way that made him think someone else was running behind him.

He barged into the room and turned on the TV, praying a news station had coverage of the outside world. He flipped to CNN, Fox News, the local channels, and even ESPN for good measure. All channels were nothing but static.

He sat on the lounge chair, all feeling draining from his legs, waves of heat radiating across his body and face as adrenaline pumped through his veins at an alarming rate. The phone lines were down, the internet cut off, the news stations obliterated into nothing. They were almost 100 feet into the Earth with no method of communication to the outside world.

Somewhere above their heads the United States was being bombed to pieces by its own military, and Kyle wondered how the events had transpired that led to this decision. Surely the death of Colonel Griffins had factored in, along with the massacre of the Pentagon, but who delivered that fateful news to the president?

An overwhelming sense of helplessness consumed Kyle as he considered what was taking place outside of these walls. Skyscrapers and office buildings were collapsing, people's screams buried beneath smoke and rubble as their final mo-ments were surely spent in terror, oblivious to what was happening. Kids in schools and daycares were silenced along with their futures, their care providers sheltering them with their own lives in a desperate, futile attempt to stay safe. Hospitals exploded, putting both an end to suffering and an end to lives that had just begun. All the innocence of day-to-day life ended with a ball of fire, the hustle and bustle of the United States falling immediately silent where no living creature could so much as utter a final breath. Neighborhoods with homes and trees and yards were now covered in gray ash. All of the monuments in the country, the tributes to history, good, bad, or ugly, were all gone. There was no longer a United States of America.

Kyle prayed his parents were safe, but knew better. His dad might have had a chance, considering his upbringing, possibly knowing the first signs of Plan D and able to take cover. But his mom wouldn't have known. She would've been at work, running her restaurant and serving a lunch crowd who received death for dessert. He tried to shake the image of his mother buried under dead bodies and remnants of her own restaurant, but he simply could not. Is it really the end of the world if you survive it?

The future was as uncertain as it had ever been. They had no way of knowing what was going on in the rest of the world, alone on a mass of land of 3.8 million square feet. The thought was chilling, sickening.

And that's when Kyle remembered perhaps the most disturbing truth of all. Sixteen hundred miles away in Denver, a living Exall remained strapped to a table far enough below ground to have survived any attack. That one Exall and laboratory housed the answers to a list of thousands of questions and would spark a thousand more, both regarding the past and the bleakly uncertain future.

With Colonel Griffins dead, Kyle was again the only person who knew about Sandra. He didn't know who to trust out of the remaining Crew members, and was reluctant to tell any of them about this heavy secret just yet. As soon as possible, Kyle would have to return home, dig his way through a lifetime of memories, and sift through the secrets trapped in that underground room, the fate of humanity relying on him.

A Poisoned Mind - Free Download

Download the free short story by joining Andre's mailing list. *A Poisoned Mind* is a spinoff story of the Exalls Attacks, focusing on the Jonathan Browne story that is referenced throughout both books of the series.

Use the link below to sign up for this story and others, in an exclusive four-story bundle from Andre Gonzalez, including other prequel stories from his *Insanity* and *Wealth of Time* series.

https://andregonzalez.net/join-andres-mailing-list/

Enjoy this book?

You can make a difference!

Reviews are the most helpful tools in getting new readers for any books. I don't have the financial backing of a New York publishing house and can't afford to blast my book on billboards or bus stops.

(Not yet!)

That said, your honest review can go a long way in helping me reach new readers. If you've enjoyed this book, I'd be forever grateful if you could spend a couple minutes leaving it a review (it can be as short as you like) on the Amazon page. You can jump right to the page by clicking below.

US

UK

Thank you so much!

Author's Note

When I published Followed Home in 2016, I didn't have plans at the time for a sequel. It was my very first book, and I was still learning the ropes of this industry. Now, nine books later, I have much more direction behind everything I do. If you happened to read these books back-to-back, you might wonder if they were written by different authors, but I can assure you it is all me! Writing is like anything in life, you can put in time and practice to become better. It is also a craft, which isn't something as straight forward as learning, but rather developing more knowledge and pushing your personal limits to try new things. I am nowhere near the same writer I was nine books ago, just like I'll surely be different nine books from now. I've learned so much in these last four years, that I'm pleased to have this sequel to really flesh out the universe and characters in more depth. Also, the story ends with a setup for a third (and final) book of what will be a completed trilogy. Look for that in 2021.

I want to take a moment to thank the team that works tirelessly behind the scenes for every book. First, my editor, Stephanie, for her fantastic work in polishing off another one of my books. This was our fifth book together, and I feel we've reached a point where we are on the same page with how each other works on projects. Thank you to Dane Low from ebooklaunch.com for another brilliant cover design. Having a solid cover is half the battle in trying to sell a book, and Dane has never let me down.

Thank you to the Dizzy Dragons, my close-knit community of author friends. We always push each other both as writers and business owners.

To my Advance Readers team. You guys play a huge role in helping the launch and consequential marketing for all of my books. Thank you for being such fast and honest readers.

Lastly, thank you to my wife, Natasha, for always keeping me motivated and moving forward. We're getting so close with every book release, and we're at the point where we can honestly ask "will this be the book that makes our dreams come true?" And of course, Arielle, Felix, and Selena, for keeping me balanced in this career that is so chaotic at times. I love you!

Andre Gonzalez
3/22/19–5/27/20

Also by Andre Gonzalez

Wealth of Time Series:

Keeper of Time (Wealth of Time Series, Book #4)

Bad Faith (Wealth of Time Series, Book #3)

Warm Souls (Wealth of Time Series, Book #2)

Wealth of Time (Wealth of Time Series, Book #1)

Road Runners (Wealth of Time Series, Short Story)

Revolution (Wealth of Time Series, Short Story)

Insanity Series:

The Insanity Series (Books 1-3)

Replicate (Insanity Series, Book #3)

The Burden (Insanity Series, Book #2)

Insanity (Insanity Series, Book #1)

Erased (Insanity Series, Prequel) (Short Story)

The Exalls Attacks:

Followed East (Book #2)

Followed Home (Book #1)

A Poisoned Mind (Short Story)

Standalone books:

Snowball: A Christmas Horror Story

About the Author

Born in Denver, CO, Andre Gonzalez has always had a fascination with horror and the supernatural starting at a young age. He spent many nights wide-eyed and awake, his mind racing with the many images of terror he witnessed in books and movies. Ideas of his own morphed out of movies like *Halloween* and books such as *Pet Sematary* by Stephen King. These thoughts eventually made their way to paper, as he always wrote dark stories for school assignments or just for fun. As an international bestselling author, Andre hopes to keep others awake at night with his frightening and thought-provoking tales. The world we live in today is filled with horror stories, and he looks forward to capturing the raw emotion of these events, twisting them into new tales, and preserving a legacy in between the crisp bindings of novels.

Andre graduated from Metropolitan State University of Denver with a degree in business in 2011. During his free time, he enjoys baseball, poker, golf, and traveling the world with his family. He believes that seeing the world is the only true way to stretch the imagination by experiencing new cultures and meeting new people.

Andre still lives in Denver with his wife, Natasha, and their three kids.

www.ingramcontent.com/pod-product-compliance
Lightning Source LLC
Chambersburg PA
CBHW051652180726
48284CB00006B/1961

9 781951 762070